"C. Matthew Smith's original, intelligent novel delivers unforgettable characters and an irresistible, page-turning pace while grappling with deeply fascinating issues of land and heritage and what and who is native.... *Twentymile* is an accomplished first novel from a talented and fully-formed writer."

–James A. McLaughlin, Edgar Award-winning author of *Bearskin*

"*Twentymile* is packed with everything I love: A strong, female character; a wilderness setting; gripping storytelling; masterful writing. Smith captures powerfully and deeply the effects of the past and what we do to one another and ourselves for the sake of ownership and possession, for what we wrongfully and rightfully believe is ours. I loved every word. A beautiful and brutal and extraordinary debut."

–Diane Les Becquets, national bestselling author of *Breaking Wild* and *The Last Woman in the Forest*

"In C. Matthew Smith's engrossing novel *Twentymile*, a park service biologist turns up dead in the Great Smoky Mountains National Park, and discord regarding annexed land fuels a treacherous chase.... a disturbing, potent thriller about ownership and trespassing, as well as unrealized dreams and aggression."

–Karen Rigby, *Foreword Reviews*

"Beauty, brutality, and heartbreak merge at *Twentymile* in this must-read debut novel from C. Matthew Smith!"

–David Tromblay, author of *Sangre Road* and *As You Were*

"Smith's spellbinding debut takes readers on a murderous journey through the backwoods of Great Smoky Mountains National Park, with indomitable Cherokee and National Park Service investigator Tsula Walker leading the way. A thrilling and evocative tale."

–Scott Graham, National Outdoor Book Award-winning author of *Canyonlands Carnage*

"A highly enjoyable read suited best to those who like their thrillers to simmer for awhile before erupting in a blizzard of action and unpredictability with a future promise of grander adventures."

–Kashif Hussain, *Best Thriller Books*

"*Twentymile* is a moody, atmospheric tale of family, vengeance, and anger too-long held, all set in the heart of the Great Smoky Mountains. Ultimately, it is the story of reaching for – discovering and recovering – home, and how such a complicated yearning can play out on both sides of the law."

–Steph Post, author of *Miraculum*, *Lightwood*, and *A Tree Born Crooked*

"C. Matthew Smith's gripping tale centers around the history of our public lands and the people who use and protect them. *Twentymile* is a tremendously entertaining first novel from a writer who knows how to spin a good yarn."

–Rob Phillips, bestselling author of *The Cascade Killer*, *Cascade Vengeance*, and *Cascade Predator*

TWENTYMILE

TWENTY MILE

A NOVEL

C. MATTHEW SMITH

Twentymile

Book design by Kevin Breen
Cover image derived from Adobe Stock photos

ISBN: 978-1-7360127-6-5
Cataloging-in-Publication Data is available upon request

Manufactured in the United States of America

Published by Latah Books
www.latahbooks.com

The author may be contacted at cmattsmithwrites@gmail.com

For Cindy and Everett

HARLAN

CHAPTER ONE

May 10

The same moment the hiker comes upon them, rounding the bend in the trail, Harlan knows the man will die.

He takes no pleasure in the thought. So far as Harlan is aware, he has never met the man and has no quarrel with him. This stranger is simply an unexpected contingency. A loose thread that, once noticed, requires snipping.

Harlan knows, too, it's his own fault. He shouldn't have stopped. He should have pressed the group forward, off the trail and into the concealing drapery of the forest. That, after all, is the plan they've followed each time: Keep moving. Disappear.

But the first sliver of morning light had crested the ridge and caught Harlan's eye just so, and without even thinking, he'd paused to watch it filter through the high trees. Giddy with promise, he'd imagined he saw their new future dawning in that distance as well, tethered to the rising sun. Cardinals he couldn't yet spot were waking to greet the day, and a breeze picked up overhead, soughing through shadowy crowns of birch and oak. He'd turned and watched the silhouettes of his companions taking shape. His sons, Otto and Joseph, standing within arm's length. The man they all call Junior lingering just behind them.

The stranger's headlamp sliced through this reverie, bright and sudden as an oncoming train, freezing Harlan where he stood. In all the times they've previously made this journey—always departing this trail at this spot, and always at this early hour—they've never encountered another person. Given last night's thunderstorm and the threat of more to come, Harlan wasn't planning on company this morning, either.

He clamps his lips tight and flicks his eyes toward his sons—*be still, be quiet.* Junior clears his throat softly.

"Mornin'," the stranger says when he's close.

The accent is local—born, like Harlan's own, of the surrounding North Carolina mountains—and his tone carries a hint of polite confusion. The beam of his headlamp darts from man to man, as though uncertain of who or what most merits its attention, before settling finally on Junior's pack.

The backpack is a hand-stitched canvas behemoth many times the size of those sold by local outfitters and online retailers. Harlan designed the mammoth vessel himself to accommodate the many necessities of life in the wilderness. Dry goods. Seeds for planting. Tools for construction and farming. Long guns and ammunition. It's functional but unsightly, like the bulbous shell of some strange insect. Harlan and his sons carry similar packs, each man bearing as much weight as he can manage. But it's likely the rifle barrel peeking out of Junior's that has now caught the stranger's interest.

Harlan can tell he's an experienced hiker, familiar with the national park where they now stand. Few people know of this trail. Fewer still would attempt it at this hour. Each of his thick-knuckled hands holds a trekking pole, and he moves with a sure and graceful gait even in the relative dark. He will recognize—probably is just now in the process of recognizing—that something is not right with the four of them. Something he may be tempted to report. Something he might recall later if asked.

Harlan nods at the man but says nothing. He removes his pack and kneels as though to re-tie his laces.

The hiker, receiving no reply, fills the silence. "How're y'all do—"

When Harlan stands again, he works quickly, covering the stranger's mouth with his free hand and thrusting his blade just below the sternum. A whimper escapes through his clamped fingers but dies quickly. The body arches, then goes limp. One arm reaches out toward him but only brushes his shoulder and falls away. Junior approaches from behind and lowers the man onto his back.

Even the birds are silent.

Joseph steps to his father's side and offers him a cloth. Harlan smiles. His youngest son is a carbon copy of himself at eighteen. The wordless, intent glares. The muscles tensed and explosive, like coiled springs straining at a latch. Joseph eyes the man on the ground as though daring him to rise and fight.

Harlan removes the stranger's headlamp and shines the beam in the man's face. A buzz-cut of silver hair blanches in this wash of light. His pupils, wide as coins, do not react. Blood paints his lips and pools on the mud beneath him, smelling of copper.

"I'm sorry, friend," Harlan says, though he doubts the man can hear him. "It's just, you weren't supposed to be here." He yanks the knife free from the man's distended belly and cleans it with the cloth.

From behind him comes Otto's fretful voice. "Jesus, Pop."

Harlan's eldest more resembles the men on his late wife's side. Long-limbed and dour. Quiet and amenable, but anxious. When Harlan turns, Otto is pacing along a tight stretch of the trail with his hands clamped to the sides of his head. His natural state.

"Shut up and help me," Harlan says. "Both of you."

He instructs his sons to carry the man two hundred paces into the woods and deposit him behind a wide tree. Far enough away,

Harlan hopes, that the body will not be seen or smelled from the trail any time soon. "Wear your gloves," he tells them, re-sheathing the knife at his hip. "And don't let him drag."

As Otto and Joseph bear the man away, Harlan pockets the lamp and turns to Junior.

"I know, I know," he says, shaking his head. "Don't look at me like that."

"Like what?"

Harlan sweeps his boot back and forth along the muddy trail to smooth over the odd bunching of footprints and to cover the scrim of blood with earth. He's surprised to find his stomach has gone sour. "No witnesses," he says. "That's how it has to be."

"People go missing," Junior says, "and other people come looking."

"By the time they do, we'll be long gone."

Junior shrugs and points. "Dibs on his walking sticks."

Harlan stops sweeping. "What?"

"Sometimes my knees hurt."

"Fine," Harlan says. "But let's get this straight. Dibs is not how we're going to operate when we get there."

Junior blinks and looks at him. "Dibs is how everything operates."

Minutes later, Otto and Joseph return from their task, their chests heaving and their faces slick. Otto gives his younger brother a wary look, then approaches Harlan alone. When he speaks, he keeps his voice low.

"Pop—"

"Was he still breathing when you left him?"

Otto trains his eyes on his own feet, a drop of sweat dangling from the tip of his nose.

"Was he?"

Otto shakes his head. He hesitates for a moment longer, then asks, "Maybe we should go, Pop? Before someone else comes along?"

Harlan pats his son's hunched neck. "You're right, of course."

The four grunt and sway as they re-shoulder their packs. Wooden edges and sharp points dig into Harlan's back and buttocks through the canvas, and the straps strain against his burning shoulders. But he welcomes this discomfort for what it means. This, at last, is their final trip.

This time, they're leaving for good.

They fan out along the edge of the trail, the ground sopping under their boots. Droplets rain down, shaken free from the canopy by a gust of wind, and Harlan turns his face up to feel the cool prickle on his skin. Then he nods to his companions, wipes the water from his eyes, and steps into the rustling thicket.

The others follow after him, marching as quickly as their burdens allow.

Melting into the trees and the undergrowth.

PART I: DRIFT

TSULA

CHAPTER TWO

October 26

By the time the two vehicles she's expecting appear at the far end of the service road, Tsula is already glazed with a slurry of sweat and south Florida sand so fine it should really be called dust. She hasn't exerted herself in the slightest—she parked, got out of her vehicle, waited for the others to arrive—but already she longs for a shower. She wipes her brow with an equally damp forearm. It accomplishes little.

"Christ almighty."

Tsula grew up in the Qualla Boundary—the one hundred square miles of western North Carolina held by the federal government in trust for the Eastern Band of Cherokee Indians—and had returned to her childhood home two years ago after a prolonged absence. This time of year in the Qualla, the mornings are chilly and the days temperate, autumn having officially shooed summer out of the mountains. In northern Wyoming, where she'd spent nearly two decades of her adult life, it takes until mid-morning in late October for the frost to fully melt. Tsula understands those rhythms—putting on layers and shedding them, freezing and thawing. The natural balance of it. But only miles from where she stands, in this same ceaseless heat, lies the Miami-Dade County sprawl. It baffles her. Who but reptiles could live in this swelter?

Tsula raises her binoculars. A generic government-issued SUV, much like her own, leads the way. An Everglades National Park law enforcement cruiser follows close behind.

She looks down at her watch: 11:45 a.m.

Tsula flaps the front of her vented fishing shirt to move air against her skin. The material is thin, breathable, and light tan, but islets of brown have formed where the shirt clings to perspiration on her shoulders and chest. She removes her baseball cap, fans her face, and lifts her ponytail off her neck. In this sun, her black hair absorbs the heat like the hood of a car, and she would not at all be surprised to find it has burned her skin. For a moment, she wishes it would go ahead and gray. Surely that would be more comfortable.

The vehicles pull to a stop next to her, and two men exit. Fish and Wildlife Commission Investigator Matt Healey approaches first. He is fifty-something, with the tanned and craggy face of someone who has spent decades outside. Tsula shakes his hand and smiles.

"Special Agent," he says, scratching at his beard with his free hand.

The other man is younger—in his late twenties, Tsula figures— and dressed in the standard green-and-gray uniform of a law enforcement park ranger. He moves with a bounding and confident carriage and thrusts out his hand. "Special Agent, I'm Ranger Tim Stubbs. Welcome to Everglades. I was asked to join y'all today, but I'm afraid they didn't give me much other info. Can someone tell me what I'm in for?"

"Poachers," Healey answers. "You're here to help us nab some."

"We investigate poaching every year," Stubbs says, nodding toward Tsula. "Never get the involvement of the FBI."

"ISB," she corrects him. "Investigative Services Branch? I'm with the Park Service."

"Never heard of it," Stubbs says.

"I get that a lot."

Whether he knows it or not, Stubbs has a point. The ISB rarely, if ever, involves itself in poaching cases. Most large parks like Everglades have their own law enforcement rangers capable of looking into those of the garden variety. Federal and state fish and wildlife agencies can augment their efforts where necessary. At just over thirty Special Agents nationwide, and with eighty-five million acres of national park land under their jurisdiction from Hawaii to the U.S. Virgin Islands, this little-known division of the Park Service is too thinly staffed to look into such matters when there are suspicious deaths, missing persons, and sexual assaults to investigate.

But this case is different.

"It's not just what they're taking," Healey says. "It's how much they're taking. Thousands of green and loggerhead turtle eggs, gone. Whole nests cleaned out at different points along Cape Sable all summer long. Always at night so cameras don't capture them clearly, always different locations. They're a moving target."

"We've been concerned for a while now that they may be getting some assistance spotting the nests from inside the park," Tsula adds. "So, we're keeping it pretty close to the vest. That's why no one filled you in before now. We don't want to risk any tip-offs."

"What would anyone want with that many eggs?"

"Black market," Healey says.

"You're kidding."

Healey shakes his head. "Sea turtle eggs go down to Central America where they're eaten as an aphrodisiac. Fetch three to five bucks apiece for the guy stateside who collects them. Bear paws and gallbladders go over to Asia. All kinds of other weird shit I won't mention. And, of course, there are the live exotics coming into the country. Billions of dollars a year in illegal animal trade going all over the world. One of the biggest criminal industries besides drugs, weapons, and human trafficking. This many eggs missing— it's like bricks of weed or cocaine in a wheel well. This isn't some guy adding to his reptile collection or teenagers stealing eggs on a dare. This is commerce."

Tsula recognizes the speech. It's how Healey had hooked her, and how she in turn argued her boss into sanctioning her involvement. "Sure, most poaching is small-potatoes," he told her months ago. He'd invited her for a drink that turned out to be a pitch instead. "Hicks shooting a deer off-season on government land and similar nonsense. This isn't that. You catch the right guys, and they tell you who they're selling to, maybe you can follow the trail. Can you imagine taking down an international protected species enterprise? Talk about putting the ISB on the map."

"So maybe that's what's in it for me," Tsula said, peeling at the label on her bottle. "Why are you so fired up?"

He straightened himself on his stool and drew his shoulders back. "These species are having a hard enough time as it is. Throw sustained poaching on top, it's going to be devastating. I want it stopped. Not just the low-level guys, either. We put a few of them in jail, there will always be more of them to take their place. I want the head lopped off."

Tsula had felt a thrill at Healey's blunt passion and the prospect of an operation with international criminal implications. Certainly, it would be a welcome break from the child molestation and homicide cases that ate up her days and her soul, bit by bit. It took three conversations with the ISB Atlantic Region's Assistant Special Agent in Charge, but eventually he agreed.

"This better be worth it," he told her finally. "Bring some people in, get them to tell us who they're working for. We may have to let the FBI in after that, but you will have tipped the first domino."

Their investigation had consumed hundreds of man-hours

across three agencies but yielded little concrete progress for the first several months. Then a couple weeks ago, Healey received a call from the Broward County State Attorney's office. A pet store owner under arrest for a third cocaine possession charge was offering up information on turtle egg poachers targeting Everglades in a bid for a favorable plea deal. Two men had recently approached the store owner, who went by the nickname Bucky, about purchasing a small cache of eggs they still had on hand. It was toward the end of the season, and the recent yields were much smaller than their mid-summer hauls. Since many of the eggs they'd gathered were approaching time to hatch, the buyers with whom the two men primarily did business were no longer interested. The two men were looking for a legally flexible pet store owner who might want to sell hatchlings out the back door of his shop.

Tsula decided to use Bucky as bait. At her direction, he would offer to purchase the remaining eggs but refuse to conduct the sale at his store. The strip mall along the highway, he would explain, was too heavily trafficked for questionable transactions. But he knew a quiet place in the pine rocklands near the eastern border of the park where he liked to snort up and make plans for his business. They could meet there.

"Do I really have to say the part about snorting up?" Bucky had asked her, scratching his fingernails nervously on the interrogation room table. "I really don't want that on tape. My parents are still alive."

"You think they don't know already?" Tsula said. "You don't like my plan, good luck with your charges and your public defender here. How much time do you figure a third offense gets you?"

At his lawyer's urging, Bucky finally agreed. The plan was set in motion, with the operation to take place today.

"So how are we looking?" Healey asks.

"Bucky's on his way," Tsula says. "I met with him earlier for a final run-through, got him mic'd up. We're going to move the vehicles behind the thicket over there and wait. I've scouted it out. We'll be concealed from the road. The purchase will take place about 12:30. As soon as Bucky has the eggs, we make our move."

"I'll secure the eggs," Healey says. "You guys reel in some assholes."

Tsula looks at Stubbs. His jaw is clenched, his eyes suddenly electric. "I'll ride with you when it's time, if that's alright," she says. "Keep it simple."

They move their vehicles behind the wall of climbing fern and ladies' tresses. Tsula exits her SUV, takes a concealed vantage point behind the brush, and raises her binoculars. To her left, a breeze has picked up and is swaying the distant sawgrass. A golden eagle circles effortlessly on a thermal, its attention trained on something below. Directly beyond the thicket where she stands, a large expanse of grass spreads out for a quarter mile before giving way to a dense stand of pine trees. To her right, that same open field stretches perhaps two miles, bordered by the service road on which Healey and Stubbs had just come in. All is silent but the soft hum of the breeze.

Bucky's rust-colored compact bounces up the road around 12:15 and disappears as it passes on the opposite side of the thicket. Minutes later, a mud-flecked pickup on oversized tires proceeds the same direction up the road, dragging a dust plume like a thundercloud behind it.

Tsula turns, nods to Healey, and climbs quietly into Stubbs's cruiser. She inserts her earpiece and settles into the seat. Stubbs looks over at her expectantly, his hand hovering over the ignition.

Tsula shakes her head. "Not yet."

CHAPTER THREE

"Go."

The cruiser cranks and shoots around the brush, lights and sirens blaring, Healey's SUV in tow. Bucky steps out of his vehicle, hands held high, and kneels to the ground. No sooner has Stubbs pulled his vehicle to a stop and opened his door than the truck throttles loudly, fishes to the right, and tears off at an angle into the grassy expanse. Before Tsula can speak, Stubbs slams his door and launches the cruiser down the service road. He's nearly standing on the gas pedal.

"What are you doing?" Tsula says over the engine's growl, gripping the ceiling handle tightly.

"You want these pricks, don't you?"

The truck's diesel roar is deafening even at this distance. Its tires, large and deep-treaded, claw the ground and leave a wake of sand and saw palmetto leaves. Black smoke billows from twin stacks at the rear of the cab. At this pace, Tsula believes the truck will reach the far end of the expanse and the road beyond before Stubbs can cut it off. They will all be on public streets headed out of the park before they know it.

Tsula wants to tell Stubbs to slow down, that they should radio ahead for assistance. That they have enough information already to catch up with them in any event. But just then the truck's front end dips down into a long depression in the grass and shoots back out the other side. The rear end follows, and soon the truck is seesawing on its oversized shocks. It yaws to the left, overcorrects the other direction, and enters a furious roll.

Something launches from the spinning vehicle's window and arcs through the air, like a flare fired from a foundering ship. A body, Tsula realizes as the object descends. Arms flailing as though to reach for something solid, legs bicycling in panic. And then it disappears in the ground cover.

"Holy shit." Stubbs brings the cruiser to an abrupt, sliding halt.

After several revolutions, the truck comes to rest on its side in a haze of dust and smoke, one front tire still spinning ineffectually in the air. A second occupant pokes his head out of the now glassless passenger window pointing toward the sky. He hoists his body out and drops to the ground. Steam from a cracked radiator briefly obscures Tsula's view of the man. Then he emerges, running in a wavering line toward the copse of pines, looking back over his shoulder at them.

Stubbs steers the cruiser into the field and pulls to a stop again a short distance from the wreck.

"You track the runner," Tsula says. Stubbs nods, and she springs from the vehicle in the direction of the body that had taken flight.

What Tsula finds when she approaches is less a human form than a crumple of its constituent parts—all purpling skin and unnatural angles from which she can detect no breath. She places two fingers over the carotid. Nothing.

"Shit," she mutters. This was supposed to be simple. Clean.

She lifts her radio to request medical assistance from dispatch, for whatever good that will do, but stops cold when she hears a pistol shot from somewhere in the distance. She looks up, her eyes scanning the breadth of the field.

The trees.

She takes off running.

Over her radio, Healey shouts for backup and an ambulance, his voice breathless and a full octave higher.

At the tree line, she hears the rustling of dirt and pine needles underfoot. The impact of bodies colliding. Muted cursing. She steps from the daylight into the shadow of the canopy, sidearm drawn. When her eyes adjust to the lower light, she spots Stubbs at a distance of twenty yards. He's standing stock still and facing her, his head hunched slightly, his eyes wide.

"Stay right where you are, bitch," a thin and raspy voice says. It comes from behind Stubbs, though the speaker is hidden by the ranger's broad frame.

"He has my gun," Stubbs says, his voice quaking. "I didn't see him and then . . . Oh, Jesus."

Tsula closes her eyes and takes a long, slow breath to calm herself. "Drop the weapon, sir," she says and takes two cautious steps forward.

"Come any closer and I'll fuckin' drop him."

Tsula breathes again deeply and takes two more steps. She has no desire for an exchange of gunfire with this man, but she wants to close the distance between them just in case. With Stubbs in the middle, accuracy will be critical. "You drop him and there's nothing between you and me. You don't want that, sir. I promise you that."

"You don't know what I fuckin' want. Where's Red?"

"Is that the other guy who was with you?"

"Yeah. He okay?"

"I think you know the answer to that already."

For a moment, silence envelops them. Then the voice returns, agitated and loud. "You bitch. He had kids, man. Little ones. He was just tryin' to make some money for them. And y'all wanna kill him over some fuckin' turtle eggs?"

"Special Agent," Stubbs calls out. "Take this shithead out, please."

"Shut up, ranger."

"That how this is gonna go?" the voice shoots back. Stubbs grimaces and nudges forward a half-step. For a brief second, Tsula sees the black metal of a muzzle angled up to the base of his skull.

"Stay calm, sir," Tsula says. "I promise you that is not how I want this to go. But you get amped up with that gun in your hand, and I start getting concerned what you're going to do next. That's bad for you. Now, let's just talk for a minute, see if we can't figure this mess out. Can you tell me your name?"

"Fuck. You."

"Pretty sure that's not it," she says. "I tell you what—we'll start with mine. It's Tsula."

"Choo-la?" he says. "What the hell kind of name is that?"

"All due respect, that's not how this works, sir. I gave you my name. Now it's your turn."

A brief silence, and then: "Eddie."

"Okay, good. I believe in straight talk, Eddie. So here's the deal. Red's hurt bad. I don't know if we can help him at this point, but we're going to try. The only thing I can tell you right now is that no one else has to get hurt. Just lay down the weapon and put your hands up, and this will all be over."

"Hell with that," Eddie says. "I'm getting out of here, and I'm taking this asshole with me."

"How, Eddie? You're not driving out. The truck is done for."

"I don't need no truck."

"You won't survive on foot," Tsula says.

"How the hell you know what I can do?"

"I know it's ungodly hot and there's no water out here you can drink. We don't haul you in, you'll be dead in two days."

Another silence. For the first time, a sliver of bare shoulder peeks out from behind Stubbs. Eddie is letting his guard down, paying less attention to his position. Progress.

"Eddie, do you have kids you're trying to feed, too?"

"None of your *fuckin' business*."

"I'm just trying to talk with you, Eddie. Remember what I said about getting amped up? I'll ask you again: Do. You. Have. Kids?"

"Three."

"You want to see them again, don't you?"

"Don't matter what I want," Eddie says. "Y'all don't shoot me, you're gonna lock me up."

"Those are two very different things, Eddie. One of those scenarios, you're still alive and they still have a father."

The sound of sirens drifts faintly through the trees. Stubbs glances in the direction of the sound and then to Tsula. She shakes her head gently to discourage whatever the young man is thinking: *Just stay put.*

"I set down the gun," Eddie says, "how do I know which option you're gonna choose? I watch the news, you know."

Tsula lowers her muzzle halfway to the ground. The sirens are growing louder. "I really, really don't want to shoot someone today, Eddie. And you don't want to die. So let's come to an agreement. You put the gun down on the ground, and I'll holster mine, and this can all be done. Deal?"

Eddie is silent for another moment. "I do that, I want you to come pick it up. This asshole gets it, he'll shoot me for sure."

Stubbs opens his mouth to speak, but Tsula cuts him off. "So, ranger, if Eddie does what I ask, you'll stay right where you are, won't you?"

Stubbs closes his mouth and nods. He swallows hard, his Adam's apple bobbing.

"Say it out loud so Eddie can hear you."

"Yes." The word comes out choked and halting.

"Seems we have a deal, Eddie," she says. "So how about we make this happen?"

Eddie lays the pistol on the ground and shoves it forward with one dingy sneaker. Half a bearded face peers from behind Stubbs's torso, watching for her next move. Slowly, deliberately, she holsters her own weapon and steps forward.

As she lifts the other gun off the ground, Stubbs bends over, gulping air, and Tsula sees Eddie clearly for the first time. He's in his forties, she figures, his bare torso rangy and leathery brown. A broad stripe of speckled bruising crosses his collarbone and descends diagonally across his chest. Sand and brown pine needles cling to the sweat of his limbs. His eyes blink and dart deep within their orbits and will not meet her own.

"Down on the ground for me, Eddie," Tsula says. Eddie complies and soon is in handcuffs. "Good," she says and helps him back to his feet. "Now let's go."

As they trudge the field's broad expanse, a long procession of light-and-siren ranger vehicles arrives. She waves her one free hand in the air and points toward where Red lies, unmoving and barely visible.

Eddie begins to weep, his body hunching over as he walks. "Shit, Red. What do I tell his kids?" Tsula gives no response and urges him forward.

Behind them, Stubbs stops, hinges forward, and retches loudly onto his shoes.

# #

Several hours later—after Eddie is gone for processing and Red is gone to the morgue, after FBI agents from the local field office have shown and begun working the scene, and after she has answered the same questions several times about where things went sideways—Tsula sits slumped in the driver's seat of her SUV. Her eyes are heavy, the adrenaline having finally worn off. To her left, the melon disk of the sun buries itself in sawgrass. The hard, flat light of the afternoon has softened and is fading.

Her phone rings, the sound startling in that quiet. A western North Carolina area code, 828, but she doesn't recognize the number.

"Is this Tsula Walker?" the female voice on the other end asks.

"It is."

"This is Nurse Eaton from the Emergency Department at Cherokee Indian Hospital. Our records have you listed as the emergency contact for Ms. Clara Walker."

A cold panic washes over Tsula. "That's my mother."

"I'm calling because she collapsed at home and was brought in by ambulance. We're trying to figure out what's going on, but given her condition, we're thinking we're going to have to transfer her to Harris Regional over in Sylva."

"Christ," Tsula says, resting her forehead against the steering wheel. "What now?"

CHAPTER FOUR

October 27

"So, unfortunately, there it is." Dr. Henderson taps the monitor with his pen. "Do you see it?"

Tsula does see it, and her body deflates.

In the two years since her mother's cancer diagnosis, doctors have shown Tsula at least two dozen CT scans of her mother's chest, abdomen, and pelvis. Initially, it struck her as an unthinkable invasion—a glimpse into secrets that her mother could not provide on her own, even if she wished to do so. But thanks to a patient oncologist and extensive research at home, Tsula has come to embrace these studies for the information they offer. She even takes pride in the facility with which, after so much practice, she can interpret the images.

The key is thinking in three dimensions, much as she does when examining a crime scene. CT scans arrange the human form into thin, sequential segments, like slicing a bread loaf from heel to heel. Scroll through these images, and organs emerge piece by piece, growing to their full, monochromatic dimensions, before shrinking and disappearing again into the ordered miracle of the body. Tsula has learned to identify the luminescent vertebrae, ribs, and pelvic bones. She can spot the ashen orb of the bladder and the scalloped and serpentine colon, their interior spaces, when empty, a shocking black. She appreciates the distinctness of the organs' borders: crisp lines separating each from each. Except where a malignancy spans the structures and obliterates their clean limits, or takes up residence in their free spaces, filling the black void with a mealy gray. Doctors call such a tumor "invasive"—a label both blunt and oddly poetic. Marauding hordes of cells ransacking the neighboring village.

Where Dr. Thompson's pen touches the screen, a new scaffolding of tissue extends from her mother's colon across to the rind of her bladder. Tsula had seen a similar form on scans two years ago, back before the surgeon removed it along with part of her mother's colon.

"So it's back," she says. Her eyes stray from the monitor to her mother. Clara Walker sits up in her bed, looking down at her sheets like she might have spilled something on them.

"I'm afraid so," Dr. Henderson says. "And I think it's actually managed to reach the bladder this time."

"The surgery, the chemo—none of it worked?"

Dr. Henderson adjusts his glasses and places his pen back into the pocket of his lab coat. "I wouldn't say that. It slowed down the progression for a while. Sometimes that's the best you can hope for. But this is why I recommended she come back in more frequently for repeat scans. You can never be certain it's not lurking somewhere else that you just can't see yet. It's been too long since the last scan. This doesn't happen overnight."

"I'm right here, Jimmy," Clara says, adjusting the pillow behind her back. "You can talk to me, you know."

He smiles and gives Tsula a knowing wink. Long before he left the Qualla Boundary for college and medical school at the University of North Carolina, James Henderson, M.D., had been known simply as Jimmy—the lanky son of Beverly Henderson and Cherokee Police Department Lieutenant Frank Henderson who lived down the road. Even after he moved back home, fresh from his hematology-oncology fellowship at Carolinas Medical Center, Tsula's mother had refused to call him anything else. It didn't matter that he had an office in a building in Sylva with "James Henderson, M.D. - Medical Oncology" on the sign out front or that the *Cherokee One Feather* had done a lengthy profile several years ago, proudly proclaiming his return to the mountains where he'd grown up. To Clara Walker, he was still just another kid from Yellowhill.

"Yes, ma'am, I know you're right there," he says. "I also know you don't listen to me, so I'm talking to your daughter. I'm hoping maybe she can get through to you."

Clara snorts and shoves her blanket down to her waist. "You'd have better luck just talking with me yourself."

"Alright, then." He rolls his stool closer to her bed until they're eye-to-eye. "I don't know if the cancer's progression has anything to do with why you passed out or why your kidneys aren't working right. We're not seeing spots in the kidneys on the imaging, so probably it's just your diabetes taking its toll, and we can give you dialysis for that." He points back toward the monitor. "But this is a significant problem. It's lucky you came in when you did. Otherwise, we may never have found this."

"Lucky," she says, folding her hands primly in her lap. "Somehow it doesn't feel that way."

"What's the plan?" Tsula says, a wave of nausea passing through her.

"Well, that needs to come out yesterday," Dr. Henderson says. "I'd like you to see the surgeon again as soon as we've got your kidney issues under control. Maybe I can get her to come see you while you're here. If not, we'll get you an appointment ASAP once you're out. I'll also need to refer you to a urologist. I don't know if the bladder can be saved. But the urologist and the surgeon can work together to determine the surgical plan. After that, I can try to get you into a clinical trial down at MUSC. They're testing out a new combination of chemo drugs for this kind of cancer that's showing some promise."

"No," her mother says. "No, I'm not doing any of that."

Dr. Henderson looks over at Tsula as though he's feared this response.

"Ms. Walker—"

"Shush," she says sharply. "I let you put me through all that once, but I'll be damned if I'm going to do it all over again."

"If you want, I'll be glad to refer you to a colleague over in Asheville. She may have some different ideas."

"That won't be necessary, Jimmy."

Tsula places her hand on her mother's shoulder. "Mom—"

"You shush, too. You may not believe it, but I've given a lot of thought about what I'd do if it came back. I don't want to spend my last days throwing up in my bed."

Tsula turns to face the back wall of the room. "Jesus."

"Ms. Walker, I want you to make your own choices about your health care," Dr. Henderson says. "It's your right, and I respect it. But first I need to make sure you are clear on what those choices are. The only treatments I am aware of that stand a chance of helping you are surgery and chemo. If we do nothing, it's going to get really bad, really quickly."

"The surgery and chemo were really bad." She reaches her hand up to pull wispy strands of her thinned hair taut. It never grew back completely, and she's complained to Tsula about it almost daily since it fell out.

"Worse," he says, his eyes pleading. "It'll be much worse."

"Mom, please." Tsula walks to the bed and places her hand on Clara's shoulder. "We can't be done trying. We can't throw away everything you've done because of one setback."

In truth, she worries that they've already thrown all the hard work and progress away, and she curses herself for her role in that waste. She had given in when her mother first begged for a break from all the scans and doctors and talk of prognoses. Given all she had endured up to that point, they agreed she could delay her next scan by one month. But in a month, they would go, even if Tsula had to tase her mother to get her in the car.

It was easier to put it off the second time, considering how the respite seemed to rejuvenate her. What would one more month mean? And wasn't her mother's improved demeanor proof that they were doing the right thing for her, on balance? So it had gone, month after month, their common resolve chipped away in increments. Now, it was nine months since her last scan—well beyond the recommended time for follow-up.

"I can be done, if I choose," Clara says. She reaches up to pat her daughter's hand. "It's still my decision, dear."

Tsula pulls her hand back and folds her arms. She's seen this face before, has heard this tone. The room is beginning to blur, and she looks down at the floor, unwilling to give her mother the satisfaction of seeing her tear up.

"Okay. I understand," Dr. Henderson says, regrouping. "This is distressing information, I know. There's no need for rash decisions. Just talk with Tsula. Take some time to think this all through."

"I will," Clara says in a tone that clearly means the opposite. "Now, what's it going to take to get me home?"

He nods and smiles weakly. "Your kidneys aren't working well, as I told you earlier. That's why you were so out of it when you came in. Thanks to the round of dialysis yesterday, your labs look a little better today, and you're obviously more alert. We'd like for you to have a couple more rounds, and then if all's well afterward, I can let you go in a few days. Deal?"

"Okay, Jimmy. Deal."

"Okay. Now get some rest. They'll come get you for dialysis later today." He pats her hands and stands to go.

Tsula follows him out the door, and he motions her down the hallway so that they can speak privately.

"She's obviously done listening to me," he says when they're far enough away. "What are the chances you can talk some sense into her?"

"I don't know," she says. For all their differences, she knows she inherited her obstinance from her mother. "You heard her. She's lumping me in with you."

"If you can think of any way we can get through to her—anyone she'll listen to—we need to do it, and soon. It's getting worse, fast."

"I was so good in the beginning," Tsula says, leaning back against the hallway wall. "I told myself, if I'm going to move back here for this, don't half-ass it. And now..."

Dr. Henderson turns and rests against the wall next to her, so close that their shoulders almost touch. "We just need to get her back on track."

"What if we can't? What happens next?"

He exhales slowly and looks over at her as though considering how much she can handle. "It'll spread further, obviously. Probably liver, brain. You're talking encephalopathy—her brain will stop working right. Bleeding issues, pain, swelling of the abdomen. It could spread to the bones. Which means you could be looking at fractures for no apparent reason, more pain. Eventually, her organs will start shutting down."

"How long?"

"Months, not years. That's the best I can tell you. It's aggressive."

"Can you guarantee her a cure if she agrees to the surgery and chemo?"

"Of course not," he says. "But it's her best shot. And the longer she waits, the less chance it will have of working. Not to put more pressure on you right now, but time really is of the essence."

At the other end of the hallway an alarm sounds, and a nurse walks swiftly into a patient's room.

"Not sure that's going to be good enough," she says. "She's stubborn as hell."

The alarm ceases, and for a moment all is quiet. The nurse exits the room, spots Dr. Henderson in the hallway, and gives him a thumbs-up.

"It was a great thing you did, coming back to take care of her," he says. "You've done so much to help her through this."

Tsula looks up at the ceiling and blinks away tears. "No, I blew this."

"You're a large part of why she's still here," he says. "She knows that, too. I have faith she'll listen to you."

"I'm glad one of us does."

When Dr. Henderson leaves, Tsula walks down the hallway to the bathroom and collects herself before returning to Clara's room. She remains at the hospital that entire day and says no more to her mother about cancer or surgery or chemotherapy. Best to let her rest and try again tomorrow.

Tsula stays until she catches herself nodding off in her chair, her head nearly slumped in her mother's lap. The prior evening, after receiving the news about her mother, she'd frantically arranged transportation for Eddie to his first appearance before the magistrate the next day. Then, after notifying the FBI case agent on the scene of her departure, she'd driven the whole night to reach Cherokee. Now the lack of sleep is finally taking its toll.

As she dozes, she dreams she's falling from a great height toward a flat, grassy clearing. The baritone buzz of the automated blood pressure cuff startles her awake just before she strikes the ground. She blinks, looks around, and waits for her heart rate to calm. Night has overtaken the room, and all is dark but for the lights on the monitors near the head of the bed. Her mother is sound asleep, her breathing soft and rhythmic.

Tsula knows she is no good to anyone in this state, so she resolves to get a few hours of decent sleep in her own bed and return in sharper condition tomorrow. Then she stands, kisses her mother softly on the forehead, and tiptoes out of the room. It is a thirty-minute drive home from Sylva even at this late hour, but the November night is bracing. In the driver's seat, she stifles a yawn and removes her fleece. She rolls down the front windows and prays the chilly air will keep her awake.

CHAPTER FIVE

November 3

After a week of long nights at the hospital and early mornings dedicated to work, Tsula allows herself a luxury. She sleeps in until 6:30. She thinks about visiting the dojo in Waynesville—she hasn't been in two weeks—but decides she's too tired. Instead, she takes a leisurely shower and drives to a restaurant along Cherokee's commercial corridor for breakfast. She orders her egg-and-cheese biscuit and coffee to go, crosses over the Oconaluftee River using the pedestrian bridge, and sits in the grass on the opposite bank.

The temperature is no more than forty degrees, though Tsula knows from the quality of the sunlight—a wide and burnished yellow, unimpeded by looming clouds—that the day will warm quickly. Her arms shiver from shoulders to wrist now, but by mid-day she'll be thankful she opted for only a fleece vest over her flannel shirt.

October color still hangs in the trees, though much diminished from its peak. Yellow birch and crimson maple leaves give way overhead and carousel slowly to the ground. Nearby, anglers wade into the river and cast lures in search of skittish trout. Tsula closes her eyes and takes in the susurrus of the stream as it flows around smoothed rocks rising up from the riverbed.

In anxious periods, Tsula takes an odd comfort in those stones. One can find them throughout this slice of western North Carolina—some small, like these, and others the size of modest homes. They were formed primarily from ocean sediment a billion or more years old and rendered strong and compact by heat and pressure. Continental collision excavated them from below the Earth's surface two hundred million years ago, leaving them to be worn smooth by water, wind, and time. They'd seen whole continents drift apart. They'd been stepped on and climbed over when her Cherokee ancestors arrived on this land ten thousand years ago. And in their presence, new people—different people— had hunted whole species to extirpation, stripped forests bare, and demonstrated a capacity for cruelty in all its forms. Slavery. War.

Removal.

Yet the stones remain, and will remain longer still after Tsula and everyone she knows is gone. On the scale by which geologic time is measured, her brief life is imperceptible. On the spectrum of calamity to which these rocks and boulders have borne witness, her own worries would hardly register. It soothes Tsula to think that her troubles, in the literal grand scheme of things, are nothing. Why, then, should she allow them much sway?

This is the conclusion she always reaches, though putting it into any meaningful practice is another matter. Her resolutions to take bad news in stride usually are forgotten as soon as the next bad news presents itself. Burned away like August dew, and just as quickly.

Her cell phone vibrates in the pocket of her fleece.

"How's your mom?" asks Brian Batchelder, Assistant Special Agent in Charge of the ISB's Atlantic Field Office. "She out of the hospital yet?"

"Not yet. Looks like later today."

"You there now?"

"No. What's up?" she says. Batchelder is a decent man and a good boss, but he is not someone who simply calls to check in. He wants something from her, and she fears what it might be.

"I know this isn't great timing," he says. "But I need your help. It's close by."

Tsula rests her forehead in her hand. "Definitely not good timing. How close?"

"Twentymile Ranger Station," he says. "Over near Fontana."

"I know it. What's going on?"

"A visitor found a body a couple hours ago. They're thinking suicide. But it looks like it's a park employee, so the chief ranger has called and asked us to take lead."

"There isn't anyone else in the Field Office who can take this?"

"The others are spread out all over the region right now. So no. I'd be happy to help out, get out of my office for a bit. But I currently have the boots of several superiors firmly implanted in my ass. You wanna know why?"

"Brian—"

"Because one of my agents was involved in a simple apprehension last week that ended with a suspect turned into hamburger. And now that the local press has picked up on it, people in Washington are starting to use words like 'accountability.'"

"What people?" Tsula asks.

"Pack-your-bags type people."

Her chest tightens. "Brian, we didn't make them run."

"But you did give chase."

She sighs. They have already been through this, more than once. "They didn't wreck because anyone was chasing them. They wrecked because they had a shitty driver. I'm sorry, but—"

"Sorry," he says. "Well, that makes two of us. We were supposed to have someone to question. The whole reason I agreed to you getting in on that investigation was the promise that we would get information on the distribution. But that dipshit y'all hauled in was clearly not the brains of the operation, and now . . ." He pauses, and when he speaks again, his voice is quiet. "You should be glad this request for help came in when it did. Otherwise, you'd be driving up here to take the abuse with me. I told you to take some time off, but you wanted to keep working, remember? So here's your chance."

Tsula looks down at her lap, and suddenly the sight of her breakfast makes her nauseated. "Mom's getting out of the hospital later today, Brian. I really need to be there."

"Look, they described a pretty basic scene. Dead guy, gun nearby. If it's that simple, you'll have plenty of time to finish up and meet your mom."

"It's never that simple, and you know it."

"Well, hope springs eternal," he says. "But it's an outdoor scene, so tick-tock."

She exhales noisily through flaring nostrils. In the distance someone hoots, and she looks up to see a fisherman thigh-deep in the river, holding his bowed fly rod steady as the line dances and darts. A companion nearby gives him a thumbs-up.

"Walker?"

"Yeah, okay," she huffs. "I'm jumping in the truck now."

CHAPTER SIX

The Twentymile Ranger Station is a humble rectangular structure situated on the sleepy southwestern edge of Great Smoky Mountains National Park next to a small creek bearing the same name. On each occasion she's found herself in this segment of the park, Tsula has wondered what purpose the station serves. She's never seen its doors open or spotted any outward signs of activity. As best she can tell, it functions primarily as a landmark—a monument marking the location of scarce parking and the trailhead for a network of lesser-known hiking trails.

As Tsula nears the turnoff onto the gravel approach, she notes cars parked on the shoulder of the two-lane road for easily a quarter mile in either direction. The narrow gravel access is similarly overrun. She drives slowly up the center of the narrow path, her tires grinding and slipping on fallen leaves and acorns. A rusting Jeep sits in the parking lot with its cloth top removed, a young man sullenly smoking a cigarette in the driver's seat. The remainder of the two small parking lots above and below the ranger station are occupied by law enforcement ranger cruisers, a fire truck, and an ambulance. They sit idle, their lights still flashing silently and bathing tree boles in pulsing colors. Firemen and paramedics mill about with nothing to offer but their presence.

The first law enforcement rangers on the scene had already strung yellow tape in a generous rectangle encompassing both the ranger station and an adjacent storage building and terminating where the ground drops down to the creek. A throng, mostly in Park Service attire, stand just outside the tape, staring across the scene toward the bobbing heads.

Bodies have been found in the park before. Only four months prior, Tsula investigated one such case just a few miles from here. A missing widower had been found well off the nearest trail, dead of what appeared to be a knife wound shaped like a coin slot in his abdomen. He was seated at the base of a wide elm as though he'd stopped to take a nap and simply forgotten to wake up. Foul play was obvious. Few people kill themselves in that manner, and a canvas of the area located no weapon. The victim's seated position would be a low and awkward angle from which to manage what, owing to the wound's vertical orientation, was likely an attack from directly in front of him. Tsula figured he had been moved behind the tree in an effort to conceal him from the nearby trail. Still, the act of placing him so carefully in a seated position had stuck with her. They just as easily could have laid him flat for the ground cover to conceal. Certainly, it would have meant less effort. So why this last gesture?

By the time she had been called in on that case, the scene was likely a month or more old, washed clean by rain and grown over as spring gave way to summer. Owing to the extent of bodily decay and the utter lack of witnesses or other solid leads, her investigation had now reached an impasse she doubts will ever be broken.

From the scene arrayed before her now, Tsula knows this new body means something entirely different. The tight bunchings of onlookers in hushed conversation. The watery eyes and mouths covered by fingers. This is how people gather when the dead is one of their own.

One small gap on the side of the gravel road, well past the ranger station, is the best she can manage for a parking spot. She velcroes on the vest announcing herself as a "FEDERAL AGENT," grabs a pack of evidence collection supplies and her digital camera from the back of the vehicle, and walks back toward the scene under the frayed canopy of red and orange. She pushes her way through the thicket of onlookers and toward a woman in green and gray posted just outside the tape. Unlike the others, she's not staring toward the back of the property. She's monitoring the crowd and the boundary they have established. When Tsula approaches, the woman introduces herself as Chief Ranger Amy Brannon.

Tsula tosses a thumb over her shoulder toward the throng behind her. "What's with the crowd?"

"Alex was part of the family," Brannon says with a shrug. "Word got out somehow, and now here they are. I've sent out instructions to stay away, but they just keep showing up. Now that they're here . . ." Her voice tails off, and she raises her hands, palms toward the sky, in a gesture of uncertainty.

Tsula studies the woman for a moment. The creases of her furrowed brow are numerous and deep, like contour lines on a topographical map. Dark bags underscore her red and liquid eyes.

"You can make me the bad guy," Tsula says, "but I'm going to need them gone unless they have some information to share. This many people just standing around the scene for no reason makes me nervous."

"I'll take care of it," Brannon says. "You want to meet the rest of your team?"

"That'd be great."

Brannon calls out: "Abbott, Cranford, Deal."

Three law enforcement rangers step forward from the front of the crowd.

"Special Agent Tsula Walker, this is Ranger Greg Abbott . . ."

A solemn block of a man, thirty-something and broad, nods to her.

". . . Ranger Levi Cranford . . ." is slight and tentative, with a salt-and-pepper goatee.

". . . and Ranger April Deal," a woman in her twenties, smiles and shakes Tsula's hand vigorously.

"First things first," Tsula says. "Let's talk roles. Who's our best photographer?"

The men point at Deal, and she nods.

Tsula hands her the camera. "Don't get creative. I just need them clear and detailed." Then she looks over at Cranford. "Can you sketch a scene?"

"Learned at FLETC," he says.

"Okay, you're it. And that means you"—she points at Abbott—"are searching for evidence with me. Now, where's . . . Alex, you said?"

"Alex Lowe," Abbott says. "Park wildlife biologist. He's down there, in the creek."

Tsula removes a small notepad and pen from her pocket and begins to scratch notes. "When was the last time anyone saw him alive? Do we know?"

"October 28. His supervisor says he left then on a solo backcountry trip for feral hog control. He was supposed to be back yesterday, but that, of course, was a Sunday. No known contact between October 28 and now."

Tsula nods and returns the pen and pad to her back pocket. "Alright, then," she says, lifting the tape. "Let's get to it."

Toward the back of the small property, Twentymile Creek flows through a ravine two to three feet deep and three times as wide. The waters of the creek, high and vigorous from recent rains, purl noisily around stones bearded with green moss and swatched with lichen.

There she finds the body, stretched across the frothing stream.

He's a little over five feet tall, Tsula estimates—certainly on the smaller side for a man—and situated prone with his boots toes-down on the bank. The remainder of him extends out toward the center of the creek, his chest resting on a flat rock barely peeking from the water and his face submerged to the corners of his eyes. A generous shock of bright red hair billows out from beneath a Park Service baseball cap and hovers above the surface. Tsula can tell from his clothing—waterproof shell covering thick underlayers, wool-lined pants with specks of dried mud around the ankles—that he'd spent recent time outside.

"So what else do we know so far?"

Abbott speaks up again. "Alex was found this morning about 7:00 a.m. by a hiker coming down to the creek to take photos. He appears deceased from a single gunshot wound to the head. There's a handgun near the body in the water."

"You're sure it's Alex?" Tsula asks.

Abbott nods grimly.

"And the hiker who found him?"

"Still here," Cranford says, "waiting in his vehicle in the parking lot."

"The Jeep?"

"That's right."

Tsula sidles carefully down the bank for a closer view of the body, then looks back up at her new team. "Have we found a backpack yet? Rifle?"

Abbott shakes his head. "Nothing yet. For all we know, he went home first and then came out here."

"Are any of the vehicles out there his?"

Abbott pauses, his lips pursed. "No," he says finally. "No. There weren't any out here other than the kid who found him."

"Probably not then, unless he had someone drop him off. We'll need to keep looking. Now, where's this gun?"

Cranford points to the creek a few inches to the right of Alex's head. Tsula steps closer and squints. There it lies, a dark, angular shadow resting on the creek bed, the shape distorting and righting itself beneath the water's surface.

She instructs Deal to photograph the weapon *in situ* and hands Abbott an evidence box from her pack. "I'm collecting the weapon."

Tsula dons latex gloves and wades into the stream. It's deeper than she anticipated and wets her halfway to her knees. Numbingly cold water pours into her boots. Her toes flex involuntarily, and her diaphragm tightens. "Christ," she groans, thrusting her arm in above the elbow. She pinches the trigger guard between her thumb and index finger and lifts the pistol out of the water.

"Revolver," she says, raising it to eye level. "Twenty-two."

Carefully, she releases the cylinder and examines the chambers. "Only one round missing."

Abbott approaches, and she secures the gun in the box.

Tsula squats then to examine Alex's head. On the right side, a small hole the width of a standard school pencil bores through his temple, surrounded by a rim of black stippling and a halo of erythema. On the left side, she identifies no corresponding exit wound. This is no surprise, given the caliber of the round. Still, she's thankful they don't have to search these surroundings for something so small as a bullet.

Tsula stands up, her knees burning, and leaves the creek. Water squishes noisily and seeps from her boots as she steps back up the embankment.

Within minutes, two men from the Medical Examiner's office arrive. The one with the scowl on his face makes his way into the creek and toward Alex's head. When they turn him over, Deal hides her expression behind the camera. Cranford gags loudly behind Tsula.

"Get out of my crime scene if you're going to do that," she barks over her shoulder.

The skin of the man's face is a marbled purple, the eyes cloudy and darkly splotched.

Tsula looks at Abbott. "Still him?"

"Jesus Christ," Abbott says, flinching. "Yeah, that's him."

Once the body is gone, Tsula instructs her team to resume their search of the area. "Let's see what we can see," she says. "Personal effects or gear, footprints, rifle."

But over the next few hours, their efforts yield nothing beyond the body and the gun. They expand the search area twice, and Cranford and Deal, having nothing further to sketch or photograph, join in. Still, they find no discarded backpack or other personal effects.

Tsula's interview with the hiker who found Alex similarly adds little, except to confirm the body was present at about 6:50 that morning. The young man puffs long on his cigarette, his hands trembling, and tells her he saw no one else in the vicinity. He assures her he touched nothing, but he had been videotaping when he came upon the body. She gives him her card and instructs him not to erase the footage or send it to anyone. She'll be in touch soon with a warrant for the camera and video.

After several hours, Tsula releases Deal and Cranford when it becomes clear the scene will yield no additional evidence. To Abbott, who has the carriage of an experienced and steady officer, she asks: "Are you able to help me with some other tasks?"

"Of course," he says. "What do you need?"

"We need whatever information we can dig up about who was here in the last two days. I'm talking backcountry permits, surveillance cameras that might have caught hikers or cars nearby, anyone who comes over here to clear trash or perform maintenance. Anyone we think might have seen anything, we need to know who. Can you assist me with that?"

He nods. "I'll get on it. You need me here any longer?"

"No, you can go."

Once she's alone, Tsula squats at the top of the bank and surveys the creek below again, hoping that a change in her vantage point might bring new revelations. A breeze picks up again and sends crumpled leaves skittering onto the surface of the stream. The water shuttles them downstream to be pressed against rocks, or else submerges them entirely. In the quiet, Tsula makes a mental list of tasks she'll need to complete soon. She needs to contact the ME about the autopsy. She needs a search warrant for Alex's residence and the witness's camera.

She needs to get out of her wet boots. She can't feel her toes.

It's then that her mother calls.

"I've tried you four times," she says when Tsula answers.

"Shit," Tsula whispers to herself, looking at the time and her phone's call history. She actually called five times, but Tsula has no appetite for correcting her. "Sorry, Mom. I got caught up with something."

"I thought you were going to be here this morning."

"So did I, but I had to do something for work. I'm on my way. I'll be there in like an hour."

"Hurry up, please. They're discharging me, and I'm going to be late."

"Late?" Tsula says. "Late for what?"

CHAPTER SEVEN

The church sanctuary smells of freshly powdered and vacuumed carpet—an unnaturally sweet smell that causes Tsula's nose to itch. She walks her mother, arm in arm, down the center aisle to the pews in the front row. "My eyes are so bad these days," Clara had said when they first entered. "I want to be able to see."

When they sit, Tsula clasps her fidgeting hands together. To distract her buzzing mind, she glances around the sanctuary. On the paneled wall behind the pulpit, a wooden board announces last Sunday's attendance (63), the prior week's (61), and the number of attendees who brought their own Bibles (26). Watercolors depicting the Bible's high points hang on the remaining walls. Adam and Eve marveling at an apple and a snake. Jesus kneeling in beatific prayer over a large stone and, elsewhere, hanging on the cross. Moses on the original Mt. Pisgah, not the one down the road, as angels reveal the Promised Land to him.

She can't help but find the last notion humorous. Of all the promises that can be made, those involving land are never to be trusted. It's history's one enduring lesson.

Beside her, Clara Walker faces forward, eyes earnest. But she has not come this afternoon for a sermon. In addition to the usual religious services, this particular church also hosts a number of gatherings organized to discuss matters of community import. This afternoon, a large screen hides the pulpit. The words projected on it are largely washed out by the full house lights, but when she squints, Tsula can barely make them out.

Stephens Cavern.

"What the hell?" she mumbles, turning toward her mother.

The woman's thin, sallow legs dangle loosely, barely reaching the maroon carpet beneath them. The rest of her is stooped but rigid, as though bracing against some unseen weight pressing down on her. No longer the force of nature who had ruled their home when Tsula was a child—the one with whom she'd fought so often and so fiercely. Clara Walker is diminished now. Fading from view.

"Mom," she whispers. "We've been through this."

"No sense in leaving now. All these people have seen you."

"I can't get involved."

Clara gives Tsula's hand a pat. "Go ahead, leave your sick mother in here alone, then. I'm sure you have calls to make or something for work. I just hope I don't have another episode while you're outside."

Tsula glares at her mother and the slight smile at the corners of the woman's mouth. At least her mind is still sharp. Tsula tries to take comfort in that.

More people file into the sanctuary behind them. A murmur of conversations and the creaking of wooden pews. A couple of women greet Clara and ask how she's feeling before taking their seats. Tsula keeps her face pointed toward the mauve carpet between her boots, praying for time to speed up.

Just before the doors close, Representative Thomas Weathers enters, doused in fresh aftershave despite the late afternoon hour. He shakes every hand as he passes down the aisle. Tsula had known Tommy Weathers in high school, though he was two years ahead of her. By the time she left for college, he was working as a paramedic for a regional ambulance company. A boy from Yellowhill turned first responder hero. When Tsula returned to the Qualla Boundary nearly two decades later, he'd made his way onto Tribal Council and metamorphosed into the consummate local politician—tidy and earnest, familiar with everyone, blessed with an uncanny instinct for what buttons to push.

To hear her mother tell it, he'd blazed onto Council like a rocket shortly before Tsula moved home, propelled by countless ideas to improve the lot of the Eastern Band of Cherokee Indians. His plans and enthusiasm often stunned the more complacent elements of the tribal government and earned him a fair share of resistance from those who preferred a more measured and compromising approach.

That, at least, is her mother's take. Tsula has heard others.

When Representative Weathers reaches the front row, he extends his hand first to Clara, his face all teeth and glinting eyes. "I understand you were in the hospital, Ms. Clara. I hope you are feeling better."

"As well as I can be, Tommy," she says, her voice suddenly lively and light.

He turns to Tsula next and tilts his head slightly. "Special Agent, a pleasant surprise."

"I'm just the driver, Representative. Please ignore my presence."

"Only a fool would do that."

Representative Weathers takes a position next to the screen and instructs someone in the back of the sanctuary to dim the lights. Then he nods, and a photo appears on the screen of a cave which, thanks to the presence of a person in the bottom right corner for scale, appears to be the width of a small gymnasium. A large industrial light has been placed in the center of the space, its aura barely illuminating etched limestone walls at the left and right edges of the frame. No stone ceiling can be seen at the top of the photograph, which gives the impression of limitless height.

"Karst," the Representative begins, his voice filling all corners of the dimmed sanctuary. "Anyone here know what that word means? Ever heard of it?"

The crowd is silent.

"Don't feel bad," he says. "Neither had I, until a couple of years ago. It's a geological term, German in origin, which describes a sort of miracle that goes on underground. See, there are springs and streams flowing deep beneath the ground we walk on. And sometimes, as it flows, that water chisels away at the layers of rock around it. Usually, the results are just small depressions in the earth, or sinkholes that open up and swallow what's on top of them. A nuisance, but nothing special. Then every now and then, you get this."

He points at the cavern on the screen and smiles, his eyebrows arching—*Can you believe it?*

"Two years ago, a man named Michael Stephens left Curry Mountain Trail on the Tennessee side of Great Smoky Mountains National Park and headed northwest through the mountains. When asked later what in the world he was thinking, he said he wanted to practice his orienteering skills and find his way down to the parking lot at the Sinks, where a car was waiting for him. More likely he'd missed the turnoff for the Meigs Creek Trail—the one that actually takes you to the Sinks—and was looking for a shortcut back to his destination. He almost made it. About a half mile from Laurel Creek Road, high on a hill, he stepped into a hole that was concealed by leaves and slid down about ten feet to a rocky ledge beneath the ground. Beyond that small ledge was a drop-off that we now know is more than a hundred feet to the cavern floor. He just missed going over, which certainly would have killed him. Mr. Stephens climbed his way back up to the surface, made it the rest of the way to the parking lot, and let a patrolling ranger know what he'd just stumbled upon. Park staff came and took a look. And so a series of underground caves just inside the boundaries of the park was 'discovered.'" He wraps quotation marks around the last word with his fingers. "The truth is, we now know this geological wonder was found at least once before, by the Cherokee."

He pauses for a moment, allowing the murmurs of a now engaged audience to rise.

"I'm sure you're wondering: Tommy, how can we be sure?" He smiles again, his eyes growing narrow and intent. "That's the good part."

Tsula already knows the answer. Inside a second entrance to the cave, hidden for generations at the bottom of that same hill, surveyors found markings on the limestone walls in the Cherokee syllabary. Since the exploration was still underway, few people beyond Park Service and Department of Interior specialists had been allowed in—ostensibly for safety reasons. However, a select few representatives of the Eastern Band—mostly members of the tribe's historic preservation department, who previously had examined similar drawings found in Alabama—were invited to examine the inscriptions. According to one participant, a scholar in the Cherokee language and syllabary, the writings suggested that a group had hidden there to avoid forced removal to the Indian Territory in Oklahoma. No official translation had yet been released, however.

In addition, in an alcove located several hundred feet behind that lower entrance lay a collection of incomplete human skeletons. Animals had made off with some of the bones, and what remained had been degraded by time and humidity. But after thorough examination and a battery of tests, forensic anthropologists believed it entirely possible the skeletons could date back as far as the 1830s and, therefore, could be the remains of Cherokee refugees.

It was an extraordinary find, covered in rapturous terms by every periodical from *National Geographic* to *The New York Times*.

But with the attention came the inevitable questions of how best to steward this new resource just inside the park's boundary. Weathers had made the issue a tentpole of his tribal council campaign, arguing that the cavern and enough land around it for ingress and egress should be deeded over to the tribe, either by means of sale or land swap. It would be simple enough logistically, he maintained, since the cavern was located just a stone's throw from Laurel Creek Road—hidden, until now, in plain sight. Seasoned leaders resisted taking such a position, cautioning that it would never succeed and would needlessly rankle the behemoth U.S. government to which too much was still beholden. Best to aim for what was achievable and not burn precious goodwill on a doomed quest.

Once elected, Representative Weathers embarked on a campaign to amass support both within the community and from those who held influence outside. He publicly asked enrolled members to shame the more conservative elements of the tribal government into joining the fight. Not content solely with the modest attendance at scheduled community club events, he found his constituents where he knew they'd be. Fairs and festivals. Twitter and Facebook. The churches that dot the Qualla's breadth. The homes of established families, where the older ladies—his specialty—held tremendous sway.

Forcing the veteran leaders' hands was a bold and politically dangerous gambit for a junior Tribal Council member, but to a small degree, it worked. The Principal Chief paired him with two elder statesmen who could smooth out Weathers's passionate edge and empowered this nominal "working group" to meet with federal government stakeholders and "explore their options."

Tsula gathered all of this from issues of the *Cherokee One Feather* her mother left lying around the house, and from the conversations she'd overheard around the Qualla Boundary but, up until now, had meticulously avoided. She knew of no instance where the Park

Service had turned land back over to the indigenous peoples who previously occupied them and had no reason to believe the federal government would approach this matter any differently. There was no sense, then, in taking any position in a dispute that inevitably would risk conflict with her employer, her neighbors, or both. She therefore maintained a veneer of ignorance and indifference, so as to avoid anyone thinking her a sister-in-arms.

"I was content, ladies and gentlemen, to play the long game in the beginning," Weathers continues. "Nothing with the federal government gets decided quickly, and the conventional wisdom is one must be patient. Push, but not too hard. Hell, some within our own government have told me, take it slow, don't rock the boat. And don't get your hopes up."

He takes a deep breath, winding up.

"What kind of wisdom is that? You know who has no hope of succeeding? Those who give up before they've even tried. And that's not how I'm built. But, ladies and gentlemen, I came here tonight to tell you that I am content to play the long game no longer. Two months ago, we received proof that park personnel are now referring to this living document of our history as 'Stephens Cavern,' after the gentleman whose only contribution was leaving a marked trail and nearly falling to his death."

He pauses again for the murmuring, this time louder and insistent.

"'Don't read into it,' the Park Service tells me. 'It's just informal. We'll allow the public lots of time to comment before we give it an official name.' That tells me all I need to know about where their heads are. Why should they be the ones giving it a name in the first place?"

Tsula knows then that she's made a terrible mistake in staying—not because she personally disagrees with anything he has said, but because she cannot risk publicly aligning herself with it. A community meeting to inform people on the facts is one thing. A rally like this is something else entirely. Those in the audience who know her mother will also know who Tsula is and who she works for. Clara Walker had made sure of that. Tsula searches in her peripheral vision for the nearest door and fantasizes about a quick exit.

"The truth is, I appreciate the park," Weathers says, and the comment elicits a smattering of hisses and boos from a back corner. "No, now, I do. It has saved part of our ancestral home from the clear-cutting and development that was destroying it. It's done some good. But it seems we have to keep reminding the federal government of our ties to this land. That we were here first. That they're the ones who made way for the timber companies and settlers the land eventually needed to be rescued from."

The audience grows louder still, a wave cresting as it nears the shore.

"It's been two centuries since the majority of our ancestors were removed from that land, and still we have to beg them for permission just to come on and harvest traditional plants that no one else gives a damn about. What do we expect they'll do with this living monument"—he points toward the screen—"unless we force them to change course? Tell us to get in line and buy passes like everyone else?"

The crowd answers the question with booming, disorganized voices. Some members clap their hands and rise to their feet.

"They have five hundred thousand acres inside the park's boundaries. They can part with this handful. Cherokee bones were found in there."

Tsula's mother seems to have found a reserve of energy and joins the clapping with vigor. Weathers nods, grinning. He's found his rhythm with the audience.

The sound is oppressive, the air in the sanctuary stagnant and hot. Someone behind Tsula pats her shoulder, but she won't turn around to see who it is. She closes her eyes and imagines she's back in Wyoming, sitting on her porch and watching for moose or coyotes in the silent distance. The morning air cold, dry, and sharp.

She hears little of what Representative Weathers says in conclusion, though she catches him looking directly at her several times. Likewise, she pays scant attention to the question-and-answer session that follows, except to wonder when it all will finally end.

When it does end, Weathers heads directly to Clara Walker. He holds out a crooked arm, says "May I?" and escorts her back down the aisle and out of the sanctuary. Tsula follows with her head bowed. In the vestibule, Weathers deposits Clara in a chair and then asks to speak with Tsula privately. Tsula glances at her mother, whose shrug of ignorance seems at odds with the grin on her face.

"Indulge me for a moment?" he says.

Tsula considers simply saying no, but she is loath to risk an awkward scene in front of her mother. Not now, after the news she's received. With a weak nod, she follows him around the corner to an adjoining hallway.

"You know," he says when they are alone, "this cavern could be the cause of a generation. I can't think of an issue on which there's been such strong support."

"Well," she replies, already eyeing her escape over his shoulder, "if there's anyone who can win over the people, I know it's you."

"That's no challenge when the cause is just," he says. "But we haven't gotten any traction with those who will make the decision. The Park Service, Interior, Congress—they give me meetings, they listen politely, they say vague things that sound encouraging. But then we leave, and no progress is made. Lately, I've come to the conclusion that the problem isn't the message, it's the messengers."

"I'm sure that's not it."

"I've been in the meetings, and I'm pretty sure it is. It's not surprising. Local tribal politicians they don't know come to their offices, asking to be given back land that was taken. Brings up uncomfortable history. Reminds them maybe we're still not square. Why would they want to admit that? It's much easier to pat us on the back, tell us they'll think about it, and send us on our way. But what if one of their own spoke out? Maybe someone with a foot in both worlds who could be the moral voice from within? That kind of messenger could get some attention the rest of us can't."

Tsula holds up a hand to stop him. "If you're about to ask me to do something that dumb, you can forget it."

"Many actions history now recognizes as courageous were once thought of as dumb."

"If it ends with me in conflict with my employer, I don't really care what you call it. I'm not interested. I don't have just myself to worry about."

A gleam enters the Representative's eyes, and he leans forward slightly as though to share a secret. "One might suggest," he says quietly, "that by working for the Park Service, you're already knee-deep in the conflict."

Owing to the advice of an early mentor, Tsula has forged a habit of avoiding outward displays of anger. *A lot of men don't know what to do with an angry woman other than dismiss her*, the mentor told her. *That's true of witnesses. It's true of suspects. It's even true of your colleagues. You gotta give some dude push-back, try smart-ass instead. Guys understand smart-ass. They've been at it since they were like five.*

It doesn't help that Tsula inherited her father's height—nearly six feet—but not his pale skin, or that her affinity for the defensive arts has rendered her frame broad and solid. Tsula is female, physically formidable, with skin just dark enough to inspire suspicion, if not hostility, from the small-minded—who, as it turns out, are everywhere. Over many years, she's honed a public persona designed to combat the inevitable assumptions about her: competent but not cocky, firm and unflappable, biting retort cocked but fired sparingly.

Still, for every rule in her life, she must allow the occasional exception.

"And some might suggest you shove that self-righteousness right up your ass."

The words come out louder than she intends, and immediately she fears others have heard her. Weathers leans back, his mouth gaping, and blinks several times as though he's just been struck in the nose.

"Tsula." The voice comes from behind her, and she turns and looks into her mother's disapproving face. The woman rests her right hand against the wall, as though steadying herself. "Shame on you."

"It's okay, Ms. Clara," Weathers says quickly. "It was my fault. My passion sometimes gets the better of me. I didn't mean to offend Tsula, though I see now that's what I've done. I'm sorry."

Tsula hangs her head and flexes her hands into fists. So much for avoiding an awkward scene. She attended the meeting and now has berated the Tribal Council member who organized it. Using such language in a church, of all places. Likely no one around them heard what prompted her reaction, just her response. Why hadn't she just left her mother in the sanctuary? She is angry with them all, but mostly with herself.

"Representative—"

"Please, call me Tommy."

"*Representative*, I recognize that my being here was a bit of a mixed signal," Tsula says. Her voice is softer now, her expression flat. "My mother neglected to tell me the topic of this meeting, or else I would not have come. I am sorry for my strong words, but let me make this clear so we never have to talk about this again, okay? Whether I personally agree with what you're doing is beside the point. I am no one's spokesperson. I am a law enforcement officer who values her job, and I am the daughter to a sick mother. That's it. Now tell me, please, you understand that."

He blinks again, then nods to her.

"Thank you."

"Let's go, Tsula," Clara says, tugging on her daughter's arm. "Tommy, thank you again for your hard work on this important issue. I would be honored to have you over to the house for dinner soon so we can continue the discussion."

His smile returns, though dimmed now. "You say the word, and I will be there, Ms. Clara. Good night to you both."

CHAPTER EIGHT

Neither woman utters a word until they are almost home. Clara Walker rides with the passenger window down, her face awash in the cooling November air. When they near the house, she turns to Tsula. "Why is it your intention to push everyone in our community away?"

"My community is you," Tsula says. "That's all I can worry about."

"Tommy Weathers is a good man."

"He just asked me to dive head-first into a dispute with the people who sign my checks. He's not stupid. He knows it's a losing battle, but he tried to pressure me anyway."

"He's not just asking for himself, you know."

"No shit. You set me up. But I have more important things I have to worry about."

"More important."

"You can sweat this issue all you want. Nobody's stopping you. But I've got to keep a roof over our heads."

The older woman snorts. The reaction takes Tsula by surprise, and its import settles and lingers heavy in the air between them. For as long as she can remember, Clara Walker has dwelled on the mundane needs and obligations of daily life. Rent. Bills. Food in the refrigerator and emergency cash beneath the mattress. She wouldn't now dismiss such concerns unless she believed she soon would be beyond their reach. Her mother, Tsula realizes, has decided she's dying.

A field spreads out on the opposite side of the road. Turkey hens bob and peck along its breadth and then stand erect as though to listen to the argument passing them by.

"You know, I understood why you wanted to leave for college," Clara says. "I even understood when you decided to stay out there for a few years after you graduated."

"You told me I should leave. Remember?"

"Because you were so unhappy here after Jamie died. You wouldn't talk. You stopped eating. You wouldn't come out of your room. It's not easy for a mother to watch her only child leave, but yes, I thought a change of surroundings would do you good if that's what you wanted. But I always figured you would return some day."

"And I have," Tsula says. "I'm right here."

Her mother shakes her head. "You're sitting right here, but you've still got one foot out the door."

"You don't exactly make it easy, you know, pulling stunts like that."

"Would you have moved back if I hadn't gotten sick?"

Tsula freezes, her eyes forward on the road, her hands tight on the steering wheel.

"Once I'm gone, are you going to stay?"

"Mom, don't talk that way."

"It's going to happen sooner or later, whether I agree to more treatment or not."

"But you'll consider it, right? The treatment?"

"Don't change the subject," her mother says. "I want you to answer the question. Will you stay?"

Tsula hesitates, then says, "I don't know."

"I do." Clara turns back to the open window. "After all this time, you're still the same girl who can't wait to leave."

Tsula is surprised by a dolorous stirring deep in her chest—one she has not known for many years. A faint movement of emotions she'd long ago packed away, entombed in graphite. She blinks away an ache behind her eyes and focuses on the road, the turns up ahead.

"You didn't need to bring him up," she says at length. "That's not fair."

They pull up to the house, and Tsula assists her mother toward the front door without another word. The twilight sky has faded to umber, and the air carries a chilly bite. From somewhere in the unseen distance comes the raspy, plaintive bugle of a bull elk in the rut. Tsula ushers Clara Walker inside and shuts the door on all of it.

HARLAN

CHAPTER NINE

May 10

They hike most of the day, stopping only toward evening when the rain threatens again. They have miles yet to go, but their packs will become impossibly heavy if they get wet. As the sky turns cobalt and the lightning flashes in the distance, Harlan Miles decides they should rest for the night. There's a large rock outcropping at the foot of a mountain just ahead that can provide adequate shelter. They've slept there before. They stop beneath the deep overhang and drink water from dimpled canteens. Now and then the wind changes direction and blows wet on their faces, a messenger bringing tidings of the deluge to come.

When the storm arrives, rivulets pour off the edge of the outcropping just beyond their feet, and they hold their open canteens beneath to refill. Water from the mountain streams carries giardia thanks to cattle runoff and will debilitate a man in a matter of hours if not boiled or properly treated. But the rainwater has not been exposed to the parasite and is potable. Harlan tilts his head upward at the edge of the overhang and allows the water to flow directly into his mouth. It tastes almost sweet, but with faint hints of the leaves and rock it has touched on its journey.

After the storm clears, the haze rises from the forest floor, but only just so high. It hangs like a shawl across the distant mountains' shoulders, obscuring all but their peaks. The men stare at the unmoving clouds and say little. They eat from bags of nuts, dried fruit, and venison jerky. For dessert, Harlan passes a jar of small gala apples he pickled last October, enough for one per man.

It's dusk by then, and slowly the gray sky gives way to night. Clouds hide the moon away and block out even its faint light. The occasional aura of lightning in the easterly distance allows fleeting views of the mountains: a sloping blackness, briefly backlit and then gone again.

The next day they'll hike a col between those mountains. On the other side, they'll follow a stream and then its branch for about an hour. They'll keep to a flat swath which a century ago was a horse path, and it will lead them home. The thought makes Harlan's heart flutter, though he is not a man generally prone to such reactions.

He reclines against his pack and looks around. The others have wasted no time dozing off. Joseph reclines against Otto's shoulder, contented looks on both of their faces. Junior snores loudly in a corner by himself. Harlan pays the sound no mind. After five years of camping with his friend, he has come to view this noise as a constituent element of the nighttime soundtrack—a rhythmic accompaniment to the buzzing cicadas, the infernal barred owl calls, and the occasional rustling of skulking creatures.

He tips his cap forward over his face and inhales deeply of the moist air. It seems to Harlan that he can smell the whole of these mountains' lives in that single breath. The gentle notes of wild herbs and grasses, of seedlings introducing themselves to the world. Also the thick and bittersweet must of leaf litter, felled trees, and decaying animals returning to the soil.

There is so much to do when they arrive at the homestead tomorrow, and his mind races through the priorities several more times. But it has been a long and draining day. In time, the ache in his thighs and hips abates, his eyelids droop, and his thoughts inevitably drift, as they often do, to the story his father told him about the homestead.

Harlan's great, great grandfather, Coleman Miles, boarded a steamship on the English coast in May of 1881 and, weeks later, set foot in the United States. He was twenty-one, bestowed by God with a strong back and a stubborn disposition. He had watched his own parents' farm in northern Britain sold off piece by piece to avoid financial ruin, and he had read the letters of those who had preceded him across the Atlantic, which gave reports of vast, untamed wilderness on which a man could build a new life. He left behind a wife named Fannie, whom he'd married the year before, and who sent him with her blessings.

Some months later, Coleman found himself in the mountains of North Carolina. He purchased his plot—nearly twenty acres—from a graying man named Meaney. Per the documents shown to Coleman at the time of purchase, Meaney's father had bought the land from a Cherokee in 1829. Black ink commemorated the acquisition on parchment paper bearing two signatures—one belonging to Meaney's father, the other a scribble that Meaney told him was the Cherokee's mark.

At the time of Coleman's purchase, a one-room log cabin and a small, single crib barn sat on the property. Meaney had long ago built those structures for a daughter and her new husband. They died in the 1830s, though, for reasons Meaney would not share. After their deaths, the old man could not bear to set eyes upon the land, much less to occupy it.

Coleman purchased the land in 1881 and immediately sent word for Fannie to join him.

I have obtained our parcel in Paradise as I promised you when I departed. Come, let us raise our children in it.

Love,

Coleman

P.S. I have also purchased an ageing horse to assist us in the fields.

It was indeed Paradise. The tract's centerpiece was a flat, grassy glade flanked on three sides by the foothills of a deep mountain range. The surrounding slopes were low and gradual, allowing for ample sunlight throughout the day. A small branch at the back edge of the property provided reliable water thanks to the plentiful rainfall the region received. While not enough to permit farming on a commercial scale, it was sufficient to grow enough crops to feed a family and still have something left over to sell. The lush land also attracted a fair number of deer and rabbit—especially once the root vegetables began to grow.

The property provided some challenges as well—chief among them, its isolation. The geography allowed for ingress and egress only from one relatively narrow hollow through the forest. The prior owner had cleared a small path which, at the far edge of the property, connected to a horse trail, which in turn connected to a larger road some five miles later, and so on. It took a half day's journey on horseback, or a full day on foot, to get to the nearest town of any size for provisions. (That town now lies beneath the waters of Fontana Lake.)

Fannie joined Coleman the following year, and they proceeded to have five children. Three would survive to adulthood. Two died within hours of birth.

With the help of some men from town, Coleman built a new cabin more suited to raising a family of five. The children spent their days trouncing around the glade and hiding from each other among the elm and birch trees. There was no school nearby, so Fannie did her best to teach them to read until the boys were old enough to take part in the many backbreaking tasks that life on the farm required.

They grew corn, potatoes, radishes, carrots, tomatoes, squash, and peas. Over time, Coleman made room for tobacco, which he found could fetch a good price in town when he didn't dry and smoke it all himself. They hunted deer, turkey, and rabbits with a rifle Coleman bought off a former Confederate soldier. And when time permitted, they trekked to a larger stream nearby to catch speckled trout on hooks baited with corn kernels.

As time passed, Coleman and Fannie were reminded that Eden is, as the Bible forewarns, impermanent. Their daughter Ruth met a man who worked for the nearby lumber mill when she was sixteen and agreed to marry him a week later. She left and rarely returned. The youngest child, Edward, was drafted by the Army during World War I and died in Europe—not of mortar shells or mustard gas, but of influenza.

Only the middle child, Lowell, refused to leave his parents' home, even when he married and had two children of his own. Coleman and Fannie gladly accommodated his family. He was what remained of their quickly shrinking world.

Coleman and Fannie died about a year apart in the late 1920s—she of pneumonia and he of a strange illness that grew lumps in his neck. Their deaths, coming as they did so close together, clouded Lowell's mind. He partook heavily and too often of moonshine he purchased from a man in town. At times he would neglect his family, disappearing into the surrounding forest and foothills for days on end, living on morels and wild blackberries. He claimed his mother and father's ghosts resided in the woods and he would commune with them there. His wife and children—one of whom was Harlan's deceased Grandpa Miller—grew concerned for the state of his mind.

By some miracle, the crops kept growing, and the family

continued to eke out a living, if only just so. In 1930, however, men showed up to inform Lowell that his land had been slated to become part of something called a "national park." He was not quite certain what the news meant, except that the men seemed to be insisting that he sell them the farm. He laughed at the men and told them to see their way back out.

But they returned several more times to insist upon the purchase. Each time he ran them off with the rifle, though the last time they threw some papers down on the ground as they fled. Those papers provided him notice that his property was being "condemned." He knew this word from reading the New Testament with his mother but thought its use strange in this context—as though land could die an unredeemed sinner.

Lowell and several other men pooled a small pot of money together and consulted an attorney in Bryson City. He explained with bowed head that there was nothing to be done. Others had filed lawsuits to protect their homes and failed. According to the courts, the States of Tennessee and North Carolina had the right to take the land and deed it over to the U.S. government. It was not a matter of whether they would all lose their farms, but how much they would be forced to accept in exchange. The only option was to bargain for higher prices.

When the sale of the farm finally closed, Lowell and his family were given a brief period of time to pack up their belongings and depart. Lowell hired a man in town with a horse and buggy to collect Lucille, the children, and their few belongings. The man would carry them to a hotel in town while Lowell tended to a few final tasks. He gave Lucille the transaction proceeds and promised to join them when he was finished.

But Lowell never made it to town. He drank his moonshine to the dregs, spent one last night with his parents in the forest, and hanged himself from a tree branch looming over the path to the cabin. When the men next arrived on their horses (for no truck could cover that ground), they had to duck their heads to avoid his body. His feet were swollen and the color of plums.

Harlan's father told him that story more times than he could have counted. Even when he was a young child, his father never omitted Great Grandfather Lowell's suicide from the telling. He said the greatest lessons lay in that act of cowardice.

"What man would rather kill himself than fight for what's his?"

But to Harlan, the fault belonged primarily to the nameless men who came upon the land uninvited, delivering ultimatums and tossing legal documents on the ground as they fled like rats. Those men brought crippling change, not just on Great Grandfather Lowell's family, but upon thousands of others who wanted nothing but to live free lives in their modest share of paradise. Yes, Lowell had surrendered the fight. But he was one man with an aged rifle. What could he have done alone, except die at the hands of others instead of by his own?

The men with their demands and papers. The governments who employed and backed them with guns and corrupt courts. The politicians who proudly proclaimed this wide-scale theft a victory for the common good. At a young age, Harlan grew to hate them all.

One night, after he'd finished the story, his father added, "You want to know a secret, boy?" Harlan was ten or eleven then, seething in his bed over the injustice of it all. He wanted so badly to hunt for deer and rabbit in those woods and to scale those mountains. He dreamed of splashing himself in cool water from the branch behind the cabin.

"What, Pop?" Harlan said.

"You promise not to tell nobody?"

"Uh-huh."

"I been searchin' for the property."

"In the park?" Harlan said.

"That's right."

"They let you do that?"

His father shrugged. "I just don't ask 'em. You get a little older, and I'll take you with me. We can look together."

"When?" Harlan shot up in the bed, his young heart galloping at the prospect. "When can we go?"

"Maybe 'round your next birthday." The man swayed at the foot of Harlan's bed and seemed ready to slide off onto the floor at any moment. Harlan smelled alcohol on his breath and his sweat. "I'll tell you one thing, boy," he went on. "We ever do find it, we're gonna take it back. And we won't let no sonofabitch kick us off it again."

CHAPTER TEN

May 11

In the morning, sunlight over the distant ridge peers in on them like the face of almighty God. They blink awake and rise, stiff from a night of sleeping on rock and dirt. None had bothered to remove sleeping bags or ground pads from their packs. They eat bruised apples and drink instant coffee heated over a small fire as the overnight cool quickly gives way to a muggy warmth. Then they pack up, shoulder their loads, and set out.

At mid-day, they reach the glade. The grass is thick, knee-high, and speckled with the bright red stalks of cardinal flower. On the opposite side of the expanse stands an indistinct form roughly twelve feet tall and three times as wide—an amalgam of graying hewn logs, stone, and Japanese honeysuckle. Harlan had hacked back the vines during their last visit in March, much as he'd done countless times over the past several years. But they'd fought back in the relative warmth of spring, clambering back up the walls like a green mouth fitting itself over prey. Years ago, the roof had collapsed. Several layers of the upper logs and virtually all the floorboards are rotted. But the sills, which had been placed high off the ground atop stacked stones, remain solid, and much of the lower structure, to his surprise, has retained its integrity. Harlan has made a small, word-of-mouth name for himself resurrecting homes in worse shape for clients from the Outer Banks to southwestern Georgia. It will be difficult, especially without the benefit of modern heavy tools and a supply of pre-prepared lumber, but he can work with it. Settlers made do with less only a century ago.

The four men drag themselves across the glade and remove their packs as they near the cabin. Harlan separates the leafy membrane with his hands and passes through. Between the exposed floor joists sit piles of additional supplies they've stacked over the last several months, organized according to purpose and covered by blue tarpaulins. Behind the cabin and hidden from sight, thirty hardwood logs, each a foot in diameter, lie on wooden supports. Previously felled from the surrounding woods and stripped of bark, they cure under the cover of canvas tenting. From the rear of the tent comes the burble of an unassuming creek branch.

Harlan steps back outside and smiles broadly to his companions. In its greed, the federal government took possession of more land than it could realistically monitor. The clearing that was his family's farm sits in an overlooked region of the park, miles from the exterior roads and interior trails. No waterfalls or high elevations distinguish it. No geological anomalies attract tourists to gawk and take photos. The horse paths and road that once led into neighboring towns have disappeared along with the towns themselves. It is, quite simply, a patch of flat land among middling mountains in an area no one else would care to visit.

It's perfect.

TSULA

CHAPTER ELEVEN

November 4

At 5:30 a.m., Tsula's cell phone rings. She's halfway through her first mug of coffee, reviewing her notes from the prior day's crime scene, when the call shatters the quiet. The sound nearly startles her out of her chair.

"Special Agent," a man's voice says when she answers, "this is Bradford Hall, Superintendent of Great Smoky Mountains National Park."

Tsula sets her mug on the dining room table and attempts to shake the last of the cobwebs from her head. "Yes, sir. What can I do for you?"

"I'm sorry to call so early," he says. "And I realize that my calling you directly is . . . well, it's not what's typically done."

Even before he has finished his last sentence, Tsula's mind is alight with worry. She knows Batchelder briefed the superintendent about the scene and her preliminary impressions last night. She doesn't know why he's calling, but it's not for the update he already has received. She knows, too, that communications with a park superintendent regarding an investigation of this magnitude and sensitivity are generally reserved for ISB leadership. It's a protocol designed to shelter rank-and-file investigators from distraction and political concerns, and one Tsula cherishes for that very reason. In fact, despite all the investigations she's overseen in this particular park, she could count on two hands the number of words she's actually exchanged with Superintendent Hall. "Not typically," she says. "No, sir."

"Even so," he goes on. "I'd like to meet with you this morning, if that's okay. There's something I'd like to discuss with you in person that pertains to this new investigation. It's a matter of some delicacy, so I'd just as soon it not be passed around too many people. I know you have a lot on your plate, but would you be able to fit me in?"

"Sir, I—"

"I've already talked with your ASAC about it, if that's what you're concerned about. We spoke just a few minutes ago. You'll hear from him soon, I expect. Just call me back after you've conferred."

He's right. Batchelder is calling even before the superintendent has hung up.

"Brian, what the hell is going on?"

Tsula can all but hear him shrug on the other end. "Damned if I know. But he insisted, and it's his park."

"And you're okay with this?"

"If it was anybody else, I wouldn't be," he says. "But you can handle yourself. Just go hear him out. Hell, take it as an opportunity to pump him for information if you can. And call me as soon as you're done."

At that early hour, Tsula encounters only a trickle of other vehicles on her drive across the Tennessee line toward Gatlinburg. She gulps down the coffee in her oversized travel mug and casts her eyes back and forth to both sides of the road, wary of elk wandering the shoulders before sunrise. The superintendent greets her himself when she arrives, no other employees having shown up yet for the workday, and leads her to his office.

Tsula appraises the man as he settles into the chair behind his desk. His tan Park Service shirt is neat and crisp, but the normally sharp contours of his face are bleary and indistinct. His hands rest folded on a desktop that's vacant except for one family photo and a smudged glass tumbler. He seems to take notice of the glass only after Tsula has taken a seat, and he sweeps it into a desk drawer with a sheepish look.

"Yesterday was hard," he says.

"We can talk later, if you'd like," Tsula offers. "When you're feeling more up to it."

He shakes his head. "I made you drive all this way. Now's as good a time as any."

"Alright, then. So how can I help?"

The man opens his mouth to answer, then stops himself. He clears his throat and looks down at the photograph, tracing the top of the frame lightly with his finger. The room is dim but for the warm glow of a desk lamp, and it gives Tsula the impression that perhaps the superintendent had remained here, in his chair, all night. Outside the office windows, the sun still has not risen, and the world is cloaked in shadow.

"I apologize, Special Agent," he says at length. "I promise I called you here for a reason. But I'm afraid it's not a comfortable one to put into words, and this whole thing has me a bit shaken."

"I understand," she replies. "Perhaps we could start with some questions I have? Basic stuff that can help me get this investigation off on the right foot. How about I see what you can tell me, and then we can return to whatever's on your mind?"

His furrowed brow softens with relief. "Yes, let's do that."

Tsula pulls her notepad from the pocket of her fleece. "I've learned some information already," she says. "But maybe you can help fill in some blanks, tell me where I'm wrong?"

"By all means."

"It appears Alex left out for backcountry on October 28 for feral hog control. I assume that would be consistent with his duties as a wildlife biologist for the park?"

"It would," he says. "Sometimes to protect the native species, you have to take out the invasive ones. Resource conservation staff had identified an area deep in the heart of the park where it looked like boar had moved in and were doing some real damage. It was Alex's idea months ago to pack in the parts to build some traps in the area. I believe his primary purpose for going out last week was to inspect the traps, see what they'd yielded."

"My understanding is he was due back November 2, but since that was a Sunday, no one necessarily expected to hear from him then."

The superintendent nods. "That's what his supervisor told me."

"Did he go alone on these trips?"

"It's my understanding he sometimes did. It would all depend on what he intended to do while out there. This time, he apparently told his supervisor he was going solo."

"When he was out there, was there someone keeping tabs on him? Maybe a GPS locator?"

Superintendent Hall shakes his head. "We didn't provide him one. Many places deep in the park, even satellite signal can be spotty. So we've not found them to be a worthwhile expenditure. Plus, Alex had been with us for several years. He was extremely familiar with the interior of the park, and he knew his way around with a map and a compass."

"Maybe a check-in protocol, then, to let someone know he's okay?"

"I'll introduce you to his supervisor," he says. "You can ask her to be certain. But there are many places in the park that nothing on the outside can reach. Not radio, not phone, not satellite. I wouldn't be surprised if the answer to your question is no."

Tsula pauses to consider this information. The lack of any ready means by which to track Alex's location for five days isn't necessarily unusual. It might indeed be, given the park's size and terrain, that GPS locators and satellite phones are simply too unreliable to merit the investment of limited park funds. But a lack of any data on his whereabouts and movements over that period of time could constitute a significant gap in the investigation. In the absence of witnesses or any communication from Alex prior to his death, proof of his activities and movements could suggest, at least circumstantially, his state of mind.

Tsula scribbles a note to determine what cell towers service the park and its surrounding towns. Perhaps connection data might help at least narrow down his movements and whereabouts. It's unlikely, given the superintendent's comments, but worth a look.

As she's ruminating, he speaks again, his words this time more tentative. "Special Agent, does your investigation into a suicide . . . does it look into the motive? Why a person might . . . do that?"

The question surprises Tsula, and she stops writing. "I actually don't approach it as a suicide," she says. "Regardless of how it looks right now."

"What else would you call it?"

"For now, it's just a death. That's all we know for sure. Labels risk coloring how we approach the investigation. I won't be prepared to call it a suicide, homicide, or accident until the investigation is complete. But yes, any investigation of a death like this will look at the circumstances, whether there was a reason he might have killed himself."

He nods in response but says nothing.

"Do you have some information that might help us with that question, sir?" Tsula asks. "Anything you saw or heard about him, maybe, that seemed out of the ordinary these last few days?"

"I do not."

"So, then, why the question?"

Superintendent Hall straightens himself in his chair, tapping his thumbs together in his lap. "Because if it turns out he did take his own life, the reason he did so may be important to a lot of people."

Tsula cocks her head and squints at him. "I'm afraid I don't understand."

"Are you familiar with the elk reintroduction effort here at the park, Special Agent?"

"Vaguely," Tsula says. "I know when I was young, I never saw an elk around here. I come back a couple years ago, you gotta keep an eye out for them on the roads."

He nods. "Eastern elk were hunted right out of these mountains probably a hundred fifty years ago. Wiped off the map. After Yellowstone reintroduced wolves in the '90s, we decided that one of our missions should be to re-fill a gaping hole in our own ecosystem. So about twenty-five years ago, with the help of some private foundations, we acquired and transplanted nearly fifty Manitoban elk into the park. Not the same as the Eastern elk, but close enough. We provided them safe grounds, we collared and tracked them, we did community outreach to try to settle the neighbors' minds and convince them not to shoot on sight."

"And this has what to do with Alex, sir?"

"He ran the whole program. It was his baby."

"What I read," Tsula says, "wasn't he a bit young for that?"

"He came to us years ago as an intern when he was in grad school, latched onto the senior biologist who helped us get the program off the ground, and he just never let go. A few years later, when that guy retired, Alex had so much knowledge already from riding shotgun, it was a no-brainer to just promote him into the role. He took the ball and ran with it. Did it all—the collaring, the data collection, the outreach, the reports to the program's funding sources. He had such a passion for it, we just let him. Best to have people involved who care, you know? Plus, budgetary issues meant we couldn't fill Alex's old position. So he was always going to be doing a lot himself."

"Sounds like too big a job for just one person, though."

The superintendent nods. "He had techs to assist him, for sure. Go out to help collar the calves, things like that. But he was a dynamo, always working, and my impression now is that he wasn't good at delegating much beyond the grunt tasks. But things seemed to work so well, I fear we may have allowed him to operate with less oversight than we should have. If it ain't broke, you understand."

"And now you think someone's got questions maybe you can't answer?"

The superintendent pulls a thick stack of paper from a drawer on the opposite side of the desk and slides it across to her. "This is an upcoming annual report Alex was working on for the reintroduction project. A draft of it, anyway. They were waiting on some more data he was gathering, and then they were going to finalize it for submission to the DOI and the private foundation who primarily funds the program. I'm no field scientist or statistician, but what I read in here is all great news. Populations are up, looking resilient. Ecological impacts all positive. The anticipated downsides still haven't really panned out. We're the talk of the Park Service. Yellowstone got its wolves, but we brought *megafauna* back to this park. Alex's life's work, a resounding success so far. But if we present this sunshine-and-rainbows report to the foundations and assure them that the money they're putting into this project was worth it, and then we have to explain that the guy who wrote the report— who oversaw the whole damn project—may just have taken his own life right here in the park where he worked. . . Well, if I were in their shoes, I'd want to know what was going on. How reliable is whatever this guy reported? Was he hiding something? If I can't give them answers, future funding is no guarantee. And, God forbid, if we learn that he was engaged in something untoward—well, we need to be able to get out in front of that."

Tsula hesitates. "Sir, I'm not saying these aren't valid concerns—"

"But you're horrified that I'm talking about them right now," he says. "Believe me, I wish I didn't have to."

"I'm just concerned you're expecting something out of this investigation that I'm not going to be able to deliver. I'm not here to reassure your funding sources. You think there may have been funny business going on, you have an OIG."

"But what you find may answer the question, right?" He leans forward over the desk, his eyes now hard and earnest. "This project is bigger than just this one park and this one animal species. This is about us unwinding the clock on things we've collectively done wrong. We can't unwind it entirely. There's a lot of bad we can't undo. But we can look for these little steps to take, and we have to see them through when we take them. We can't leave them half-done."

"Unwinding the clock." Tsula repeats the words absently while her brain grasps for a plan to gracefully exit this conversation. She can ask the rest of her questions to Alex's supervisor, likely with far less discomfort.

"You, of all people, must surely understand that."

Tsula pauses and looks at him. "I'm not sure what you mean."

"I know you were at the community meeting yesterday," he says, his voice lower, a co-conspirator's whisper. "About the cavern."

Her body flashes cold, and it feels as though the floor has disappeared beneath her. "I'm sorry?"

"I don't call it Stephens Cavern, by the way. That's a stupid name. But what are you going to do? Someone said it, and it's out there now."

"Let me stop you there," Tsula says, holding up her hand. "I just drove my mother to a meeting she wanted to attend because she's too sick to drive herself."

He eyes her skeptically across the desk. "Is that right."

"Where did you hear that, anyway?"

"I receive phone calls from a . . . well, let's call him a 'concerned citizen.' He lets me know when community meetings happen and how unanimous the support among the Eastern Band is for deeding the cavern over. I would expect unanimous support, of course. It's completely understandable. But he calls to tell me all the same. He let me know that last night that an enrolled member who works for the Park Service was among the crowd. Not the park, you understand. The Park *Service*. From there, it wasn't all that hard to figure out. Not really a long list as far as I'm aware."

"Is this 'concerned citizen' perhaps a thirty-something blowhard on Tribal Council?"

He shrugs and tilts his head in a manner that suggests she's on the right track. "I'm not sure I'm at liberty to say."

Tsula's neck and face flush with heat. Tommy Weathers was going to drag her into this conflict one way or another. "Sir, despite what anyone else may have implied to you, I was simply the chauffeur."

"So you don't have an opinion on what happens with the cavern? I would have thought—"

"Yeah, there's a lot of that going around right now," Tsula says, her irritation bubbling to the surface. "My opinion is I work for the Park Service, and it's not my job to take sides. Once it's decided how it's going to be, what the rules are, I'll help you enforce them."

Superintendent Hall stares at her for a long beat, then a smile crawls slowly across his face. "Fair enough."

A dewy perspiration has gathered on Tsula's forehead and arms, and she's acutely aware of it cooling on her skin. Is this the true reason he wanted to speak with her personally—to confront her about what he'd heard? This investigation is going to be difficult enough without the park superintendent questioning her loyalty.

She wonders if he intends to share his knowledge with anyone else, but she dares not ask.

"Maybe we should get back to Alex, sir," she says finally.

He nods and leans back in his chair. "I apologize for getting us off track."

"I can't promise you the answers you're seeking," Tsula says. "Let's be clear on that. But to conduct a proper investigation that might uncover them, I'll need your support. I'm going to require access to a lot of information, and I may need your help in getting some of it."

"Just say the word, and you'll have it."

They stand, and Tsula shakes the man's hand hastily. She reaches the doorway in long, quick strides, then stops and turns back toward him.

"Sir, there's no telling where this may go. You say you want answers to your questions, but if there are answers to find, you may regret knowing them."

"The speculation that comes in their absence could be worse."

"You don't know that," she says, and she heads for her vehicle.

CHAPTER TWELVE

November 5

The front door to Alex Lowe's rental home swings open with a guttural croak.

"After you," the landlord says. He gestures with the hand holding the search warrant. "Make yourself at home."

Tsula steps in and flips a light switch just inside the doorway. An opaque glass lamp flickers on the ceiling and illuminates. It hums faintly and casts a dim, almost pink light over a small living room containing one fraying couch, a futon, and a small television sitting on a plywood stand. She pulls open the vinyl shades covering a series of windows along one wall, and a warm, late afternoon amber floods the living room and attached kitchen. The space—one half of a small duplex located about ten miles outside the Oconaluftee entrance to the park—is modest and compact. The kind of space a man rents when he means to spend as little time in it as possible.

On this particular afternoon, it also gives the impression that its occupant has left for a period of time but will return. Coffee maker dutifully unplugged, the pot resting in the sink, its dregs now dried to a brown ring. A single white ceramic plate crusted with dried marinara and shrunken, petrified noodles. Trash can emptied of contents to avoid ripening in the period of absence. Shades drawn to prevent the detection of vacancy. Central heat and air turned off so as not to run up the power bill. Long-johns and parcels of dehydrated food no doubt initially packed but then reconsidered and left on the made queen bed.

Four framed photographs punctuate the otherwise barren walls of the living room. A capacity crowd at old Turner Field. A grizzly bear tracking a salmon in the air. Lou Gehrig despondent before the microphone, bidding his fans farewell. Clingman's Dome in full autumnal glory. In the center of the room stands a small, round dining table which appears to double as Alex's home work space. A laptop, also unplugged, sits lifeless on the tabletop.

The landlord clears his throat and removes a crinkled pack of American Spirits from the pocket of his snap-button shirt. "If you don't need anything—"

"I don't, thank you." Tsula does not turn to look at him. "Take your time."

A half-dozen or more composition notebooks are piled upon a bookshelf against one wall, the stack propping up paperback volumes of Muir, Thoreau, Abbey, and Kephart. A similar notebook rests on the table next to the laptop. Tsula dons latex gloves and flips its cover open. In broad marker strokes which bleed through to the back, the cover page inscription simply states the year. The following pages are replete with dated, handwritten notes, written single-spaced and without regard for margins, recording Alex's daily activities in the park.

Tsula sits at the table and reads. Some entries briefly document days spent in the office recording data and drafting reports. Others describe unexpected excursions into the field to address a nuisance black bear that had ventured too near campsites or to direct visitors' automobiles when elk grazing on grass on the side of the park's roadways brought traffic to a halt. Still more recount longer sojourns deep into the park to collect data on elk grazing activity or to tag new calves with radio collars.

The last entry details a planned excursion to hunt feral hogs, complete with a description of the traps he would inspect and their locations by longitude and latitude. He had each day of the trip mapped out by miles to be covered, by traps to be inspected, by destinations to be reached before the sun set and the water sources he'd pass along the way. Alex, it would appear, was organized to the point of obsessive.

"Beautiful rod."

Tsula looks up to find the landlord, back from his smoke break, examining a fly rod and reel propped up in the corner of the living room. It is still assembled, as though the owner frequently had need of it and so did not bother to break it down. The landlord runs an admiring finger down the shaft. "Must've been a gift."

"Please don't touch anything," she says.

He snaps his hand away like a scolded toddler and hides it behind his back.

"Why a gift?" Tsula asks.

"The inscription on the rod—it's a guy in Franklin who hand makes them out of bamboo. I've seen the prices. It's not a thing you buy for yourself."

"You fish?"

"You've seen where we live, right?"

She shrugs. "I grew up in Cherokee. Never took up fishing."

"Nobody's perfect." He turns back to the rod. "Speaking of which: It looks like Alex was a lefty. You know, I don't think I've ever noticed that before. And I've been fishing with the guy."

"You know that because. . . ?"

He points. "The reel's set up on the right." He pauses, but Tsula just stares at him, waiting for more. "You use your dominant hand for casting and reel with the other. With this setup, he'd be casting with his left hand, reeling with his right."

"You're just noticing this now?"

"You really haven't ever fished, have you?" He snorts and shakes his head. "Only thing you're paying attention to out there is the water."

Tsula's eyes return to the open composition book. This time, she registers the faint slant of the letters—top left to bottom right. It's subtle, perhaps owing to years of corrective practice, but the efforts had not righted the tilt completely. Alex wrote with his left hand, too.

"Yep, there you go," the landlord says. He's standing now in front of an acoustic guitar resting in a stand nearby. "That's also set up for a lefty. The strings are backwards." He plucks each string in succession with his forefinger, right to left. "E-A-D-G-B-A." Then, as if this knowledge requires validation: "I have more than one hobby."

The collection of tones—not quite a chord, something dissonant in the mix, perhaps strings in need of tuning—stands the hairs on Tsula's neck straight. She walks over and places her gloved hand lightly across the strings to halt their vibration. "What did I say about touching things?"

"Right. Shit. Sorry."

Tsula photographs and gathers the laptop and the stack of composition notebooks into evidence bags. Then she turns her attention to the remainder of the apartment. Opened cabinets, drawers pulled out, boxes slid from beneath the bed—all suggest an anodyne existence remarkable for little other than the nature of Alex's work and, now, the circumstances of his death. What strikes Tsula most is the utter lack of personal photographs—of his family, his friends, even himself. So stark is the absence that Tsula searches the apartment twice to be certain. No frames on tables or hanging on walls. Not even a magnet on the dimpled white refrigerator.

"You knew Alex personally?" Tsula asks.

The landlord nods. "Friend of a friend. He's rented from me for, what, five years now? We didn't hang out a lot. Beer here, a little fishing there. I don't like to get too close to the tenants, in case I have to kick 'em out. But yeah, I knew him some."

"Did you note anything unusual going on with him the last few months?"

"Not that I noticed or he told me about. But he'd been real busy with work, I think. Told me so when I said it was high time we go fishing again. I hadn't really seen him since August, except when he dropped his rent checks off."

"Any reason you can think of he might want to hurt himself?"

He starts, as though the question catches him by surprise. "Is that what you think happened?"

"Did I say that?"

The landlord stares at her expressionless face for a moment, then shrugs. "Last I knew, the guy loved his work and I'm pretty sure was seeing somebody he liked. So no." He pauses and shakes his head. "But then, my brother took a whole bottle of oxys one night, and he'd just had his first kid. Maybe I'm not the best judge of those things."

"Do you know who Alex had been seeing?"

"No," the man says. "He just hinted at it from time to time. Like if he mentioned he was going to a concert or out of town, and I asked him if he was going with someone, he'd just give me a goofy smile and say yes. That's all he ever told me."

The sun has set by the time they leave the duplex, the front yard veiled in a mid-autumn black. The aura of distant streetlamps nibble at the night's edges. Next to her, the pale blue flame of a lighter appears with the grinding click of the flint wheel and is replaced a moment later by the orange rim of a cigarette.

"Feels fucked up," the landlord says from the darkness. "Someone you've known that long, lives in your place, you get used to them being there, you know? And then . . ." He takes a long drag and exhales slowly.

Tsula waves her hand to clear away the smoke and thanks the man for his time. "I'll likely be back," she says. "So please don't disturb anything for now, and don't let anyone in who doesn't have a warrant. I'll call you when I'm ready."

His silhouette grunts and turns to lock the door. "I'll be here."

CHAPTER THIRTEEN

November 6

"You'll have to forgive me, Special Agent, but I'm in a bit of a crunch." The Medical Examiner drops his corpulent frame into the desk chair. His heavy eyelids and slouched carriage suggest a man who has not slept well in days. A coffee stain archipelago floats in the white sea of his lab coat, the fabric's wrinkles like looming waves. "I'll need to make this quick. We can arrange to meet again later once I have labs and pathology back."

"Busy day?" Tsula settles into a guest chair across from him.

"Busy year." He lifts a stray napkin from the desktop and wipes a sheen of sweat from his brow and jowls. "These opioids will be the death of me."

He rifles through a pile of folders stacked high on his desk, pausing when his mind catches up with his words.

"Well, you know what I mean," he says, shaking his head. "It's a damn wildfire out there."

He removes a folder from the pile, opens it, and slides out a stack of photographs. Bright trapezoids skate across them under the fluorescent ceiling lights.

"I appreciate you letting us go ahead with the autopsy last night.

I can't keep up if we don't work into the wee hours. I'm busting my budget this year with overtime for staff."

"It's alright," Tsula says. "Why don't you just tell me what you found."

He arranges the photos before her on his desk, setting them atop a litter of reports marked DRAFT, chewed-up pens, and crumpled snack bar wrappers. "To begin with, there's no question the cause of death was this bullet wound," he says. "The rest of the body was pristine. No other signs of trauma, no fatal disease process that I could identify."

He pulls a photograph out of the stack and hands it to her. The image shows the right side of the skull, its yellow sheen splotched focally with red. At the edges of the photograph, she can make out the two crumpled halves of his scalp, brushy red hair retracted almost out of the frame. One small black void punctuates the skull's surface like a quarter-inch pilot hole.

"Bullet trajectory was right to left," he continues, passing over another photograph. "I'm assuming you saw the stippling around the entry wound. That and the residue pattern around the wound are consistent with the shot being close range. The swabs confirmed residue on both of his hands, not just the right. I'm not sure what you make of that."

"We believe he'd been out hunting before this. Though we haven't yet found the rifle."

"Then there you go, I suppose," he says. "The bullet trajectory was more or less level at first. Not the most common trajectory if self-inflicted, but consistent with it. Slight deviation anterior to posterior as it traveled through the skull."

He lifts a series of images of the exposed organ to the top of the pile. The first shows it whole, the tight gray and pink coils of the surface wending around each other and dipping away into countless dark ravines. The entry wound black and angry.

Tsula leans forward in her chair and studies the image. "You said 'at first'?"

"I'm sure you noticed the bullet didn't exit. Didn't have enough force left for that, so it just bounced off the left side of the skull and ricocheted around in there for a bit. Made a big old mess."

He lays out the next several photographs and taps them with a chapped forefinger. The organ has now been dissected at the level of the bullet wound. Angry gashes char the surrounding tissue like strafed earth.

"You got a time of death?"

"That's tougher," he says, slumping deeper into his chair. His expression is one of pained disappointment. "Part of him sitting in cold water like that can throw everything off. Rigor, body temp, decomposition rate. I have more to do, but right now, my best guess is within a day or two."

Tsula nods and scribbles some notes. "Anything else I need to know?"

"Toxicology is still pending. And I've got some medical records I've subpoenaed and am waiting on. I doubt they'll tell me anything, but I'll let you know."

CHAPTER FOURTEEN

The last squares of sunlight from the surrounding windows stretch, slide across the conference table's lacquered wood, and disappear. The evidence bags Tsula received from the Medical Examiner's staff lay splayed out before her, along with those she'd collected herself. The sum total of this stranger's known life slowly dissolves with the fading light. Waterproof athletic watch still dutifully keeping time. Topographical map of the park, its folded creases fraying like cotton. Smartphone, the display dark and lifeless behind its waterproof case. Compass still keeping to its singular purpose.

Alex's phone and laptop call for specialized skills she does not possess. But she knows who does. She dials a number on her cell and waits.

"Special Agent Harris," the voice says.

"Harris, it's Walker."

"I know it is," Harris says. "My phone told me. They can do that now, or haven't you heard?"

"You guys miss me out there?"

"Like the plague."

"Is it snowing where you are?"

"It's Colorado," he says. "So yeah, now and then."

Tsula puts Harris on speaker as they talk and opens the photographs stored on her phone. She has put off a scheduled replacement of the device largely because she still has pictures of her home in Wyoming on it and hasn't yet figured out how to transfer them over to a new model. She prefers having them handy when homesickness overtakes her as it is threatening to do now.

She scrolls back to a collection of images she took from her back porch the day before she left for North Carolina. The vast, flat expanse stretching out toward a distant crenellation of white-tipped peaks. It would be snowing in Wyoming, too, now and then. Morning frost would coat the grass and the roofs, like the world was growing a delicate new skin. Yellowstone should have just closed off most roads in the park, and the elk, bison, and mule deer soon would be migrating toward their wintering grounds in lower elevations or in other states entirely.

"What are you really calling about, Walker?" Harris says, interrupting her reminiscence. "Much as I'd love to shoot the shit, I've got something I gotta get to."

"I need your skills, Harris. Why else?"

"I've told you before, I can't erase your browser history for you. It's against policy."

"What is wrong with you?"

"With me?" he says. "It's your browser history."

"You're an idiot."

"Agree to disagree."

"Are they still letting you hold onto the Nerd Box, Harris?"

"Now we're getting down to it," he says.

"Is that a yes?"

"Of course I have it. None of you Neanderthals would know what to do with it. What you got?"

"I've got a body found dead in Great Smoky Mountains of a gunshot wound to the head," Tsula says. "Has the look of a suicide, and it probably is. But no one had eyes on him for a few days, and we don't have any clear motive."

"Guess a note would be too much to hope for? Manifesto? Disturbing journal entry?"

"No such luck."

"So what are we looking to analyze?"

"I've got a laptop and a cell phone. Texts, calls, internet searches, e-mails, social media. I need to cast a wide net."

"Password locks on the phone and laptop, I'm assuming?"

"I don't know," she says. "I haven't tried charging or powering them up. You yell at me when I do."

"Good girl."

"Don't be an asshole. I'm not a horse."

"Fine. Good *Special Agent*," Harris says. "Moving home has made you touchy."

"It's not home."

"It ain't a two-year vacation. What's our authority for all this snooping?"

"Search warrants for everything. I'll get them to you."

"Time frame?"

"You know I'm impatient," she says.

"In that, you are not unique. What's the *actual* time frame?"

"Investigation's new, but I need the info to point me in the right direction. Could you maybe get me cell phone calls and texts and e-mail data in a week and the rest later?"

"Next week?" Harris exclaims. "Hell, why not this afternoon, Walker?"

"I mean, if you want."

He exhales heavily, as though struggling under the weight of this imposition. "I'll see what I can do, but I can't promise anything. I have my own cases to run, you know."

Tsula smiles and shakes her head. He says that every time.

"You're the man, Harris."

"Tell my wife. You remember where to send everything?"

"I do."

"Then I gotta go. Stay off those sites, Walker. It's really inappropriate."

"Goodbye, Harris."

HARLAN

CHAPTER FIFTEEN

September 19

Going on ten years since her death, Harlan has found that his wife comes to mind less these days. This realization usually comes laden with a healthy dose of remorse. But it's understandable, he tells himself, with a home to restore before winter sets in and four mouths to feed. The current needs of survival leave little time for luxuries like sentimentality. It is, he figures, a kind of mercy. No time to dwell on what was lost when there is more yet to protect.

Even so, as Harlan stands beneath the flat September sun and surveys the still-wet chinking between the hewn logs, he cannot help but think of Janie. Joseph has failed to sift out the remaining chunks of burnt wood from the ash before mixing it with the other materials, resulting in lumps in the paste. Harlan counts at least a half-dozen small bulges in the otherwise smooth, white surface, like bubbles that just won't burst. Like the nodules just beneath Janie's skin that had been the first sign of her illness.

He'd like to say it went quickly after she found the first one. People so often pray for more time, not knowing what that will actually entail or how bad it can get. They speak of "quality time" without realizing that often there's little quality to be found in an endless cycle of chemotherapy, nausea, pain, waiting, and setbacks.

Harlan might have even prayed for it himself when they first sat with the doctor in his sunlit office in Asheville, frightened and naïve, discussing Janie's prognosis. Everything that followed has blurred those early days in his mind, and what he recalls of them now has no doubt been filtered through the agony that came after. Their experience gave the lie to any hope they'd once felt, so much so that now he can't remember feeling it at all.

He remembers Janie's last days clearly enough. He recalls when the same doctor, a sallow man with a twitch in one of his eyes, told them she'd run out of options. "We've taken the conventional treatments as far as we can, but she's just not responding."

Harlan has always resented how he phrased that. *She* wasn't responding, like somehow, despite the dozens of appointments she'd attended, the blood draws and imaging to which she'd routinely submitted, and all the infusions she'd received, still it was Janie who hadn't done enough.

"There must be something else," Harlan responded, gripping the handles on the guest chair lest he reach across the desk and grab the man by his collar.

The doctor nodded solemnly. "There may be one other option. It's not widely used, and I doubt Medicaid will cover it. But if you can swing the cost, I think it'd be worth a shot."

"What do you mean, you doubt Medicaid will cover it?"

"I mean it's experimental," the doctor said. "It's a matter of using drugs for a purpose they weren't initially intended. What they call an 'off-label use.' And the medications they use are costly."

"I don't give a damn what they were intended for. If it works, why won't Medicaid cover it?"

"We've spent everything we have on the co-pays and deductibles," Janie said. "We got nothing left." These were the first words she'd spoken since they arrived, and she slumped back in her chair, taxed by the effort.

"Medicaid, Medicare, Tricare," the doctor said. "The government payors tend to be slow to accept new treatment modalities."

Harlan's fingers dug into the upholstery until the edge of the cracked vinyl pricked the skin below his nails. He'd initially resisted the notion of enrolling Janie in Medicaid, but after exhausting her medical leave and paid time off, she'd lost her job at the textile plant. The cost of continuing her employer's coverage was simply too high—especially since the southeast was still clawing its way out of the recession, and Harlan had been struggling to find new work. Healthcare coverage policies available on the so-called "marketplace" offered no realistic alternative, considering her pre-existing diagnosis. The insurers might be required to cover her condition, but the mandate meant little when they could impose an annual deductible higher than Harlan could hope to make in two or three years. To compound matters, they had two growing boys under the age of ten to feed and clothe.

"How slow?" Harlan said.

"Years and years slow," the doctor said. "Multiple double-blind studies and FDA approval slow."

Harlan rubbed his cheeks roughly with his hands and cleared his throat. His neck and face flushed. Janie's cold fingers touched his forearm, and she looked down. The skin on the back of her hand was papery, and a recent IV infusion had left a bruise that was still blossoming purple and yellow at the edges.

"Harlan," she said.

He shook his head. "What the hell will they pay for at this point, doctor?"

The doctor's right eyelid clamped shut briefly, and he looked down at his clasped hands on the desk. "Hospice."

Janie placed her head in her hands.

Harlan leaned forward. "Excuse me?" He could barely hear the words over the storm brewing in his head.

"Medicaid pays one hundred percent of hospice care costs."

"They'll pay the costs of her dying?" Harlan slammed his hand down on the armrest, and Janie jumped in her chair. "Well now I feel better. I was worried all those tax dollars weren't getting put to good use."

"I don't make the rules, Mr. Miles."

"Who does?"

"Mr. Miles—"

"*Who?*"

"The State makes the rules, Mr. Miles," the doctor said. "The Department of Health and Human Services."

"Give me a number. I'm going to call and get this straightened out."

"Harlan," Janie said.

"Give me a goddamn number."

Harlan emerges from this memory as though from deep and turbulent water. His pulse races, and his scalp tingles. He breathes in deeply and blinks several times before he remembers why he is standing there, staring at the cabin's newest logs.

"Joseph," he says at last. "A word?"

"Yeah, Pop?" Joseph sets down his trowel.

Harlan digs his finger into the wet chinking and removes a chunk of burnt wood the size of a marble. He walks over and places it in Joseph's hand.

The boy freezes.

"What was our purpose in moving here to the homestead, Joseph?"

"What, Pop?"

"I asked you, why did we move all the way out here?"

Joseph hesitates. "To live as free men and reclaim what's ours, Pop."

The skin of Joseph's face is drawn tight over its cheek bones, owing to four months of honest labor and eating only what they can hunt and cultivate themselves. In the life they'd left behind, people likely would say he looks gaunt, that he's starving. But Harlan knows the truth. Joseph is simply shedding the last remnants of a world that didn't care about him in the slightest.

"Is it our purpose," Harlan says, "to die out here in the cold?"

"What, Pop?" Joseph furtively eyes Otto, who has descended from his makeshift ladder at the other end of the structure.

Junior continues hewing a new log in the front yard, grunting quietly with each swing of the axe. He does not look up.

"Something wrong with your ears, boy?"

"No, sir."

"Then kindly answer my question. Is it our purpose to die out here in the cold?"

"No, sir. It's not."

"Then perhaps you have forgotten the purpose of the chinking?" Harlan says. "Otto, would you like to remind Joseph what purpose it serves?"

"Pop, I'm sure he rem—"

"*Remind* him."

Otto looks at his brother and then at the ground. "It fills the gaps between the logs."

"And why is that important?"

"It keeps the cold out and the warmth in."

"Very good," Harlan says. "Joseph, what did I tell you to do with the ash before you mix the chinking?"

"Sift out the chunks of wood, Pop."

"Do you know why?"

"So it looks better?" Joseph says, shifting on his feet uneasily.

Harlan puts his hand behind Joseph's neck and leans in toward his son's face. "Certainly, a smooth surface looks better. But that's not the reason I told you to sift carefully." He claps Joseph's neck hard and turns to address both sons. "When it gets cold, materials like to shrink. When it gets warm, they expand. Same thing with dry and wet conditions. Contract, expand. That puts stress on your materials, and they can crack if they were not prepared properly in the first place. If there is inconsistency. Where do they crack, Otto?"

"At their weakest points."

"That's right. Things break at their weakest points, like spaces filled with chunks of burnt wood and not a carefully mixed chinking. It cracks, this lump falls out, and now there's a gap. The cold and the wind and the bugs are that much closer to the inside of your home."

A slight breeze picks up, carrying with it the bright, gummy scent of the flowering kudzu they have yet to clear behind the cabin.

Otto speaks again. "Pop, I—"

"What are we supposed to do here, Joseph?" Harlan says, ignoring his eldest son. "I asked you to sift the ash and remove the leftover chunks of wood. But it would appear that you did not think I was serious. Or perhaps you decided that I don't actually know what I'm talking about?"

"No, Pop. I tried. I spent a long time, I swear. I don't know how I missed it."

"Carelessness, then," Harlan says. "You are still too used to things being done for you. That's what *they* want—dependents who cannot do for themselves, who look to them for everything. Please, almighty government, do for me. Please, society, I don't care what I must give up so long as you take care of me." He lifts Joseph's hung head with his finger until they're face to face. "It's all a lie, boy. The only people that give a damn about you are right here. We are on our own."

"Yes, sir."

"But don't worry. I will teach you to do for yourself, and to do it properly."

Harlan walks behind the cabin to the tent and finds the rope of dried and braided grapevine coiled on the ground. When he returns, he holds the rope out for Joseph to see. "How many will it take to ensure you are more careful next time? Twenty?"

Joseph sets his jaw. His eyes have grown filmy and red. "Five," he says.

"Fifteen."

"Ten."

Harlan nods. "Ten it is."

"Pop," Otto says, stepping between them. "I did the sifting with Joseph. What we used right there, I sifted it. I'm sure of it. It was my fault."

Joseph shakes his head. "No, Otto—"

"That right, Junior?" Harlan calls out.

Junior releases the axe from his hand, wipes his brow, and looks up. "What?"

"Otto says it was he, and not Joseph, who failed to sift the ash properly. I figured since you've been out here all day, maybe you could enlighten me."

Junior frowns, picks the axe back up, and resumes his work. "You want someone watching over your kids, that's up to you. I don't babysit."

Harlan sighs and turns back to his boys.

"It's true, Pop," Otto says. "The punishment should be mine."

Harlan smiles, the display of brotherly loyalty filling him with an unexpected pride. It isn't the lesson he's intending, but it pleases him all the same. "Your brother's taking up for you, Joseph. I suspect he's lying, but now I can't be certain. I guess you'll both have to share in the punishment, then. Five each. Now lift your shirts."

Otto and Joseph both comply. Across their bare backs, raised scars in crisscross patterns tell of prior infractions, of teenage insubordination and attention not paid. His gut feels momentarily hollow at the sight, but he shoves that reaction aside as quickly as it arises. Harlan's father had taught him in the same manner when he was of age, and he knows its effectiveness intimately. The first time Harlan used the rope on them, they flopped like fish dropped on dry land. But now, as young men, they've learned to accept these lessons without movement or protest.

"Okay, then," Harlan says, uncoiling the rope. "Let's begin."

TSULA

CHAPTER SIXTEEN

November 9

Three days after their conversation, Special Agent Harris
sends Tsula a file of the call and text data recovered from
Alex Lowe's cell phone. "The rest will have to wait," his
message says. "Hope this is enough to get you started."

It is.

The day before he was found dead at Twentymile Ranger
Station, Alex Lowe received a series of texts from a number simply
labeled "Bobby" in his contacts—no last name, no assigned photo,
no "ICE" or other moniker attached. Alex responded to none of
the messages.

Good morning. U missed a great party.

U ok?

Gps lost u i think. looks like u r not moving?

Alex r u hurt? u havent moved. txt me pls.

Baby pls pls pls text or call me if u can.

Im freaking out. r u mad at me?

Im getting drunk i cant take it y wont u txt?

God nite asshole.

The time stamps suggest that they all were received within the
same two-minute span on the morning of November 2. But given

their content, Tsula knows that can't be right. They must have been sent previously over some longer period of time but only received by Alex's phone later and all at once—probably because of the poor cell service available in the park's interior. Still, the absence of a response, even when Alex reached Twentymile where service would be more reliable, puzzles her. This may have been his last contact from someone who cared for him, and it is common investigative experience that people who take their own lives tend to reach out to a loved one in the end.

Tsula recalls the landlord's suspicion that Alex was seeing someone, and now it appears that she has found that someone. It also appears that Bobby has the first solid information regarding Alex's location and movements on November 1. Such information might also be the first contemporaneous clues regarding Alex's activities and mental state shortly before his death. A chill darts down her neck and out the length of her arms—the thrill of the investigation's first break-through.

Tsula picks up her phone and dials the number. A man's voice answers on the fourth ring.

"I'm trying to reach Bobby," Tsula says.

"Speaking?"

She introduces herself and adds, "I'm investigating the death of Alex Lowe. It appears you and I need to talk."

Bobby audibly catches his breath. Then comes his voice, low and tremulous: "When?"

"What are you doing this afternoon?"

# #

Tsula notices Bobby's fingernails first. She sees them when he opens his front door, cupping his fingers around its edge as though he might have to resist some intruder's entry. A few minutes later, when he brings her a mug of coffee, she clocks them again.

They're chewed down to nubs, only scant, ragged traces of black polish remaining.

Bobby settles tentatively on the other end of the couch and crosses his legs underneath himself. He's of average height but muscular—a gym rat, she figures—with swooping hair the color of straw, except at the roots. A chocolate Labrador named Leroy pants hot breath on Tsula's leg. His yellow eyes have locked on her like she's his new best friend. Tsula rubs his ear, and he lowers his head onto her knee.

"Let me know if he's bothering you, and I'll put him up," Bobby says.

"He's great." Tsula switches to Leroy's other ear, and the dog groans and nearly sinks to the floor.

Bobby examines the fading Biltmore House inscription on his mug for a long while before asking, "How did you find out about me?"

"Alex's phone. We recovered your texts to him."

"Just mine?"

"Were you thinking there would be more?"

"No. But you never really know, do you?"

"I suppose not," Tsula says. She sips coffee slowly from her mug. Light roast, hints of vanilla. Bobby has good taste. In fact, the entire apartment, situated above a studio in an art deco building in downtown Asheville, gives the impression of someone with strong preferences and money enough to satisfy them. "Bobby, as you might imagine, I have a number of questions for you. I'm sorry to have to ask you, but they're necessary for the investigation."

"What's there to investigate?" he says. "They found the gun next to him, didn't they? At least, that's what I heard."

"We did."

Bobby's eyes grow wide, and his head droops. "You were there?"

"I was."

He shudders and looks up to the ceiling, blinking. He opens his mouth as though to ask something, then stops himself and shakes his head clear of that thought. "What is it you want to know?"

"I'd like to start with the text messages, if we could." Tsula removes a folded printout from the front pocket of her fleece. "Do you still have them on your phone? I need to confirm something."

Bobby lifts the phone from an end table next to him. He swipes and taps, scrolls, then hands the phone to Tsula. On the screen are the same messages, but stamped with the times they were actually sent. The series began late in the morning of November 1 and continued sporadically throughout the day, finally ending late that night when Bobby apparently had succeeded in getting himself drunk enough to be capable of sleep.

Tsula removes her pen and writes the correct times next to the messages on her printout.

"Okay if I send these as screenshots to my phone?" she asks. "This may be pretty important."

"Sure."

When she's done, Tsula hands the phone back. "So why in one of the messages did you ask if Alex was angry with you?"

Bobby clears his throat before answering. His expression tells her he'd expected more warm-up before they reached the meat of the questions. "We had a fight the night before he left," he says finally. "A pretty big one. And when he didn't text me back, I thought maybe he was still mad at me."

"Why not just assume he was out of cell range? A lot of that wilderness doesn't have good cell service. I'm betting you know that."

"Because, Special Agent, I'm insecure, and I have a habit of assuming the worst." He smiles wryly and adds: "Though I guess in this case I really didn't assume the worst, did I?"

"What was the fight about?"

"Halloween."

"Halloween?"

Bobby nods. "At least, that's where it started."

"I don't understand."

"When Alex first told me he was going to be gone into the park over Halloween, I got upset. We were supposed to be going to a Halloween party here with some of my friends. He said we didn't actually agree on that, and I said we did but he never listens, and then it all went downhill from there. He accused me of making up the conversation, and I told him an uncomfortable truth."

"What truth was that?"

"That he would rather run into the woods to hide than be seen out in the world with me."

"Why would he be hiding?"

"Because I'm a gay man, Special Agent. And so was he."

Tsula sets her mug down on the coffee table in front of her. "Was Alex closeted?"

"He wasn't exactly out. I think only one person he worked with knew. I knew, of course. His family didn't. He said they wouldn't have approved."

"How did you two meet if he wasn't out?"

"I found him at a nightclub here in town," Bobby says. "He was sitting alone at the bar on a Saturday night. Big red flag, right? I knew I should have kept walking. But he looked so cute and lonely." Bobby's voice falters, and he brushes a finger beneath his eye.

Tsula waits until he's gathered himself before continuing. "Last week, after the fight, how did you two leave it?"

"We said all the things we shouldn't, and then I hung up on him. Or maybe he hung up on me. I can't remember. Anyway, the next morning, we talked before he left and both said we were sorry, and then he promised he'd make it up to me for missing the party when he got back." Bobby picks a tuft of Leroy's undercoat from the arm of the couch and lets it fall to the floor. "Liar."

Tsula scribbles a few notes and reviews her printout again. "Your texts also mention something about GPS," she says. "But Alex's bosses have told me they didn't provide him with one."

"Alex knew how nervous I got when he was in the woods for so long. He told me it was silly, but you read stories, you know? To put my mind at ease, he bought one of those devices himself and figured out how to share the data with me. He downloaded some program on my laptop, linked it with the device, and showed me how I could follow along."

Tsula's heart quickens. "You have location data from that trip?"

Bobby nods. "He said he did it so he could have a record of his trips. But I knew it was to make me feel better. If he just wanted that kind of a record, he could have shared it with his own computer or with a co-worker."

"And when you said that it looked like he wasn't moving . . ."

"Just that," Bobby says. "The little marker that's him on the screen, it was in the same place all day. A lot of times he'd enter an area where he just couldn't get whatever signal is required, so his position wouldn't change until he got somewhere better, and then it'd suddenly catch up. I was used to that. And, of course, he would stop to camp overnight. But this time, it's like he didn't move for almost a whole day. I knew that couldn't be right, unless he was hurt or something. I don't remember when I first noticed it. The Halloween party was the night before, and I was in pretty bad shape. But when I figured it out, I texted him. I knew it probably wouldn't go through, but there was nothing else I could do, and I was hoping maybe, you know? And then some hair of the dog later, I guess I forgot that maybe he couldn't receive them and I started taking it personally."

"Where's your laptop now?" Tsula asks.

Bobby lifts a carrying case from the floor beside the couch and holds it out to her. "I had a feeling."

"You haven't deleted the program or the data, have you?"

"Wouldn't know how," he says. "I haven't been able to touch this thing since I got the call they found him. I don't care if I ever get it back."

Tsula takes the case and sets it beside her. "I'm curious—if you were concerned about Alex, why not call someone?"

"Who would I call?" Bobby says. "911? 'Hi, my boyfriend is deep in the woods and won't write me back and I'm scared. Can you please go check on him?'"

"So how did you learn what happened?"

He slowly picks a fleck of polish from his thumbnail. "There's a friend of his from the park. Mandy. She gives tours of . . . something. I met her a couple times when she came to town and joined us for dinner or a night out. She was the one person at Alex's work who knew about me. She called me the next morning, told me."

"Bobby, I suppose you can give me some people who will confirm where you were on Halloween?"

"The party, you mean?"

"As much of the day as you can."

"I'm sure I can. I worked that day, so I was with people for most of it."

"November first and second, too, if you saw anyone?"

"You making sure I didn't Rambo my way into the woods and kill my boyfriend?"

"It's a standard question," Tsula says. "An 'i' I have to dot."

"Someone ends up dead, you look at the husband or the boyfriend first. It *is* like TV." Bobby stands and walks to the kitchen. "Would you like some more coffee?"

"No, thanks. Can't have too much."

"I shouldn't, but I drink it all day long." Bobby fills his mug almost to the rim and returns slowly to the couch. When he finally settles back into his seat, he says, "You don't think Alex shot himself, do you?"

"I didn't say that."

"Yes, you did. Just not in those words."

Tsula shakes her head. "I have no idea yet. And until I do, I have to cover all possibilities. Was there anything going on with him that you observed was new or unusual? Was he depressed? Going through a rough patch of some sort? Anything that might help explain what happened?"

"If he was going through something, he didn't tell me about it. He had his issues like all of us, but nothing unusual."

"Issues like what, exactly?"

"Like I said, he was still coming to terms with who he was. Wasn't sure people would accept him. But when you spend that many years trying to be someone else, that comes with the territory. That's not a new story."

"Anything else you can think of? However small or innocuous it might seem to you."

Bobby considers the question for a moment, then says, "You wouldn't know it when you first meet him, but he could have a real temper."

"How so? Did he get in fights with people or something?"

Bobby chuckles. "I never saw him actually fight. But if something set him off, he'd make you think he would."

"You saw this happen?"

He nods.

"Can you give me an example?"

"A few months ago, he gave a talk to some community group in Waynesville about what he did for the park. I drove over and sat in the audience. I liked to see him speak. Afterward, some guy came up and started bitching at him about the elk. Said he had a farm near the park and he had had to put up extra fencing to keep them off his land, keep them from eating up his pasture or crops—I can't remember which. Nothing Alex hadn't dealt with before, he told me. You'd be surprised how many people have a problem with those elk."

"I'm sure I would not," Tsula says. "So what happened?"

"This asshole tells Alex that if he sees any elk at the edge of his property, he's going to shoot it right through the fence."

"What did Alex do?"

"You would've thought the guy had threatened to shoot Alex's child. He was up in this man's face, finger almost in his eye. And this guy was probably a hundred pounds heavier than Alex, several inches taller. But Alex is face to face with him, telling him that if he did anything like that, he'd better hope the cops get to him first. I thought the guy was going to take a swing at Alex, but someone else stepped in and pushed him away and out the door."

"You saw this go down?"

"I was right there, maybe ten feet away," Bobby says. "It was hot."

Tsula hesitates for a moment, considering how best to approach her next question. "Do you think when he left on his trip, he was over the fight you two had?"

"You mean, do I think he got sad and killed himself because I yelled at him about a party?" Bobby cants his head and squints at her. "How did you imagine I'd answer such a question?"

"I was hoping for honesty," Tsula says. "You just told me he can get pretty upset. And that it was about much more than a party."

"Do you know how many people were at Alex's funeral?" Bobby asks.

"I wouldn't have any idea."

"At least two hundred," he says. "Packed church. Not a damn one of them knew who I was, other than Mandy. I sat in the back, couldn't even *see* the front row where his parents sat. Where I should have been. The parents he barely spoke to, who didn't know

I existed. Can you imagine? After more than a year together? This man who will risk getting his ass beat for an animal couldn't even admit to the world I existed. Of course, I thought about it, was he still upset? Did what happened between us send him down some spiral, make him do it? I couldn't stop thinking about it at first. But after the funeral, I knew the answer was no. I wasn't important enough to him for that."

"I'm sure he loved you, Bobby."

"Really?" Bobby's eyes narrow, and he leans forward. "What makes you say that?"

Tsula looks at him, then shakes her head. "Just something you say, I guess."

"Did you see any hint of me before you saw the text messages? Picture of me on his phone, maybe?"

"I'm still waiting to get the photos from his phone back."

"What about at his apartment? You searched it, didn't you?"

"I did."

"Did you see me anywhere? Wall? Desk? Screensaver?"

Tsula briefly considers telling him she didn't find pictures of any person in Alex's apartment other than a long-deceased baseball player. But whatever that says about Alex might not prove much of a consolation to the one who'd fallen in love with him. Instead, she chooses silence, laboring over a sip of room temperature coffee.

Bobby blows at the steam rising up from his mug and nods. "That's what I thought."

JUNIOR

CHAPTER SEVENTEEN

November 1

Junior finds what he's seeking in a swale between two ridges. He glasses down at the elk from a hillside aflame with autumn color. The animal strides through the clearing about five hundred yards due east, dipping its head now and then to nibble on receding grass that soon will disappear for the winter.

Well, I'll be damned.

He had come out here, half a mile east of the cabin over the surrounding rim of hills, in search of hogs. Two months or so ago, he'd seen the first signs of their presence this close to the homestead: swatches of dried mud thigh-high on tree boles, a wallow the size of a compact car beneath an old oak. Bad tidings for the local plants and the animals that fed on them, but good for putting food in their pot. Since then, he'd bagged three boar and set out this morning intent on bringing home a fourth.

He had been following a thin trail trampled through the grass and undergrowth when he'd heard the bugle. He'd stopped and listened. It came again, and he'd set out in search.

The two curved spikes of antler tell him it's a young bull, no more than a year or two old. He estimates it at three or four hundred pounds. Between the lean muscle and organs, it would last the four of them a good while. Some would spoil eventually, no doubt. But if they dried it right, they could enjoy jerky for weeks, perhaps even months.

A gentle breeze blows up the hillside and kisses his face. He sidesteps slowly down the slope, remaining downwind of the beast's keen nose, until he finds an unobstructed line of sight three hundred yards out. In one smooth but silent motion, he removes the rifle from his pack, sets the pack flat on the ground in front of him, and lowers himself to his belly. He drops his eye to the scope and maneuvers the barrel until the crosshairs come to rest several inches above and behind the animal's front shoulder. Aiming for the lungs.

He sucks in a full breath, exhales half of it, and squeezes the trigger. The stock pulses against his shoulder, the sound of the rifle echoing back like thunder.

The bull startles, takes a half-dozen steps as though to flee, and collapses slowly onto its side. Junior stares at the heap through the scope for several more breaths, just as his daddy taught him. "It gets some second wind, you want to be ready to put another one in it before it gets away." He can still hear the man's words with every kill, even all these years later.

It was his daddy who first called him Junior, though not for the usual reason. Not because the two shared a name. The nickname came in his teenage years, when father Leonard Holiday first taught son Jacob how to drive. From the beginning, Jacob displayed a fearlessness behind the wheel that reminded his old man of Junior Johnson, the 1950s bootlegger turned NASCAR champion. He took corners and curves with abandon, drafted the neighbors' cars on straightaways, and avoided brakes except when absolutely necessary. In the driver's seat, he both impressed and frightened his father in equal measure.

But if there was one pastime in Junior's upbringing that could compete with his love of speed, it was hunting. Ever since his daddy showed him how to work a turkey at age thirteen, he was hopelessly hooked. Each new season gave cause for celebration—black bear, deer, pheasant, quail—and brought its own unique challenges. And unlike driving, it allowed him to spend long stretches of time with his father without inducing panic. When he wasn't stalking live prey on weekends and summers, he sped out to his uncle's property near Sylva and shredded everything he could turn into a target.

Junior enlisted in the Army as soon as he was able, thanks to a recruiter who came to the high school and promised him better guns, more interesting targets, and maybe, if he played his cards right, something to drive. The recruiter was right. The year was 2000, and he served much of the next decade deployed. It was there that he discovered that one "extra gear" his father maintained everyone had buried deep within them. Junior found it conducting sweeps through shitty little villages and tear-assing down potholed roads in pursuit of insurgents, his massive frame shoehorned behind the wheel of the Humvee. Real stakes, life or death, sent adrenaline coursing through his veins like cocaine, washed his brain in jet fuel.

As he stands and packs away his rifle, it occurs to Junior that, of the dozens of animals he has killed, this is his first elk. He was overseas when the park transplanted them in the early 2000s, and he has never seen them anywhere but along the sides of the road cutting north from the Oconaluftee entrance. He prays that this pleasant surprise is a sign of more bounty to come, perhaps a change in their patterns of movement. Surely a bugling male means females are close by.

The yellow jackets are already on the carcass when he reaches it. He waves his hands to shoo them, but it doesn't work. They flit about and return just as quickly, nibbling at the rim of the entry wound. One stings his left hand, and he slaps it dead.

"Little shit."

Junior rubs at the welt that begins to form and takes stock of his unexpected blessing. The usable meat is simply too much for him to carry alone. He'll need to return to the cabin and lead one or two of the others back here with him. He removes a bag stuffed with white cloth strips from his pack and gives the elk one last look. He crosses the clearing westbound and starts up the rise, tying white ribbons on tree branches in intervals as he goes.

He returns an hour later with Harlan and Joseph in tow, urgent to dress the carcass before any predators find it. His companions whistle and hoot when they lay eyes on the bull. "You're earning your keep," Harlan says, clapping a hand on his shoulder. "That's got to be worth a couple logs right there."

Junior shifts on his feet and shakes his head. "Shit."

When Junior had finally agreed to join Harlan and his boys on their mission, it was based largely on a promise. In exchange for his labor on the restoration project and his assistance in eking out a subsistence in the surrounding wilderness, Harlan and the boys would help him build a cabin of his own.

"Think about it," Harlan had said. "No more run-down apartments with domestic squabbles next door. No more landlords kicking you out for smashing something up in one of those . . . moments you sometimes have. And no more cops coming by and hauling your ass off to the hospital for a day or two because they don't like how you're acting. Your own place means you can tell anyone who gives you a hard time to go to hell. Except you won't have to, because no one will know where you are."

When they shook on it, Junior had figured both structures would be done by winter. But Harlan's methods were so exacting that each task took much longer than Junior had anticipated. Junior knew it'd be a slower process without modern equipment, but Harlan obsessed over every detail as though he were restoring a gothic cathedral. At the rate they were going, they'd be lucky to complete the project by winter. Construction on his was unlikely to begin before spring. As a consequence, Harlan's banter about what each fresh kill or foraged plant was worth had grown increasingly tiresome. Like IOUs he wasn't sure would ever be honored.

"Hog got me a couple logs," Junior says, spitting into the grass. "That there's worth a whole damn wall."

"I don't know," Harlan says. "It's not the biggest I've seen."

"Bullshit. It's the *only* one you've seen around here."

They work quickly, stuffing the edible portions into carcass bags, removing the cape, and skinning the skull. The latter, Harlan says, will make a fitting wall decoration once cleaned and sun-bleached.

Junior feels a tickle of irritation on his scalp and in his throat. Once his cabin is done, he's taking the skull with him. If Harlan wants one on his wall, he can shoot the damn thing himself.

Joseph slides the tracking collar off the elk's neck and says, "What do we do with this?"

Harlan nods toward the far hillside. "Take it up that way and leave it."

After they've hauled what remains into the trees at the edge of the field, Harlan hands Junior the cape and fastens the skull to his own pack. Junior narrows his eyes but clamps his mouth shut. He's had a good hunt. No need to spoil that feeling now with disagreements that are not yet ripe. There will be time for such discussions later.

When they're nearly across the clearing, Harlan halts and holds up one hand. He lifts his binoculars and scans the easterly rise.

Junior looks as well but sees only a swell of orange, red, and yellow climbing up toward the sky. "What?" he whispers finally.

Harlan lowers the binoculars, shakes his head, and turns to go.

As they walk, the details of the hunt return to Junior's mind, the sequence replaying over and over. "Was a good kill," his daddy would've said. "You put food on the table today." He's too occupied with his thoughts to remember the white ribbons he'd tied on the branches earlier. The ones that lead back to the cabin. He trudges on, weighted down by the cape and the meat and his thoughts, leaving the markers blowing in the stiff breeze.

TSULA

CHAPTER EIGHTEEN

November 20

Tsula met Jamie Johnston when she was sixteen—he, the swaggering athlete a year ahead of her in school, shouting at her to "look out!" as she carelessly walked across the court in the middle of a game of pickup basketball. She felt him before she saw him, his hands gripping her shoulders to keep her upright as he twisted his body around her mid-stride. When play was stopped and he had retrieved the ball, he returned to her, now scooted back beyond the sideline by a friend but still in shock. Shocked by the sudden fright, but also by the touch of someone's hands on her person—which, except by her mother and a small circle of relatives, did not happen. In that moment, a boundary had been breached, and it thrilled her.

He was beautiful in all the ways television shows said a boy should be beautiful. Wide, mischievous smile always at the ready. Hair so wild and fulsome that his mother, Tsula later learned, constantly begged him to make his way to the barber shop. A broad frame bearing the promise of, but not yet quite achieving, manhood. But what attracted her in that instant was not so much his looks as a capability he seemed to embody. It was a quality he communicated tactilely as he gripped her to protect her, as he bent his body and momentum around her and somehow remained upright. He was not among the scores of high schoolers wondering how they would make it through the next day successfully and without embarrassment. Praying their uncoordinated feet and awkward brains wouldn't plunge them into minor catastrophe.

To her surprise, he did not berate her for interrupting the game as others might have done. Instead, he gave her the first glimpse of that smile, asked if she was okay, and asked her name. From that early moment, she was his, and up until his departure from the Qualla Boundary ten months later, she spent every moment she could with him. Their courtship initially consisted, thanks to the watchful eyes of her mother and his parents, of a long series of chaste walks along the river, ice cream, and high school football games where she waited in the bleachers to greet him when it was over. She didn't mind. The prospect of the physical intimacy some girls in school spoke of in hushed tones, and that boys high-fived over, terrified her. And, in any event, she didn't need him in that way at first. She needed the answers he possessed, his key to walking through the world with such ease and confidence.

Jamie seemed to understand this, and he didn't demand any more of her than she was ready to give. But he also had no real answer to the question she asked of him in so many different ways. "I just know that it's all on me," he once said when she pressed him directly. "Whatever I want to do, whatever I want to become, no one can give it to me. I work as hard as I can, do the best I can. And I tell myself I'm good enough, because I have to be." This response seemed to her of no more value than vague and ancient parables, but she did not blame him. She resolved that, in his youth, he did not yet have the words to explain what he possessed or how he had acquired it. It fell to her to investigate it, to define its contours and divine its origin for herself.

One hot afternoon that summer, Jamie persuaded Tsula to let him drive her north, out of Cherokee and across the Tennessee line, to a waterfall on the northern edge of the park named the Sinks. This was not the destination they had announced to their parents, and Tsula initially resisted the suggestion. But he persisted. "It'll be my birthday soon, you know. Your gift to me is to trust me, let me take you somewhere cool. It'll be fun."

When she entered the car, she noted that he had placed two folded towels in the back seat. He had known, before he ever even brought the idea up to her, that she would agree. This realization both irritated and excited her. "You think you're so slick, don't you?" she said.

He smiled and shrugged. "I'm an optimist."

An hour later, the car skirted the Little River, the sunlight gilding the stream's surface in the deeper, calmer stretches. Tsula knew, based on the signage, that they were within the boundaries of the park, though probably only just so. In time, the water reached a roiling, whitewater cataract followed by a series of calm pools downstream where heads bobbed on the surface. Jamie parked in the lot straddling the river and grabbed the towels.

"We're going swimming?" she asked.

"You can swim anywhere," he said. "This is the Sinks."

She did not ask him anything more, preferring instead to relish this small mystery. She followed him onto a trail high above the downstream river and looked up at an electric blue sky that seemed to scorch the few clouds that dared cross it. A breeze lifted a sweet and herbaceous scent to her nose, and the ground was bursting with Queen Anne's lace. A small swarm of Spring Azure butterflies rose from the edge of the trail like confetti in reverse. In a moment, they came upon a rocky bluff hanging over the gulch, and it no sooner came into view than a man flipped backward off the far edge and disappeared into the void.

"What the hell?" Tsula shouted, causing Jamie to laugh. "You're not serious?"

"Of course I am! Come here."

He led her by her elbow to the edge and pointed down to the man treading water in a still pool, high ripples radiating out from him in all directions. The man hooted, and someone clapped and hooted back.

"See?" Jamie said. "It's deep right there. Look how much darker the water is. Look how still the surface is next to everything else."

"You're crazy!" she said, sidling back from the ledge. Her knees were trembling.

"Wait a minute." He stepped toward her, a look of recognition on his face. "Are you afraid of heights?"

"No," she said much too quickly. It was a lie, and she was certain Jamie could see it in her eyes.

The truth was, Tsula had few true phobias, but heights had always been the most potent. Even climbing into the low branches of her backyard's maple trees or onto the rooftops of her friends' homes used to turn her stomach sour and make her mind go blank. Years later, in her mid-twenties, two friends with graduate psychology degrees would promise to cure this fear with what they called "immersion therapy"—by which they meant they would take her out to climb Colorado rocks for hours until she got too tired to freak out anymore, and then feed her margaritas as a reward. Their plan would not work. Even with a harness and top rope rigged to one of the friends belaying, she would spend a half-day sweating but not moving far, clinging to the rocks like a spooked lizard, the muscles in her flexed legs twitching uncontrollably.

But that day nearly a decade earlier, standing with Jamie on the outcropping, she realized the only outcome she feared more than falling to a watery death was spoiling the day's adventure. That anything could subordinate so deep-seated a fear was itself an astounding revelation. So she repeated her lie and added by way of explanation: "I'm just scared of breaking my neck or leg on the river bottom."

"You won't," he replied. "I've done it a bunch of times, and see?" He spun around slowly as though on display. "I'm still in one piece."

"You're a liar and a bad influence," she said, laughing despite the pounding in her chest.

"You can trust me," he said. "I would never lie to you." He stepped closer and took her hand. "Do you?"

"Do I what?"

"Do you trust me?"

She did, though in this moment both reason and her reptile brain counseled against it. "Yes."

They removed their shoes and placed them on the towels. She giggled nervously, and he winked his reassurance. Then he grabbed and gently squeezed both of her shoulders. "We'll go together," he said. "Stick with me. Jump where I jump, and you'll be fine." She breathed in and out heavily, then nodded.

In the years that followed, Tsula would find that she could not recall that walk to the edge or the thrust of her legs into the air. Her clearest memory more than twenty years later is of the long, breathless wait as she fell, seemingly forever, and the water swallowing her at last. When she burst from its surface, unhurt, her mind noisy and electric, she grabbed for Jamie and kissed him hard.

Later, in the fading light, they lay together in a secluded field amongst seeding dandelions and surrendered to each other as they had not done before, paying no attention to the mosquitoes that circled their bodies or the faint sound of cars on the road just out of sight.

Toward the end of July, Jamie turned eighteen and announced to Tsula that he had visited the Army recruitment office in Sylva and decided to enlist. "It's a great opportunity," he offered as Tsula blinked back the burning haze in her eyes. "I'm not the student you are, and college just isn't for me. But the recruiter told me I can learn all kinds of new skills toward a bunch of different careers."

"But . . ." Her voice trailed off as she searched for some argument or incantation which might reverse time, might un-seed this idea from his brain before it could take root.

"You know I can't just stay here and do nothing," he said. "Working odd jobs, whatever I can find on a high school diploma? That's not a future."

"But people live here. They work here."

"It's not about here or there," he said. "It's about chasing your opportunities. Are you telling me that you're not planning on leaving when you graduate, going somewhere else for college?"

She hesitated. There were universities within an hour's drive. The truth was, she had not once considered a future which involved leaving for a place he would not be. The fact that he had done so felt like a betrayal.

"Because you should be," Jamie continued. "With your grades, you can go anywhere you want."

"But . . . the Army?"

"My cousin Davey, he enlisted like five years ago, learned how to be an electrician while he was stationed in Georgia. Now he's out and going to NC State, studying to be an engineer. If you'd known him in high school, you would've never guessed that's how he'd end up. It taught him some things, and it made him grow up a lot."

Through panicked eyes she saw he had made up his mind, and now she was fighting the tide. She turned away to hide the tears she no longer could contain.

"Tsul," he said, using the nickname he'd given her. In his mouth, the first consonant came so close to a *j* that she could believe he was calling her something precious and beautiful. "I need to make something of myself we can both be proud of." He placed a hand on her shoulder. "Tsul, look at me. Please."

If she said anything to him after that, those words, too, were lost to the intervening years. Her memories of the remainder of that summer reside now in the realm of the sensory. The moist smell of coming rain. The chapped pain of sunburned skin. The pang of imminent loss always lingering just below the surface, like a bruise. She and Jamie remained inseparable until he departed for basic training; she knows that is true. Still, she can't recall a single day with him after this conversation in any detail. The summer ended, she returned to school for her senior year, and just like that, he was gone.

He wrote to her at first. Simple letters detailing the grind of basic training, the nicknames and personalities of the other trainees. The ever-changing plans of a young man who felt his limitations had been lifted and for whom all was now possible. Then, on a nondescript morning in early September, Tsula stood watching two smoldering skyscrapers collapse on television and knew it all would change. His last letter told her he was shipping out for Afghanistan soon. "I'm not sure how much I'll be able to write you while I'm there," the letter said. "I'm not sure what it'll be like. I'm pretty sure you won't want to read about all that. But with any luck, I'll be home sometime next year."

The following January, Tsula returned from school one afternoon to find her mother sitting at their small, round kitchen table, her face pale and grave.

"Sit down, Tsula," she said.

# #

When Clara Walker spoke Jamie's name almost three weeks ago, it was the first time Tsula had heard it said aloud in nearly two decades. He is not a subject she volunteers, and her mother typically knows to avoid it. After Clara's indiscretion on the drive home from the church, memories long shut away had returned to confront Tsula and would not be denied. There had been other men since him—one in college, a handful in subsequent years. But none had held her interest for long, and none could inspire in her the passion she once had felt for Jamie and she now feels for her all-consuming job.

It takes her a couple of weeks of aimless driving whenever her schedule permits before she finds the field that she and Jamie shared that evening. The years have worn away the sharp contours of even that memory. What remains is more an impression of the event— the feel of the grass on skin, their languid repose after as crickets chirped, her mother waiting up for her when she returned long after dark. The look on her face.

Eventually, Tsula locates the clearing tucked away in a sparsely populated corner of the Qualla Boundary, less than five miles from Jamie's family home. It looks smaller to her now than she recalls— roughly two acres, she figures, far deeper than it is wide. That evening years before, it had felt as though they had a whole valley to themselves. Also absent are the summer dandelions and golden aster, replaced by desiccating yellow and orange leaves blown in from bordering trees. Even so, she recognizes the place from a bend in the road near the dirt entrance, which Jamie swore had been the site of more than one fatal car wreck.

As she props herself against the front grille of her vehicle, a whitetail doe and her fawn step daintily into the field to feed on the withering grass. The mother mainly stands watch, her black eyes trained on Tsula, ears twitching, while her offspring noses the ground. Tsula returns the doe's gaze and does not move. For a brief moment, her mind is still.

Her phone breaks the silence like cannon fire. She jumps, and the deer disappear back into the trees.

"Sorry," Tsula calls out to them, fumbling in her pocket for the phone. "Hello?"

"I'm going to be transferring some files to you," Harris tells her.

"Anything good?"

"I was able to capture that GPS data. Hopefully you'll know what to make of it."

"Here's hoping," she says. "Thanks again for your help, Harris."

Tsula hops up onto the hood of her SUV and lies back, looking up at an overcast sky. She pinches the bridge of her nose with her fingers, and the pressure relieves a dull throb behind her eyes. Nearby, a chimney belches the acrid smoke of still-wet wood, and it burns her nostrils.

CHAPTER NINETEEN

December 1

Thirty minutes into sparring, Tsula lands flat on her back, every wisp of breath expelled from her lungs. Her partner mounts, rocking his heft up her torso, his knees and thighs prying her arms up and away from her body. Soon he'll have a forearm across her neck.

These are precisely the moments when Tsula's mind used to excite with fear. The reaction was so sudden and overwhelming that she'd tap out without giving it so much as a thought, or freeze up until exhaustion overtook her. "You're panicking," her instructor would say. "You can get out of these holds if you just relax and think about your next move." Easier said than done, she'd thought. But after years of practice, she'd learned to recognize the fear, to grasp it with both hands and set it aside.

Tsula closes her eyes, draws in what breath the pressing weight will allow, and thrusts her hips off the mat with firmly planted feet. Near the crest, she twists her hips to the right, and the man's body tilts with them, toppling to the mat. The tangled mass of them keeps rolling, and soon she's mounted him, her arms grappling for an advantage.

Her phone sounds with the ring assigned to her mother's

number. She taps her partner on the arm to pause the sparring and trots over to her bag to retrieve her phone. "Yeah, Mom?"

"Tsula," her mother said. Her voice is weak and ragged.

"Mom, what's going on?"

"I'm not feeling so good."

# #

Dr. Henderson rolls a stool up next to Clara Walker's bed and takes a seat. He looks somberly at her sleeping face, the clear venti-mask fogging with each breath, and then at Tsula, who hovers near the foot of the bed. "This is probably what we can expect as the disease goes untreated. Has she been going to dialysis?"

"Yes, she's been going," Tsula says. "She doesn't like it, but she's been going."

He nods, his face long and slack. "It concerns me that she's still having these episodes even with regular dialysis. Now I'm wondering if the cancer isn't in her kidneys after all. I'm still optimistic we can have her back up and running in a few days. But I'm worried she'll be back here sooner the next time, and even sooner the time after that."

Tsula rubs her eyes with the heels of her hands. She feels suddenly exhausted. "When will we know about the cancer?"

"Results of the scans will be ready soon," he says.

"So you'll be by later?"

"I'll round on her again this afternoon. We should know a lot more by then."

Knuckles rap out the rhythm of "Shave and a Haircut" on the hallway door, and both of them look up. Tommy Weathers stands at the threshold with flowers in his hand.

"Doctor. Special Agent."

Tsula resists the temptation to slam the door in his face. "Representative."

Dr. Henderson looks back and forth between the two and promptly excuses himself from the room. Weathers steps aside to allow him to pass, then enters.

"I hope I'm not intruding."

Tsula sighs. "Well, you're here now."

"Ms. Betty called me, very worried," he says. "How's she doing?"

Tsula gestures a hand toward her mother, toward the array of lines and leads. "You're looking at it."

Weathers searches the room for a place to set the bouquet down. Tsula watches him but says nothing, in no mood to play host. Finally, he shrugs and lays them in a guest chair against the wall.

"Is there anything I can do?"

It's a perfunctory question, Tsula knows. What one asks under the circumstances. But the worry in his eyes catches her off guard and tempers her bubbling anger.

"This is the second time in a month Mom's been here," she says finally. "Her kidneys aren't working right. They've recommended surgery and chemo because the cancer's back, but she's refusing. She's doing dialysis, thank God, or else she'd probably be dead already."

He opens his mouth to speak, but she continues.

"All of this," she says, motioning around the hospital room, "plus the dialysis when she's not here, the scans to check progress, the surgery and chemo if she'd allow it—whatever she needs that doesn't come free, I'm paying. Plus the rent, utilities, food. So I can't—I *won't*—allow anything or anyone to endanger my job. I won't take that risk."

She allows these words to settle around them before stepping toward him and lowering her voice.

"I know you told the park superintendent I was at that meeting."

His face blanches, and he swallows hard. "I never said it was you."

"You said it was someone from the Park *Service*, not the park. You didn't think that would narrow it down?"

He takes a breath and appears ready to reply, then lets the air out and shakes his head. "I guess now that I think about it . . ." He drops his eyes to the floor.

"You're lucky this is the first time we've seen each other since I found out," Tsula says. "I was really going to crawl up your ass. But now"—she looks back at her mother in the bed—"I just don't have the energy."

He reaches behind his head and scratches his neck nervously. "I'm sorry. I never meant to implicate *you*. I just wanted—"

"I know what you wanted," she says. "But now I need you to recognize what I have at stake."

Tsula can tell from his pained expression that he wants to turn away, but still he maintains her gaze. "I understand."

A nurse knocks lightly at the door, takes stock of the room, and departs just as quickly.

"I can't decide," Tsula says, "if you pulled this stunt because you really believe you have a shot at winning this fight, or if you just keep going because you can't give up without losing face."

He furrows his brow and tilts his head. "I'm not nearly as cynical as you think I am, Special Agent. I keep going because at least if I press, then maybe they have to respond, explain themselves to us and to everyone who's watching. Do I think the federal government has suddenly grown a conscience after all these years? No. But I've read the articles, and I've seen the TV coverage. We have public support. So maybe, with that support and the right strategy, we can shame them into a different answer."

Tsula examines his face for a long moment. Something in the set of his jaw, his narrowed eyes, tells her he means what he says, and the earnestness surprises her.

"Okay," she says. "Fair enough. But you're going to have to

figure out a strategy that doesn't involve me."

He nods, and the two fall into a heavy silence. Just outside the door, a therapist in aquamarine scrubs escorts a frail patient down the hallway, offering him encouragement as one would a child first learning to walk. The shuffle of the man's feet and walker drag out their own plodding rhythm.

"Now, since you asked what you can do," Tsula says once they've passed by. "And because I think we can all agree you owe me."

He straightens his slouching body and looks at her. "Anything."

"Come back this afternoon when Mom's awake, and see if you can talk her into the treatments they've recommended. She won't listen to me, but she adores you. For whatever reason."

"Of course. Whatever I can do. She is one of my favorites."

"I know," Tsula says. "Mine, too."

CHAPTER TWENTY

December 5

The house is set back in the woods down a single-track gravel drive, nearly a mile from the paved road. Over that gravel path looms a canopy that reminds Tsula of the rainforests in Oregon. Inside, a full fifteen degrees colder than the world around it, the moisture thick and dank on still air. Dusk all day long, until it is night again. Green moss and mushrooms the shape of cantilevered steps cling to the trees, ferns arcing above the roots.

In front of the house curls a drive of fresh ballast in the shape of a teardrop that eventually returns to the same single-track path she's just come in on. Trees rise up from the island in the center of the drive, reaching for the sunlight. Tsula drives almost the full circle and pulls to a stop with her SUV aimed back toward the single-track path. In unfamiliar surroundings, she prefers her vehicle pointing toward the exit. She looks down at the property records sitting in the passenger's seat and the driving directions on her phone. Then she peers over her left shoulder out the back driver's side window. This is indeed the place.

The last recorded sale of the .22 revolver that killed Alex Lowe was in 1984 to a man named Carl Miles. The dealer who sold it to Mr. Miles had long ago gone out of business and shipped all of its records to the Bureau of Alcohol, Tobacco, Firearms and Explosives, where they've remained in paper form, gathering dust. It was a minor miracle that the sale records were located this quickly, or at all. But since nothing can ever be that easy, Tsula next learned that Carl Miles died thirty years ago while serving a prison sentence for robbing a pharmacy. The man's last known residence has long ago been razed, and his wife also is deceased. That leaves an adult son, named Harlan, as his only surviving next of kin.

The house she now sits in front of is this son's last known address. She hopes he can help her account for the more recent whereabouts of that revolver. Perhaps he found it while cleaning out his father's belongings and placed it in the stream of undocumented commerce that flows all around them.

Tsula opens her driver's door but stops before stepping out. From somewhere in the trees comes a rumble, the low growl of some form of motor growing near. It occurs to her she may have passed trail cameras affixed to the trees along the single-track. Someone knows she has driven up and is coming to check her out.

An ATV noses its way out of the tree line and onto the circular drive. A silver-haired man in jeans and a Carhartt jacket, no helmet, gooses the engine and comes around the drive, cutting the vehicle off just behind her SUV. Harlan Miles is around fifty, if her memory serves her, but this man appears closer to seventy. Perhaps he's the landlord, Daniel Willis, who according to local property tax records lives on an adjoining ten acres. The man hops off the vehicle, spry for his apparent age, and stands looking at her truck. Tsula steps out, credentials in hand, and turns to face him.

"Can I help you?" the man says.

"Are you Mr. Willis?"

"I am. And you?"

"I'm Tsula Walker. I'm a Special Agent with the National Park Service Investigative Services Branch."

"That's a mouthful."

"Wears me out just saying it."

A smile briefly cracks his taciturn demeanor. "What can I do for you?"

"I'm here on an investigation," she says. "Need some info."

The old man slowly spins a full rotation until he's back around and squinting at her again. "I don't see no park around here. Just my property."

"I do apologize for being a bother. I'm just hoping to speak with a man I think lives here. Harlan Miles?"

"You got a warrant or something I should see?"

"No warrant," she says. "I'm not here to search anything or arrest anybody. I was just hoping to have a chat with Mr. Miles, ask him some questions."

Willis smiles again, broader this time, and sets his arms akimbo. "He ain't here."

"Do you know when he'll be back? I can wait."

The man swivels his head to the side and launches a long stream of brown tobacco spittle toward the ground.

"Won't do you no good to wait. Harlan Miles moved out like six months ago."

"You got any idea where he went?"

"It ain't like that with me. You don't want to live here no more, that's fine. So long as you pay me the last of what you owe and leave the place as you found it, where you go after is none of my business."

"He didn't leave an address to forward his mail?"

"Do you see a mailbox anywhere?" Willis says. "Ain't no mailman comes back here. If Harlan had a box up at the Post Office, that wouldn't be my concern. You could check with them."

"And I take it you didn't have a security deposit to send back to him, either?"

"Harlan's a builder," the man replies. "We agreed when he moved in, if anything broke, he'd just fix it. I didn't ask for no deposit. I knew he was good for it."

"Did he happen to leave anything behind when he left?"

Willis eyes her again, pauses. "Anything you're looking for in particular?"

Tsula doesn't answer.

After a moment, Willis shakes his head. "Place was cleaned out when they left."

"They?"

"He had two boys," Willis says, then corrects himself. "Men now, really. And a wife at one point, but she's been dead a while. What did you say you're investigating exactly?"

Tsula hesitates before answering. In the event the man is lying about having no contact with his old tenant, she doesn't want him knowing anything specific he could pass on. If Mr. Miles does have information on the revolver, he'll surely be more reluctant to speak with her knowing the gun has been involved in a death. "I didn't," she says at last.

Willis glares at her, as though this response violated some tacit agreement they'd reached. "So that's it, huh? You come up on my property uninvited, and you're the only one gets to ask the questions?"

"Mr. Willis—"

"No," he says, cutting her off. "I've run out of hospitality. It's time you head on back where you came from." He climbs back onto the four-wheeler. In the motion, his jacket swings open, revealing the grip of a holstered pistol. "You come back up this way, make sure you got somethin' like a warrant."

Tsula nods and turns back to her vehicle.

Driving back down the road—not too quickly, lest Willis think he'd gotten to her—she spots the trail cameras. Camouflage rectangles affixed to trees at the edge, angled toward the house so that drivers headed up the single-track path won't see them. Willis follows closely behind her, just his head and shoulders visible through her rear hatch window. He peels off toward his own property only once she reaches the end of the drive and turns onto the blacktop beyond.

CHAPTER TWENTY-ONE

December 15

'You told me it was going to be simple. Dead guy, gun nearby. Remember?"

Tsula wipes sweat from her brow with a wadded-up napkin. The small Sevier County diner is uncomfortably hot, the air tumid with butter and bacon grease sprung from a griddle barely hidden behind a swinging half-door. She glances down at her bowl of oatmeal—instant, she figures, judging from its mealy texture—and imagines a cap of aerated fat congealing on its surface if she were to sit here long enough.

This establishment is not, to put it kindly, Tsula's kind of place. The patrons are surly and surprisingly vocal about their standards, given the food being served. The staff are by turns outwardly indifferent, impatient, and jittery for reasons unknown but worthy of suspicion. But it's Batchelder's favorite venue for an in-depth morning discussion—whether because he likes the food or because he feels certain no one can hear them over the chaos, Tsula isn't sure.

Batchelder watches as a tangerine glob of over-easy egg slides off the tines of his fork and splashes back onto his plate. "I know we've talked about it in pieces. But how about you take me from the top, give me the whole thing, and I'll be the judge of how easy it is." He scans his shirt for any splatter of orange. "So, victim found dead in the park—"

"Alex Lowe, park wildlife biologist."

"Okay. Alex Lowe."

"Found dead of a gunshot wound to the head."

"ME confirmed that was the cause of death?"

"Yes."

"Time of death?"

"One to two days before he was found. Best he's been able to do."

In the far corner of the diner, a plate shatters on the tile floor, and patrons clap and jeer. Batchelder looks over his shoulder briefly, then turns back to her.

"He was out there twenty-four to forty-eight hours, and no one saw him?" Batchelder asks.

Tsula shrugs. "He was down an embankment in the creek behind the ranger station. I'm not all that surprised."

"Tell me about the gun."

"Twenty-two revolver, snub-nose. One round missing from the cylinder."

"And found in the victim's skull?"

"Too beat up for a ballistics match, but the recovered bullet did come from a .22."

"What range?"

"Very close. Stippling and a ton of residue."

"Residue on his hand as well?"

"Yes, but—"

"Starting to add up to me."

A thin, pock-marked waiter approaches, presenting his coffee pot like a question. Both shake their heads, and the man floats past to the next table without a word. Batchelder watches him until he's out of earshot, then turns back to Tsula.

"I interrupted you. 'But' what?"

"Well, that's where things start getting hard. He'd been out in the park for a few days hunting hogs, so he had residue on both his hands. That doesn't actually tell me much, I don't think."

"Entry wound on the right side of his head, residue on his right hand—that's not nothing."

"Except he was left-handed."

"And?"

"Come on," Tsula says. "Who shoots themselves with their non-dominant hand?"

Batchelder places his napkin on his plate and pushes it away. "When my son, Logan, was young, he used his left hand for everything. I was so excited. I was already researching how young I could put him in Little League, planning his career as a middle reliever for the Braves. But then when he was like two, Logan tipped a small marble-top table over onto his left hand and broke it. Spent two months with a cast on it, couldn't use it at all. In just two months, he learned to use his right hand because he had to, and that was it for him being left-handed. Never went back to it, even when the cast came off. *Except* he eats with his left hand. Does everything else righty. Eats lefty, even ten years later."

"Using a fork and shooting a gun aren't the same thing," Tsula says.

"I'm just saying people aren't always consistent with the hands they use." He sips his coffee. "Does this gun have a serial number?"

She nods. "Last evidence of a sale was to a local named Carl Miles who's been dead a long time."

"How long?"

"Twenty-plus years. Died in prison."

"In prison for what?"

"Robbery."

"That kind of entrepreneurship can run in a family. He got kids?"

"One adult son who used to live in the area. No record to speak of. Pretty under-the-radar kind of guy. The landlord at his last known residence says he moved out in May. No idea where he went."

"We can't find him?"

"Not yet. Still looking."

"All we know for sure, then," Batchelder says, "is the last recorded purchaser didn't kill our victim. Owner died in prison, and the gun went on walkabout. Maybe this son found it and pawned it, bartered with it, whatever. Could have ended up in anyone's hands. We don't know because those transactions aren't the kind people keep records of."

"You think Alex Lowe got this .22 off some pawnbroker or street corner sale?" Tsula shakes her head. "There's nothing else about this guy that suggests he's the type. Why would he do that?"

"Imagine you're thinking of ending things but all you have is a rifle," he says. "That'd be a bitch. You want to get something else more user-friendly, and quick, no waiting period, where do you go? But fine, for the sake of argument, I'll give you that one. He doesn't seem like the type. Answer me this: Did you find any red flags for suicide?"

"Friends and family don't report he was withdrawn or acting strangely. His work performance was steady and good. Nothing concerning in e-mails, texts, social media. He looked like a normal guy doing normal things. Only one thing even comes close, but I honestly don't know what to make of it."

"Okay?"

Tsula stares down at her coffee mug and spins it slowly on the table with one hand. "He was gay but not really out, and he and his boyfriend had a big fight about it the night before he left."

"About not being out?"

"The boyfriend says it was taking a toll on their relationship."

"I can imagine."

"I'm not thinking that's much of a red flag," Tsula says. "But I'm open to more . . . informed perspectives."

Batchelder eyes her for a moment, then leans back in his chair and shrugs. "Lots of people are still in that boat, I imagine, no matter how far things have come. And not all places"—he motions his hand around him—"progress at the same rate. I was worried about coming out where I grew up. Jeffrey'd tell you the same. The futures we were able to imagine didn't involve getting married and having kids, I can tell you that. It took a long time before any of that was conceivable. We didn't take our lives over it, but we knew someone who did."

"Did you see it coming, with the person you knew?"

"It shocked the hell out of me. I guess for some it simmers a long time before it boils over, and maybe from the outside you don't get a lot of warning. Best I can say." He motions to the waiter for the check. "What else you got?"

Tsula pulls a map from the pocket of her fleece. "The big thing that I can't understand, the thing I need to show you, is Alex's path."

"Explain."

She clears the dishes out of the way and unfolds the map on the table facing him. On the map she's placed a series of Xs in black ink marking the locations of feral hog traps which, according to his last journal entry and the well-worn map found on his body, Alex had intended to scout. Tsula has also placed red dots wherever Alex's GPS locator picked him up along the way. One final red dot toward the bottom of the map marks where he was found behind Twentymile Ranger Station on November 3.

"According to his records, he was going to visit three collections of hog traps in the westernmost segment of the park. He entered the park through the tunnel off Lake View Drive, hiked north a bit, then worked his way west. Most of the trip, it looks like he followed his plan. But then, on November 1, he did something I can't explain." She indicates a red dot about a mile southwest of his planned route. It sits in what appears to be a small clearing between the bunched contour lines of several surrounding hills. "GPS next picks him up down here. He's off course."

"He was hunting," Batchelder says. "Maybe he was chasing a hog."

"Maybe. But then it looks like he just stops moving. He has more traps to inspect, more of his route still to go, but it doesn't look like he got there. The GPS stays put at this last spot until it goes dead the next day, November 2. Then the next morning, without any explanation, he shows up dead a full day's hike to the southeast, down here at Twentymile. There are no trails that people can take between these two points. He would have had to leave what he was doing and find his way around all these mountains and ridgelines to make it to Twentymile. And the GPS wasn't on him when he was found. For all we know, it's still back here." She points again to the dot in the clearing a full day's hike or more to the northwest.

"So while he's out there, he decides he's had enough. For reasons yet to be determined. He leaves his route. Ditches his GPS out there somewhere, probably so no one knows what he's up to. Comes back and checks out."

"He would have had to ditch more than his GPS," she says. "We didn't find any of his gear. Backpack, tent, water, food. Rifle. None of it. Not at Twentymile, not at his apartment, not at his office."

"So?"

"That's too tough a hike, and he's too experienced out there to just dump all his gear."

"That'd be true if you're talking about someone who wants to stay alive. But if he doesn't, you move faster without sixty, seventy pounds of gear on your back. You're looking for the red flag? There you go. He quits the job he's doing right in the middle, ditches all the gear he'd need to keep himself safe, goes off everyone's radar. That sounds to me like a person in crisis."

The waiter appears and sets the check on the table.

"Look, bottom line," Batchelder says. "Either he put a bullet in his own head, or someone else did it for him. You've given me some reasons why you think maybe he didn't do it. Fair enough. But you've given me nothing yet that makes me think someone else did. No forensics that indicate it was someone else, right?"

"That's true," she says.

"No witnesses saw shit, other than the kid who found him, and he didn't see anything other than a body."

"True again."

"You pulled surveillance video, backcountry permits?"

"We did. Dead end."

"What about boot prints, fingerprints—anything that puts someone other than our witness at the scene?"

"One partial print near the body, but not enough to cast. The leaf cover was a bitch. There were prints on the road and the trail just beyond, but it was autumn. You'd expect a bunch of hikers going through there."

"What about the tip line?"

"Nothing useful."

"Any reason you've uncovered that someone else might want him dead?"

She shakes her head.

"Then where's this headed?" He leans back, places his hands behind his head, and raises his eyebrows expectantly.

Tsula taps a brief, nervous rhythm on the table, then says,

"There's something I need to do."

"Need?"

"Okay, want very, very badly."

"I'm all ears."

Tsula points at the red dot in the clearing between the mountains, Alex's last known location before Twentymile Ranger Station. "This is where it all changed. I want to go take a look."

"You want to what, hike a full day or more into the backcountry, just to take a look?" Batchelder shakes his head. "And what do you think you're going to find out there after all this time?"

"Honestly? I don't know. But this meticulous person threw out his plan right here. Why? It's the last thing we know for sure before he shows up dead. Whatever it was, it must have been big. Maybe I'll find something that explains it. Maybe I'll find all his gear ditched out there like you said. Maybe . . . who knows? But I won't feel like I'm through with this investigation until I've done it."

"That's a pretty thin rationale. When were you wanting to make this journey, Meriwether Lewis?"

"ASAP. I'm here the next couple of days."

"You do realize there's a massive winter front headed this way soon? They're talking feet of snow, not inches."

"All the more reason to get out there now," she says. "If there's something to see, I need to see it. Lord knows what the snow will do to anything that's still out there."

He hesitates before asking, "What about your mother?"

"What about her?"

"You sure you want to be out there away from her right now?"

"It's no different than flying up to Acadia or driving to Mammoth Cave, both of which I did recently. She's got friends who'll check on her. It's a couple days at most."

Batchelder screws his lips and shoves them to one side of his face.

Tsula doesn't wait for him to answer. "The way I see it, it's a win-win. If I find something that helps, great. I'm doing my job. If I don't, I'll have to come back and admit you were right and that it was a waste."

"I do like being right."

"And rubbing it in," she says. "I know."

He crushes his napkin into a tiny ball and squeezes it several times in silence. "Tell you what. I'll let you go if someone goes with you. I can't spare anyone, but I'll call the chief ranger to see if she can."

Tsula shakes her head. "I don't need a babysitter."

"You're talking about going backcountry with biblical weather right around the corner. I'm not about to let you go alone."

"I'll move faster on my own," she says. "I grew up in these mountains."

"Have you made the hike you're talking about now?"

She doesn't answer.

"Of course not. Because there's no trail. Plus, you've spent almost two decades out west in between. Forgive me if I don't consider your distant memory of some other place an asset."

"Brian—"

"I'm not negotiating. You go with someone, or you don't go."

She leans back in her chair and shoves her hands deep inside the pockets of her fleece. "Fine. But get me someone who knows what they're doing at least. I'm not running a guide service."

"Whatever you say."

Batchelder swipes up the check, the paper nearly translucent with grease, and strains to read the total.

"A couple other things," he continues. "One, you're carrying a GPS tracker. I know there are lots of places out there where it won't work, but I want tabs on you as much as I can. Two, I don't care how much you do or don't get done, you get out before the weather gets bad. Deal?"

"Fine."

"Look in my eyes, please, and see that I'm serious. If I have to send out a search party to look for your frozen ass, I'm going to be pissed. More pissed than I was about that shit show down in Florida."

"You need to let that go," Tsula says. "They cleared me, you know."

"Don't push my buttons, Walker."

"Okay, okay." She raises her hands in surrender. "I got it."

"Good," he says, laying cash down on the table. "Now let's go. I need to find you a babysitter."

CHAPTER TWENTY-TWO

That afternoon, Ranger Greg Abbott calls Tsula and asks her to meet him at a bar in downtown Bryson City. "Apparently you and I are taking Alex's investigation on the road," he says. "We need to talk details. But it's my day off, and my fiancée's at work, so that's where I'll be for the foreseeable future."

Tsula takes the two-lane highway west from Cherokee, past abandoned motels disappearing into the kudzu and rusting neon signs of teepees and tomahawk warriors, to the tiny town straddling the Tuckasegee River.

"How'd you get so lucky?" she asks him, settling into a chair across the table and sliding a beer toward him. Daylight pours in through the front windows. The ceiling of the bar's main room arches above them, reminding Tsula of a small air hangar.

Abbott leans forward and catches the can. "The Chief knows I used to be a guide."

"Backcountry?"

"That's right."

"Bullshit."

He sips at the foam rimming the can. "It's true. Anything from day hikes to a week or two camping."

"Around here?"

"Here, north Georgia, Tennessee, Virginia. Wherever the work was. I pretty much lived out of my truck."

"How long ago was this?"

"Whole other life ago," he says. "Back when showers and grooming weren't quite as important as they are now."

Tsula cocks her head, as though viewing him from a new angle might help her discern the wilderness nomad behind the high-and-tight haircut and the stern countenance. "I'm having a hard time seeing it."

"You're not alone. Most people's heads explode when I bring up the ponytail."

"Mine's exploding right now," Tsula says. "How did you go from that to park police?"

He shrugs. "I decided I wanted more steady pay and got tired of moving from place to place. But I still wanted to be outdoors, you know? Seemed like the natural choice."

"But there are lots of other jobs you could have applied for that would have let you spend your time outside. Why law enforcement?"

Abbott taps at his can absently, looking toward Tsula but not at her, as though mulling something in his head. Finally, he says, "I knew a girl, Sarah, who got attacked on the AT. That was my last season guiding."

Tsula leans forward. "I'm sorry," she says.

"She was a guide, too, and I'd met her the summer before. We were . . . friends."

The way Abbott says *friends* suggests that perhaps they'd been more than that—or, at least, that he'd wished for them to be. "How bad?" she asks.

"Bad as it can be," he says, shifting uncomfortably in his seat. "They found her body still in her sleeping bag just yards from her campsite. They figured he'd come up on her in the middle of the night. Dragged her out of her tent and off into the brush."

"Did they ever charge anyone?"

Abbott inhales deeply and holds it, shakes his head. "She was camping alone. I begged her not to do that, but she wouldn't listen. Said she'd been doing it for years and enjoyed her time by herself. Anyway, no one was around to see anything, and the DNA didn't match anyone anybody knew about. They never came up with any suspects."

Tsula nods slowly and allows her perception of Abbott to clarify. The carefree existence gutted by loss; purpose later forged from rage and grief. She's heard variations on this story from any number of law enforcement officers over the years—almost always, like this one, recounted in the confessional of a bar.

"So you wanted to make sure no other Sarahs got hurt," she says. "Or at least make sure the guy who does it gets caught."

Abbott grimaces slightly. "Sounds silly when you put it like that."

"No, it doesn't."

For a moment, the only sounds are those of the bar around them. On the television suspended above the bartender, three suited men passionately debate the coming weekend's football games and the results from the prior weekend. Somewhere behind them in the recesses, a cue ball breaks a nine-ball rack.

Abbott clears his throat and picks at a Nantahala Brewing Company sticker affixed to the tabletop. "So, Special Agent—"

"Call me Tsula," she says. "Or Walker. I'll answer to either."

"Okay, Tsula. How about we get back to why you're here? Where are we going and when?"

She nods, unfolds the map, and lays it out on the table facing him. "We're going here," she says, pointing at the same clearing she'd shown Batchelder.

"That's pretty deep into the park," Abbott says, furrowing his brow, "with no trails close by. You think Alex was there?"

"GPS says he was."

"Gonna take a while to get there. You know about the forecast, right?"

"I've heard. That's why I want to get out there as soon as possible. Whatever's still out there to see, I don't know what that kind of weather will do to it."

He studies the map at length, dragging his finger back and forth between their destination and the park's southern border. Finally, he asks: "You any good on a horse?"

"It's been a while, but I'm alright. Why?"

He turns the map around and walks around the table beside her. "If I'm reading this correctly, it looks like maybe there's a route we can take through the mountains, not over them, here. You see this?" He runs his finger in a serpentine line along the map.

She squints, concentrates for a long moment, and then sees it. Between the opposing groupings of irregular, concentric rings, each representing a rising mountain or ridge, his finger traces one uninterrupted lowland route to the clearing. The path briefly follows a small branch, then parts ways with the stream, winding between the ancient peaks until, several miles into the interior, it reaches the small cul-de-sac marked in red. With Abbott's finger on the map, she sees the route plainly. A moment later he lifts his finger, she blinks, and it's gone.

"Wait, show me again?"

"You got a pen?"

She pulls one from her back pocket and hands it to him. "It's here," he says, lightly committing the route to ink. "Looks like it stays somewhere between fifteen and eighteen hundred feet elevation the whole way."

"That's incredible."

"I wouldn't be surprised if people used this as a road before the park took the land over. Back when people lived there."

"So . . . horses?" Tsula says.

Abbott's nod is tentative and suggests he's trying to convince them both of his plan. "We could cover ground faster with them. Plus, they can carry the gear. With the storm coming, we'll want to pack more, for contingencies."

"It's not supposed to be here until Thursday, right? Why not just head out tomorrow on foot?"

"The forecast keeps moving up," he says. "On foot, there and back is a two-day trip minimum, and that's hiking full-tilt. We don't want to cut it that close if we don't have to. If the storm shows up even a little early, we're out in it, and maybe for a while. My guess is, if we leave out at first light on horseback, we can be back here before sundown, and we'll miss the weather entirely. If we absolutely have to, we can camp somewhere for the night, head back at first light, and hopefully still miss most of it. Either way, at least we wouldn't be out hiking in it."

"But how would we get horses for first thing tomorrow morning?"

"I know a guy who runs an outfitter," Abbott says. "It's the middle of the week with shitty weather on the way, so he should have some available. I gotta run this by him, though, to make sure he thinks it's doable for his horses. I'll need your map for that."

"Of course. Take it with you."

He folds up the map and places it in his front fleece pocket. "You good on gear for this?"

"I'm good."

"Alright then. We both have some packing to do. I'll go see about the horses. If they're not available, or if he tells me I'm crazy, we'll do it your way. We'll go on foot and pray the weather has mercy on us."

He stands and pulls his wallet from his back pocket, but Tsula shakes her head.

"These are on me. I'm interrupting your day off. It's the least I could do."

He shrugs. "Tomorrow I'll be in the woods instead of a patrol car. I'd say that's a fair trade."

JUNIOR

CHAPTER TWENTY-THREE

November 1

They're nearly to the fire pit in front of the cabin, the leaves and lacy greens of winter vegetables flanking them in the garden, when they hear the man approaching behind them. The sound, unobtrusive as it is, strikes Junior with all the violence of an earthquake cleaving the land. He knows instantly that their time in this place, however long it will be, has now split in two: what has been, and whatever will come next.

"Stay where you are!"

The voice bellows, but buried beneath the bluster, Junior detects a hint of something else. A tremor of uncertainty. Fear, perhaps.

Junior, pulling up the rear of their procession, turns to find a small man in a Park Service ballcap. He's marching as quickly as his large backpack will allow, his rifle up and aimed at them. When he's nearly within arm's length, Junior notices a white strip of cloth dangling between the fingers of the hand holding the forestock.

Shit.

The three men exchange glances, and Harlan speaks first. "If you think you're going to scare me with that rifle, son, you'd be wrong. My Pop used to point one at me just to get me used to the feeling."

"What the fuck is that?" the little man says, casting his head toward the carcass bag in Junior's hand.

"Food," Junior says.

The little man shifts uneasily on his feet, his shoulders jittery, his head swiveling between the men. "Put it down," he barks. "All of it."

Junior bends slowly and sets the bag on the ground. When he stands again, he lifts his hands shoulder-high. Their assailant's jumpiness has him uneasy. It reminds him of the children he sometimes encountered overseas, the ones waving around the AK-47s they'd been handed days, or maybe minutes, before. Putting on a tough show but pissing their pants the whole time. They were the wild cards who transformed an encounter from manageable to *who the hell knows.* They didn't know enough to understand the true risks of their conduct.

A high whistle sounds, loud and sudden as a boiling kettle, and all heads turn toward it. Otto is stepping off the porch some thirty yards away, his eye to the scope of his own rifle.

Junior knows Otto to be a poor shot, just as likely to hit him as this intruder. But he has the man's attention. Before the situation can devolve, Junior lunges forward, grabbing the forestock and lifting it toward the sky. The rifle discharges, bucking from both men's grips and clattering into the grass. The little man bends toward it, but Junior shoves him backward until he totters, backpack and all, onto his ass.

"Stay the fuck down!"

The man blinks and gasps but doesn't move.

Junior swipes up the rifle and the strip of cloth from the ground, handing the former to Harlan and stuffing the latter surreptitiously into his pocket.

Harlan makes a long, slow show of admiring the gun before slinging the barrel over his shoulder. "What's your name, son?"

The little man glares at him, his face flush and trembling. "Alex."

"Alex, you want to tell me what this is all about?"

TSULA

CHAPTER TWENTY-FOUR

December 16

Tsula sits in her vehicle at the trailhead parking lot, fingers wrapped tightly around her insulated thermos. The temperature gauge reads thirty-five degrees and, unlike most mornings, the number is dropping. A cobalt ceiling of cloud admits only the faintest aura of daybreak. Over the radio, an earnest voice announces the latest forecast.

"To repeat: The winter weather is now expected to arrive by six p.m. at the latest, though some areas could see sleet or flurries well before that. It is a fast-moving storm which already has dumped feet of ice and snow over the Midwest. The Governor has declared a state of emergency for all western counties as far east as Buncombe and Madison, with more likely to come. Schools in those counties will be closed tomorrow and for an unknown number of days after."

In the warmth of the cab, Tsula presses her bare hand to the driver's side window and questions why she must be so damned curious. The risk-to-reward ratio for this outing is rapidly changing.

Headlights swing onto the access road and come to a stop behind her. The lights darken, and Abbott steps out. She rolls down the window as he nears, his breaths puffing moist clouds.

"Good morning."

"You heard the latest?" he says, nodding toward the radio.

"We'll be fine," she replies, though without conviction. "In and out, right? Kinda the only option at this point."

"Better be." He pulls a satellite phone from his jacket pocket and holds it up. "If not, someone on the other end of this is going to give me hell."

"If they can reach you," Tsula says. "Who gave you that?"

"Chief Ranger Brannon. She likes to take some pretty wild vacations, apparently, and this is her personal sat phone."

Tsula cranes her neck out the window to look behind him. "Where are the horses?" From her seat in the warm vehicle, the cold is not yet bothersome. But suddenly she finds the notion of making the trek on foot intolerable.

"They'll be here," he says. He leans forward, resting his wrists on the driver's side door, then flicks his nose toward a long, rusted white canister sitting next to her in the passenger's seat. "What the hell is that?"

"Bear spray. Why?"

"Looks like the bottom is about to fall out. How old is it?"

"I don't know," she says. "A few years."

"Who was president when you got it?"

She shrugs. "Not the current guy. Best I can say."

"There are no grizzlies here, you know. No mountain lions."

"I know. But that thing goes with me everywhere. I'm not going to let this be my first trip without it."

Abbott squints at her and adjusts his toboggan. "Just keep it away from flames, okay?"

"What flames? We're going to be back before sundown. We better not be building any fires."

"Today, tomorrow, a month from now, I don't care. Keep it away from flames. You don't know what accelerant this relic has in it."

Tsula shrugs again. "Okay, dad."

A pickup pulling a long horse trailer crawls its way up the access road and joins them. A tall, bearded man named Randy steps out of the vehicle and approaches.

"Thanks for accommodating us on such short notice," Tsula says, stepping out of her SUV.

"I owe Greg a favor or two," Randy replies. "Let me introduce you to the horses real fast. I'm sure y'all will want to get going."

He opens the back trailer and leads out the first horse, handing the reins to Abbott. It's a brown gelding with a white stripe down the middle of his nose and muscular haunches which seem nearly as wide as the horse is long.

"This is Thor."

Next comes a jet-black mare with only slightly smaller proportions.

"And this is Freya."

Tsula takes Freya's reins and strokes the horse's placid face.

"I know they're on the big side for trail horses," Randy says. "But they've got the surest feet I've ever seen, and they don't spook at difficult terrain. Greg will vouch for it."

"That's true," Abbott says, nuzzling Thor.

"You'll need sure feet where you're going."

"Any special instructions for them?" Tsula asks. "It's been a while since I rode something other than established trails."

"Let Thor lead, and Freya will follow," Randy says. "Pretty simple. He'll go just about wherever you tell him to. But if he tells you not to go somewhere, it's best to listen."

Tsula and Abbott pack their gear in large saddle and cantle bags that Randy straps to the horses. Abbott directs the organization of the various items with a particularity that surprises Tsula. "Doesn't matter if you end up using it or not," he says. "If it turns out you need your stove, it doesn't make sense for your fuel or lighter to be somewhere else you gotta go looking for it."

She doesn't bother disagreeing. She simply checks her watch and the sun's slow rise through the barren trees. The cold breeze on her neck feels like the storm taunting them, making its imminent arrival known.

"We'll leave your tent here, save some room," Abbott announces, closing the hatch on her vehicle. "We can bring mine. If the worst happens and we need it, it's small, but it'll sleep two. Just don't let Amy know."

"Oh, I'll let Amy know," Randy says. "Maybe then she'll come to her senses and marry me instead."

The three shake hands once more. Abbott promises he'll call upon their return, and Randy nods and drives away.

Before they depart, Tsula packs away the items she wants in her pockets, close at hand: compass, annotated map, GPS locator, six-inch spring-assisted knife, water bottle, trail bar, Ziploc bag of deer jerky, and bear spray. She stuffs the water bottle inside her layers, closer to her body's heat, to keep it from freezing.

Abbott pulls out the marked map Tsula gave him the night before and holds it up. "I'm going to hold onto this unless you want to."

"You're the guide."

He unfolds it and presses a finger on the dot he's added in blue ink to mark their starting point. He looks at the trailhead sign and nods. "Okay. Last chance. You sure you want to do this today?"

She isn't sure of much anymore. But she knows the questions plaguing her will never let her be if she turns back now. She breathes in deeply and nods.

"Then let's roll out."

Tsula mounts Freya falteringly, her leg not quite clearing the cantle bag on the first attempt. Once she's situated, Abbott hands her the reins. Then he swings himself onto Thor and steers him toward the trail they will follow for the first couple of miles. Tsula cinches up the hood on her coat as Freya falls in behind Thor.

The wind has picked up, and it's beginning to mist.

PART II: COLLISION

HARLAN

CHAPTER TWENTY-FIVE

January 16, 1988

Much too early one Saturday morning, Carl Miles shook his son awake. Harlan, then twelve years old, lifted his head from his pillow, blinked hard, and rubbed a string of spittle from the side of his face.

"Pop?"

"I got somethin' to show you," Carl Miles said. For once, his breath didn't carry the astringent scent of liquor. "Get up."

"What time is it?" Harlan asked, still not entirely certain he wasn't dreaming.

"Time for you to learn somethin'. Go on and get dressed. Meet me outside."

Harlan rolled down his two blankets, and icy air washed over his bare hands and feet. Their home was old and ragged, with uninsulated floorboards, siding on the verge of falling off, and windows that kept everything out but the wind. The one source of heat inside, a wood burning stove, had reduced its contents to ash and cooled overnight. There was no warmth to be found anywhere.

In a move he practiced every winter morning, Harlan leapt from the bed and slid yesterday's pants and flannel shirt over his long-johns. He took no time for socks, but his boots were insulated with wool that would keep his feet warm. A puffy, hooded jacket purchased at Wal-Mart last year was already too short for his arms, but he'd not gotten a new one for Christmas as requested. To avoid snide comments from his classmates, he'd learned to cover up his wrists by shoving his hands deep inside the pockets.

The house that morning was sepulchral. Harlan's mother had disappeared the week prior, leaving only a short note to say that she loved her little man and she was so sorry. In the blackness of that early hour, it appeared she'd taken all light and sound with her.

The prior afternoon, Harlan had returned from school to an empty house. That his father was gone did not surprise him. He often disappeared for hours or even days at a time, only to return later without a word of explanation. But his mother's absence disoriented Harlan and made the walls and space feel unfamiliar, like he'd entered the wrong residence by mistake and now had to make the best of it. He waited that afternoon at the round kitchenette table for someone to return and finally decided, well past sunset, that no one would. Then he made himself a bologna and ketchup sandwich, lit the cast iron stove using a note from his math teacher for a starter, and put himself to bed.

Outside on the porch, the air was still but sharp, and he stood there for a moment while his eyes adjusted to the inky black.

"Come on, then," his father's voice said from the darkness beside him. It startled Harlan, and he hoped his father had not seen him jump. A small flashlight illuminated, and Carl Miles led the way to the storage shed behind the house. When they reached it, Harlan held the light while his father slid open the padlock.

"You ready to become a man?"

Harlan felt a tightness in his chest, like a fist thrust just behind his sternum. "Yeah, Pop," he said, though his words felt more like a question than an answer. He had no idea what his father's question implied, but its tone left him cold.

The door swung open silently, and Harlan caught the faint, sweet smell of WD-40. Had his father oiled the hinges to the door? Normally, they croaked like a toad.

The chain to the one naked bulb mounted in the ceiling clicked, and then Harlan saw the man. His hands extended above his head and were bound together with duct tape. A length of rope also encircled them in a knot and extended up and over the base of a roofing truss, holding the man upright by his arms. The other end of the rope descended at an angle into the rear darkness and anchored back there to something Harlan could not see among the silhouettes of fishing gear and neglected lawn tools.

More duct tape covered the man's mouth, and his nostrils flared with panicked breaths. His right eye and forehead were swollen and purple. Blood trickled down his face from somewhere in his hair. He was stripped to the waist, his arms and bare torso blue from the cold and shivering. His legs were taped together at the ankles, and his toes reached for but barely touched the blue tarpaulin spread over the floor.

"Pop," Harlan said. "Who is that?"

"This, son, is the reason your mama ain't home right now."

Harlan's pulse scudded in his temples, and his mind strained to make sense of his father's words. "He kidnapped her?"

"In a manner of speaking," his father said. "No woman in her right mind just up and leaves her husband and child behind. And you know your mama is a right-minded woman. Only conclusion I can reach is this piece of shit here done somethin' to her. Got her under some sort of spell."

The man jerked and made a long, high noise beneath the tape. Carl sunk a fist in the man's gut, quick and sudden as a timber rattler. "Shut the fuck up."

The man wheezed, his nostrils sucking air rapidly, and was still.

Carl removed a hunting knife from a sheath at his hip, gripped the blade, and offered the handle to Harlan. "Whatever spell he put your mama under, boy, it's time for you to break it."

Harlan backed up against the door frame, his breaths now quick and shallow, his stomach churning hot and sour. "Pop, no."

His father's free hand struck the top of Harlan's head. It was a glancing blow, but it sent his head back into the frame. Lightning shot down Harlan's neck into his shoulders, and his eyes welled immediately with tears.

"A man does not let someone else take what is his," Carl said. "Come on, now."

Another hand to Harlan's head. Another pulse of electricity down his body.

"A man will fight those who try to take it. Will kill, if necessary."

Harlan tried to speak, but his chest was convulsing, sucking air in and shoving it back out. His words would not come. He felt himself on the verge of collapse, and a small part of him prayed he would just lose consciousness. He knew what would come next if he kept resisting.

"Do I need to get the whip?" his father said.

Another hand, and sparks began to dance before Harlan's eyes.

"He took your mama. What's more precious than that?"

His eyes darted around the shed as the walls and the man tilted back and forth.

"Maybe you don't deserve the mama you got then, if she don't matter a lick to you."

Another hand, this one removing the breath from his lungs entirely.

"Maybe she knew it. Maybe that's why she left, her kid don't give a shit about her. Take it!"

Harlan stood paralyzed, his cheeks slicked with cooling tears, shaking his bowed head. "Pop, I can't."

His father let out a slow exhalation and squinted at his only boy. He gently tousled the boy's unkempt hair until his sobbing subsided. Then he spun and thrust the knife into the man's belly.

The man bucked like a hooked fish as blood pattered onto the tarp below and steamed in the cold. His head bobbled, and a strange, high keening forced its way from beneath the tape over his mouth. It probably took only a couple of minutes, but to Harlan, cowed in the corner by shock and shame, it felt like hours. Finally, the man was still and the whole of his weight pulled tight on the rope and his slackening shoulders.

Carl Miles turned back and loomed over his son. "You do not let others take what is yours. Do you hear me?"

Harlan clamped his eyes and covered his ears, but he nodded.

"Now get your ass in the house."

Later, Harlan stood before the cracked bathroom mirror. He held his hands under the sink's lukewarm water and stared at himself. His face was sallow, his eyes swollen and bloodshot. The gash in the reflection ran from his ear down his jaw and across his neck. His whole body shook.

The rumble of a truck approached outside. Harlan turned the faucet off and listened. The truck bed opened and clanged shut a couple minutes later. Two muffled voices exchanged brief words. Then the same rumble faded back into the night. Harlan walked to his room, doffed the boots and coat, and lay awake the rest of the morning on top of his blanket, oblivious to the cold.

His father returned after the sun had risen, smelling of gasoline and smoke. Harlan shut his eyes and pretended to be asleep, but it fooled no one. His father ambled into the room and sat on the edge of Harlan's bed. The weight of the man's stare was oppressive.

"That business in the shed," his father said finally.

"I'm sorry, Pop. I just . . ."

Carl put a sooty finger to his son's lips. "Time for you to listen now."

Harlan clamped his lips tight.

"Good. I need you to understand, that was for your mama. And I'd do the same for you if I had to. You know why?"

"Because I'm your boy?"

"That's right. You're my boy. And I'm your Pop. But what makes us family isn't our blood. Not really. What makes family is what one person's willing to do for another. Sometimes it's doing something hard to protect each other. And sometimes it's just staying quiet. You follow me?"

"Don't say nothing."

"Because if doing right by each other means you're family, well, doing the wrong thing . . ."

"Means you ain't?"

"That's right." Carl looked down and absently picked at blackened spot of blood on his pants. "And I don't have the same loyalties to those that ain't family."

Many years later, Harlan would hear whispered stories about a local florist who had lived on a preserve his family owned for generations and was rumored to have taken up with more than one man's wife in his time. The remote plot allowed for privacy and reportedly had several points of entry and departure, so it was hard to know with certainty who was coming and going. The florist disappeared one evening in early 1988 and never returned. The police found his truck abandoned on the side of a county road near Murphy a week later. People figured some husband had found out about him and taken matters into his own hands. Harlan would hear names bandied about of women he did not know and the spouses who might have been capable of such a thing. His parents would never be mentioned.

Carl Miles was right about all of it, of course. Harlan knew this for certain when he returned from school two days later and found his mother sitting at the kitchenette table. She smiled at him with trembling lips and told him she was so sorry, that she didn't know what she'd been thinking. Her eyes were bleary, her voice choked, and he fell asleep that night to the sound of her crying softly.

Still, the spell the man had cast over his mother was broken. His Pop had fought for what was precious to them both, and he'd won it back. Before Harlan closed his eyes that night, and for every night that came after, he swore that next time he would do the same. He would never fail like that again.

CHAPTER TWENTY-SIX

November 1

"Jesus, Pop."

"Stop your whining."

Harlan sits on one of the horizontal logs arranged around the fire pit and looks down at Alex's body in the grass. Only minutes before, Alex had been seated right next to him at the log's edge, imploring them all to let him go. "I won't say shit, I swear."

It was out of the question, of course. Alex's attire told them who he worked for, and Harlan doubted the assurances of discretion. In any event, Harlan lacked an appetite for taking unnecessary chances.

It had been Junior's idea to tie the little man with cloth strips instead of the rope Joseph fetched for them. Rope rubbed the skin raw and left fibers, he explained, and duct tape would leave residue. At the time, Harlan didn't ask Junior where he'd come by this knowledge or why that was his primary concern. But now it occurs to Harlan that his friend had been the first one to recognize what they must do. He'd known, even before Harlan, that they would need to ensure Alex's body was found and that it showed no signs of apprehension or struggle. But the cloth bindings were hard to get right, and even after several attempts by Harlan to cinch them sufficiently tight, the little man had bucked and spluttered and nearly squirmed one of his hands free. So Harlan put him down with the .22 in the back of his waistband before he'd fully devised a plan for what would come next.

Alex's head jerked with the report of the pistol, the whole of him tilting to the ground like a toppled domino. He came to rest on his side with his hips flexed and his knees bent as though still seated. The small hole behind his eye smoked and frothed, then the blood settled and formed a thick, black rim.

But for that hole and the cloth bindings, Alex's corpse gives the impression of a child peacefully napping.

"That's two," Otto whimpers, drawing Harlan's attention away from his thoughts. He paces just outside the circle of logs, his gaze aimed down toward his shuffling boots. He rubs his hands together so forcefully Harlan's sure he will leave them raw. "That's two. That's two."

Harlan stands from his seat and is in front of his son in three swift strides. "I said shut up, goddammit. I can't think with you going on like that."

Otto halts and stares wide-eyed at his father, his mouth clamping shut with a dull clack of his teeth.

Though he's nearly two inches shorter than Otto, in his anger Harlan looms over his son. "You think if we'd let him go, he'd just go home and forget about us?"

"No, Pop," Otto says. "It's just . . ." He waves a tentative arm toward the body, and his eyes follow.

"And when that little shit went back and told them what he'd found, what do you think would happen next? They'd just let us be? Let us while away our lives out here?"

Otto shifts uneasily on his feet. "You never said anything about killing people," he mumbles. "Now that's two."

Harlan grips his son's face with one clenched hand and forces his gaze back. "That sonofabitch pointed his rifle at me. You think I ought to just let that go, hope next time he comes around acting nicer?"

Otto just stares at him.

"You do not survive by being kind to those who want to harm you. You do not survive by letting others threaten your home, your food, your family. Do you hear me?"

Otto swallows hard and gives a weak nod.

"Now stand up straight and stop whimpering like a fucking dog. You get soft now and you're as good as dead. I'm as good as dead." He leans in until he's inches from his son's face. "Your brother's as good as dead."

Otto looks down at his feet and says nothing.

"I didn't think I had to ask you this," Harlan goes on. "But if you can't do what is required to keep the family safe, boy, I need to know now."

His firstborn glances again at the body, then returns to studying his boots. "I'm good, Pop."

Harlan shakes his head and walks back toward his log but doesn't sit. He sets his arms akimbo and leans back with his face toward the sky, summoning the focus he had lost.

He's certain Alex came alone; any companion surely would have intervened. Even so, Harlan has to assume someone will know where Alex was headed, why he was out there, and when he was expected back. This is someone whose disappearance would prompt search parties on foot and helicopters overhead, and their home surely would be discovered in the process. Alex needs to be found before such a search can commence.

Joseph approaches with a shovel in each hand and stands next to Otto. His face is earnest and bears none of the uncertainty etched into his brother's. "You want we should bury him, Pop?"

Harlan dons his work gloves, squats down, and takes hold of

the man's boots. He torques the body prone and pulls the legs out straight before rigor mortis can set in.

"No," he says, untying the knots at the man's hands and feet. "We're not burying him."

Joseph glances over at Otto's pallid face. "What'll we do with him, then?"

Harlan stands and flexes and straightens his right arm. His elbow's been bothering him lately. "I want you both to go pack. We'll be gone a couple days. Bring your gloves and your headlamps. Bring out my sleeping bag, too. We'll carry him in it."

"Carry him, Pop?"

The pistol rests on the log next to Alex's rifle, and Harlan picks it up. He opens the cylinder to prevent the gun from discharging and wipes the whole thing down vigorously with the sleeve of his shirt. He looks around as he rubs. "Where'd Junior go?"

"Out back," Joseph says. "He went to have a smoke."

Harlan places the grip in Alex's cooling palm and closes the fingers around it.

"Tell him too. We'll need everyone."

TSULA

CHAPTER TWENTY-SEVEN

December 16

Tsula and Abbott spy the cabin in a clearing beyond the trees. It appears almost spectral through the gossamer mist—at first, just a hint of a shape. A blocky shadow rising from the ground.

They urge their horses beyond the tree line for an unobstructed view. Tsula pulls her binoculars from one of the saddlebags draped across Freya's haunches and scans the small glade, taking inventory of the environment. As they draw toward the center of the clearing, Tsula can make out the structure more clearly. A porch spans the front façade, and hinged wooden shutters are opened to reveal two glassless windows. Wooden shakes adorn half the roof, naked boards the rest.

A vegetable garden flanks the cabin on one side. Behind the structure but visible from their angle of approach, a canvas tent stands seven or eight feet tall. Nearby, two smoothed logs are planted vertically in the soil, rope strung between. An improvised water catchment basin abuts the side of the building. On the opposite side, well away from the building, sits an outhouse. Directly out front, a fire burns high and hot. Horizontal logs encircle the fire pit, and between two of them lies the wiry brown heap of a boar.

The seeming normalcy of this scene nearly trumps its audacity. In almost twenty years of working on federal lands, Tsula has encountered her fair share of individuals seeking to take up residence within their boundaries. Tents, RVs, shanty lean-tos—she's seen all manner of attempts at establishing a home. Most are characterized primarily by an intention to remain concealed. But this settlement is an effort of an entirely different character—open and unafraid, as if she and Abbott have stumbled upon a living museum.

"Is this some new park project I need to know about?" she says quietly.

Abbott lowers his binoculars and shakes his head. "I didn't tell you about our squatter reintroduction program?"

"Must have slipped your mind. Can I see the map?"

Abbott hands it to her, and she spreads it out in her lap.

"We're in the right place, aren't we?" she says. She pulls out her GPS locator. It has worked only intermittently all day, but now, at the edge of this clearing, it shows them exactly where they are. She hands the device to Abbott.

"Looks like it," he says, handing it back. "So Alex was here?"

"Seems like it. But why? Why leave what he was doing to come here?"

He shrugs. "Maybe something caught his interest?"

"So he comes here, and then . . . what?"

Abbott raises his binoculars again and says nothing.

A man emerges from the cabin. He stretches his neck to both sides, steps down from the porch, and makes his way toward the fire. As he does, he casts his eyes toward Tsula and Abbott and pauses, his expression flat and frozen for a long moment. Then a broad smile overtakes his face, and he waves, beckoning them to approach.

"Shit," Tsula whispers under her breath.

Abbott keeps his binoculars to his eyes. "Guess we're going to talk with this joker?"

"Or we leave it for now, call for back-up."

"What back-up?" Abbott says. "It'd take them as long to get here as it did us. Longer with the weather. We disappear now that he's seen us, what are the chances he's here when we get back? Don't we want to know if he saw Alex?"

Tsula hesitates, but decides he has a point. "Alright, we'll go introduce ourselves." She looks at him and says, "Take your toboggan off."

"What?"

She taps her forehead to demonstrate. "It says Park Service."

"You think he won't know?"

"Just humor me."

About twenty yards from the fire pit, they dismount. Tsula hands Freya's reins to Abbott. "You hang back a little bit behind me and just keep an eye out. I'll talk with him," she says.

Abbott opens his mouth to speak. Just then, two younger men file out of the cabin and join the first man around the fire. One carries knives no doubt intended for dressing and preparing the hog. They exchange words with the older man, then look up toward their new guests.

Tsula glances over at Abbott. His face has hardened.

"Stick to the plan," she says.

He shakes his head slightly. "I don't like the numbers anymore."

"Just keep a sharp eye."

He breathes in and nods.

Tsula trudges forward across the remainder of the clearing and greets the men as she nears the fire pit. "G'mornin'. How are you gentlemen doing?"

"Just fine," the first man replies, smiling warmly. She figures he's in his late forties or early fifties, tanned and broad, with shaggy salt and pepper hair. He motions to the land around him and then to the sky above. "How could we not be?" He extends his hand. "I'm Harlan Miles."

Harlan Miles.

Pieces of the puzzle slam noisily into place in Tsula's mind. An uprush of panic fills her, like she's unwittingly stepped off the precipice of a deep pit. A twitch takes up in her thighs, as though urging her to move. *Breathe*, she tells herself. *Think.*

Her instincts tell her to play dumb. They have weapons of their own, and they're capable of using them. The hog tells her that. Alex's death probably does, too. If her gut is right, the best outcome she can hope for is a graceful exit from this encounter that doesn't result in more violence or alert them to what she knows.

"Tsula Walker," she says, shaking his hand. "And that gentleman behind me with the horses is Greg."

"Well, I'm pleased to meet you both." Harlan waves toward Abbott, then motions to his two companions. "These are my boys, Otto and Joseph."

Neither moves or speaks, and Tsula regards each of them individually. Otto appears to be the big brother, several inches taller, with a somber face. Joseph looks to be a few years younger, with unkempt hair and darting eyes. His fidgeting hands hint at a barely corked energy.

"You must be cold," Harlan says. "Lord knows I am. Come join us around the fire, warm your hands a bit."

"Maybe just a minute." Tsula steps into the circle of logs as Otto takes a seat behind her. She turns and eyes him over her shoulder, her hands extended out toward the flames.

"The temperature's been dropping," Harlan says, looking toward the sky. "If I didn't know better, I'd say a storm is coming."

"So they say. Supposed to bring lots of snow overnight." Tsula takes a step closer to the fire. Even under these uncertain circumstances, its warmth is a welcome relief. "You'll probably want to take shelter soon."

"You hear that, boys?" Harlan says, looking at them. "Told you we'd need to hurry up with the chores today."

"Quite the setup you've got here," Tsula observes, motioning around her. "How long y'all been out here?"

Harlan shrugs. "Oh, a few weeks, I'd say. My boys have really taken to it, you know? I wanted them to get the full experience."

"Looks like mission accomplished," Tsula says. "That y'all's handiwork on the cabin there?"

He looks back toward the structure and smiles. "That cabin belonged to my great granddaddy, if you can believe it."

"Is that right?"

"It is. State of North Carolina took it from him a long time ago, gave it over for the park, and I guess they forgot all about it. I just hated to see what had become of it. Shameful, really. We decided to fix it up a bit while we're here."

"Looks like y'all really know what you're doing. The park should be grateful."

"It was the least we could do. Keeps the boys busy, teaches them some new skills. Plus, in this weather, no tent can compare with four solid walls."

Tsula nods her head toward the garden plots. "I see you've done some planting as well?"

"One must eat, of course. Granola and jerky can only get you so far."

"Guess that explains the hog too?"

"Invasive species," Harlan says. "They destroy everything. This one came rooting around the gardens, looking to eat our vegetables. Now the world's down one pest, and we get to fill our bellies. Win-win."

The wind picks up and shifts direction, blowing a thick plume of campfire smoke into Tsula's face. Her eyes burn, and all else disappears. The blindness spikes her anxiety.

Through tears and haze comes Harlan's voice: "What brings you all the way out here today?"

"Just wandering," she says, coughing. The taste in her mouth is earthy and astringent. "Figured we'd take the horses out and all stretch our legs before we get cooped up with the snow."

"I hate to say it, but I think you might be a little lost."

The smoke eases, and Harlan briefly comes back into view. Has he moved closer?

"There aren't any horse trails around here that I know of," he says.

"Are we lost?" Tsula gives Harlan a conspiratorial smile. "Nice thing about a park this big, you can break a tiny rule here or there and no one's the wiser. Who's it hurting, right?"

"I like the way you think, Tsula Walker." He smiles broadly. "Though I am curious: How did you end up right here? I mean, half a million acres you could wander, and you end up in our front yard."

How indeed. Tsula's mind races.

"We saw the smoke," she says finally, though she fears she's taken too long. "I'm sure you remember the fires a few years ago? We just decided to come over, see what was up."

"Is that right?"

The wind shifts its direction, and the world again is pungent and gauzy nothing.

Tsula ticks through her remaining options. She sees little likelihood that she and Abbott can arrest and haul these three men on foot and horseback several hours over this terrain and in these conditions. They're armed, and she's certain they would resist apprehension. In this environment, Harlan clearly is capable beyond the skills of most men. She doesn't yet know what to make of saturnine Otto, but Joseph looks poised to bolt or attack at the slightest provocation.

She concludes it would be wiser, if possible, to withdraw and leave them here. She could return with more officers later, once this storm has passed through and the conditions improved. It appears Harlan and his sons intend to make this settlement much more than a campground, so they likely will still be here when she returns in a few days. Assuming they survive the coming storm, she can arrest and question them about Alex then.

"Well alright," she says. "I know you've got chores to get done, and we probably need to keep moving so we can make it home before the storm. I sure do appreciate a couple minutes by this lovely fire."

"Is Greg there not cold?" Harlan asks. "He's welcome to come on over and warm himself, too, before y'all take off."

"Oh, I'm sure he's fine." She turns to Abbott and calls out through cupped hands, "You good to go?"

He nods. "Let's roll."

Tsula looks back to Harlan and waves. "Thanks again. Y'all stay warm out here."

She turns to go, and behind her Harlan speaks. "Otto."

Otto stands up from the log where he's been sitting and steps forward to block her path.

"What's going on, Otto?" Tsula says.

His expression is uneasy, pained, and he won't look at her directly. "I'm sorry," he mumbles to his feet.

She takes a step back from him into the center of the ring of logs and pivots so she can look back and forth between Otto and his father.

Abbott releases the horses' reins and takes several steps forward. His eyes are narrow, his body tense as a bow's string. Tsula holds her hand out, low and level, signaling him to remain calm. "Harlan, what—"

"It was the GPS, wasn't it?"

Tsula remains still, struggling to keep her face placid.

Harlan laughs ruefully, shakes his head. "That's my fault, really. It didn't even occur to me to look through his backpack until we got back. It was dead when we found it in the pack, so I hoped maybe . . ." He pauses for a moment, as though reliving his error, then shrugs. "Well, that's too bad. I preach attention to detail until I'm blue in the face, and here I'm the one who makes the careless mistake. You live and you learn. Right, boys?"

His sons glance at each other but say nothing.

Tsula's pulse bounds in her temples. "Harlan, I don—"

But Harlan interrupts her again: "Speaking of details, I can see the outline of your sidearm beneath your coat. Sig, right? That's what they give you guys? And I've seen Ranger Crew Cut there before, when he came around Deep Creek asking everybody with a rod for their fishing licenses." He looks over at Abbott directly and raises his voice so the man can hear him. "I'm sure you don't remember me, ranger. But I certainly remember you."

Just like that, the good options have dwindled to zero. There is no practical way to run from whatever is coming next. Dismounted as they are, making a quick break on horseback will be next to impossible. And the clearing will provide nowhere close to shelter if they take off on foot. If these men want a fight, it's going to happen, one way or another.

Tsula prays they don't want it.

"Harlan, whatever you're thinking right now, I want you to look at your boys and ask yourself how you think it will actually turn out."

"That sounds like a threat to me, Tsula Walker," Harlan says. "Are you threatening my boys?"

"I'm not threatening anyone." She turns to face Harlan fully, her back toward his son—a gesture that she intends Otto no harm. "But you know we're armed and trained. So are you, I'm sure. If this goes bad, it goes bad for everyone."

"Is that a fact?"

"You know I'm right. The only way everyone here is guaranteed to live through the day is if we ride away and you let us go."

"Just let you ride away, huh?" Harlan says. "And I guess you'll just forget all about this, right? I won't have scores of cops and rangers at my doorstep in a day or two?"

Tsula considers lying to him, promising they'll not tell a soul what they've seen and heard. But she knows he won't believe her even if she means it. "The only thing we can guarantee each other now is getting through this day right here," she says. She takes a step backward as though preparing to go around Otto—a test—but he sidesteps in front of her again.

"I'm afraid that's not going to be good enough for me," Harlan replies. "We didn't go to all this effort just to get one more day."

"Fuck this," Abbott says. He removes his pistol from beneath his unzipped coat and trains it on Otto. "Put your hands up now and step back from her," he shouts, stomping toward the campfire.

"Abbott," Tsula says.

Harlan's face darkens, a cloud casting a deep shadow over his features. "Ranger, you really didn't need to do that."

Otto looks at his father, his eyes wide, but doesn't move. "Pop?"

"I said step back from her, asshole. And put your hands up, all of you." Abbott swivels his torso, training the pistol on all three men in turn.

"Pop," Otto says again.

"You come onto our land uninvited and you threaten my family—"

"Abbott, holster your—"

"I said put your hands up now!"

"Pop!"

"Okay, ranger," Harlan shouts suddenly, loudly enough to be

heard above the other voices. He raises his hands over his head. "You win. My hands are up. Otto, Joseph, do what the man says."

Harlan's eyes appear to cut toward the cabin, but when Tsula's gaze follows, she sees nothing but the structure. It occurs to her he might have all manner of weapons inside. Perhaps he's calculating how long it would take him to sprint to the door.

Otto and Joseph raise their hands, eyeing each other anxiously.

Harlan chuckles to himself and shakes his head, as though enjoying a joke only he has heard. "Now I guess it's only fair to warn you," he says. "This is not going to go the way you want it to."

JUNIOR

CHAPTER TWENTY-EIGHT

December 15

Junior approaches the ginseng consolidator seated at the fold-out table and removes his pack. The old man squints at him with eyes sunk deep in a pie-shaped and jowly face. He's given every person in line before him the same glare. It's probably a consequence of his occupation, formed over years of straining to ferret out the criminals among the legal harvesters. Ginseng means good money, but immature roots could result in fines, and poached ones mean potential jail time. Caution is likely a helpful default attitude for men in his position. Even so, the man regards Junior just that much longer than the others in line—taking in, perhaps, the unkempt beard, the smears of grime that a quick bath of cold creek water and lye couldn't fully clean away.

The old man coughs to clear his throat. "You, uh . . . You been out all night digging?"

"What?"

"You got a little . . ." He motions with his hand to the side of his neck, to the wattle beneath his chin. "Just a little dirt is all."

"We doing business or going on a date?"

The old man rocks back on his heels and nods. "Fair enough. Let's see what you got."

Junior removes his pack and tips it over. Roots pile onto the table so high that the old man's gaze leaves the mound and returns, stunned, to Junior's smirking face.

"Go on, check them out," he says. "Four prongs at least. They're old enough."

The consolidator lifts one from the pile. The central root is thicker than his thumb, several smaller tail roots sprouting away from the body like drooping tentacles, thinning as they descend into even smaller fibers. It gives the impression of some strange creature plucked from the sea and left too long in the sun.

Ginseng grows wild in the park, and poaching has been common on its outskirts for years. As a result, resource conservation staff began injecting dye into the roots of plants where illegal harvesting is known to occur. The blue-black splotches on roots mean no reputable consolidator will touch them. To avoid this hazard, Junior had hunted for roots north of the cabin, deeper into the interior where few poachers would dare venture and park personnel would not have focused their work. The results of these efforts are an impressive collection of the oldest, thickest roots he has ever seen, with no evidence that they hail from an unlawful source.

The man holds the root at eye level, turning it over in yellowed fingers. "Where'd you get these?" he says. "I haven't seen roots this old in years. People aren't usually willing to wait this long before selling."

"My aunt lives over in Hanging Dog," Junior lies. "Got a couple acres, but she doesn't leave the house much. She didn't even know they were out there until I found them."

"I'm surprised nobody's stolen them."

"People know they steal from my aunt, they deal with me."

The man clears his throat again. "I'm sure your aunt gave you permission to harvest those roots?"

"She told me I could pull them if I split the money with her and replant the seeds."

"You got that permission in writing, I hope?"

"Of course." Junior pulls a folded sheet of paper from his front shirt pocket. On it, he has scrawled a short note allowing himself onto property that doesn't exist, signed and dated by an aunt he doesn't have. The man glances at it, then back to the mountain of roots, and once again, briefly, at the note. Weighing, no doubt, the money this haul could yield on the one hand and the likelihood it'll bring him trouble on the other. Junior expects him to begin salivating at any moment.

"I'll need to make a copy of this for my records," the man says.

Junior nods. The man bobs up on the balls of his feet, grinning, and thrusts out his hand.

Four hours later, a farmer in an aged but immaculate pickup truck drops Junior off at the Fontana Village parking lot. On the radio, between the breathless rantings of some political commentator he doesn't recognize or care to know, a calmer voice discusses the massive snowstorm that should arrive in a couple of days.

"Hope you got all your errands done," the old man says. "You'll be wanting to hunker down somewhere soon."

Junior's mind is elsewhere, and he doesn't reply. He's thinking, with some reluctance, that he might need to move inside the cabin with the others until the storm passes. After the new trusses were finally erected and roofing boards were planed and nailed into place, Harlan and his sons had moved from the rear tent into the structure itself. He, on the other hand, had elected to remain on a sleeping pad in the tent among the menagerie of tools, curing logs, and already shaped lumber. The canvas walls were familiar and comfortable enough for the time being, and he didn't want the others getting accustomed to his presence and forgetting he was owed his own living quarters. Even so, the now-looming threat of hypothermia might require him to soften his stance—at least until the worst of the weather is past them.

Junior retrieves the backpack from the bed of the truck and pats the side panel hard enough for the old farmer to hear. The truck pulls away slowly, and he waves his thanks. For purposes of this mission, he's carrying the internal frame pack they confiscated from their unexpected visitor, so as to attract less suspicion. The compartment, which previously contained only the roots, now holds a ponderous collection of supplies he purchased with the cash the ginseng consolidator paid him: new draw blade for stripping bark; linseed oil for staining; an array of batteries for headlamps and flashlights; bag of salt for curing meat; bags of dried beans for when the meat runs low. The weight of the pack ignites a sharp stinging in his right shoulder and a throbbing in both knees. All those marches years ago with a hundred-plus pounds strapped to his body have rendered his joints arthritic and prone to inflammation. But the success of the day has bolstered him with a surprising lightness of spirit, and he forgets the pain as quickly as he does the feeling of the boots on his toes or the cap pulled low over his head.

He proceeds back out of the parking lot, scanning for onlookers, his trekking poles ticking lightly on the concrete. As he walks, he remembers Harlan's admonition when he'd prepared to head out yesterday morning. "Don't fuck this up, Junior," Harlan had said, with no hint of humor in his expression or voice. Harlan was nothing if not an asshole. Still, buried in this exhortation was a belief that he had it in his power *not* to fuck up, so Junior saw within it a respect few others had shown him since his enlistment had ended.

As the forest embraces him again, his mind drifts even further back to the day the two men met. They'd come to blows within only a matter of hours. Junior's cousin had brought him along as part of a crew for a restoration project Harlan was managing over in Jackson County. Harlan quickly took exception with how slowly Junior was carrying lumber and other supplies off a truck.

"The owners will be dead before you finish," Harlan said. "I'd like them to still be around to pay us."

Junior kept moving at his pace and said nothing. He knew once he said something, once he gave in, his temper would take over and then he'd be out of a job.

"Jesus, look how hoss you are," Harlan kept on. "You can haul faster than that."

Junior was, and he could. He just saw no reason to move faster. So far as he knew, he was getting paid either way. Still, those needling comments in the morning led to greater recriminations in the afternoon and, eventually, to the fists he initially had thought to avoid. But as they lay in the yard after the scuffle, panting and wiping blood from their noses, Harlan laughed and said, "See? I knew you had something more in you."

The suggestion that Harlan somehow had figured him out, had found the buttons to push, enraged Junior. He hurled profanities at the bastard before stomping away toward the road. But he returned to the site the next day, having no other immediate prospects for money and a lingering curiosity about the man who had angered him so.

Harlan walked directly up to him and, to his surprise, did not send him away. Instead, Harlan smiled before asking, "Anybody ever teach you how to roof, Junior?"

#

The next morning, he wakes under the rock outcropping, shouting his way out of a nightmare about the first man he ever saw die. It was Afghanistan, some tiny shit town, 2002. The kid who died was from just down the road in Cherokee, as it turned out, fresh out of high school and basic training. Private Johnston, if Junior remembers correctly, though some of the others had taken to calling him "Chief" on account of his heritage. The way he smiled—more of a grimace, really—Junior didn't think the kid cared much for the nickname. But he said nothing, just did his job.

Then one day, the sole road running through said tiny shit town suddenly rose and spewed smoke and rock into the air as though birthing a new volcano. Several others nearby were injured, but they passed away later in hospitals after evacuation, and Junior didn't count them among the men he'd watched die. Private Johnston was killed in an instant, scattered for yards in every direction.

Once, while camping, Harlan witnessed Junior emerging from this same dream, thrashing his arms and screaming like a ghoul. Sharing a tent or overhang allowed for very few secrets. The following morning, over coffee and bananas, he felt compelled to explain the memory that had stalked his sleep for so many years.

Harlan sat quietly until the story was over, sipping absently at his mug. "He was young," he said finally. "He probably still believed he was on the right side. It's not such a bad thing, to die for what you believe in, while you still do believe in it."

Junior had never thought about the incident from Private Johnston's perspective, but he doubted the young man would find in it the consolation Harlan offered. Nor could he be certain what the kid believed, or how strongly. Private Johnston might have been, like so many Junior met in boot camp, simply in search of an opportunity. A clear and acceptable path forward. The only thing Junior knew for certain—the one truth he could distill—was that Private Johnston's death had cracked him wide in ways he still did not fully understand.

"You kill anyone while you were over there?" Harlan once asked him.

"I did what I had to."

Harlan studied his face for a long time before replying. "I understand."

"Do you?" Junior said, the question precariously situated somewhere between challenge and wish.

"In fact, I do," Harlan said, though he did not elaborate further.

Unlike others, Harlan didn't pretend to see his friend's path past the trauma of his deployment, didn't tell him to be a man and get over it already. He didn't recommend a verse or a prayer to mend his spirit or offer him drugs that would make him forget for a while. Didn't make him drive to the VA clinic in Franklin to bare his shame and fear to a know-it-all who in fact knew none of it—at least not from experience. Harlan simply gave Junior wide berth until the moments of fury and panic passed and then, when he was able to hear it, returned to speaking of the future he was planning for them all.

Harlan spoke with such conviction of building a life in the quiet of those mountains that Junior came to believe it was possible. "I've got the property, and I know how to build," Harlan said during one of their first discussions. "You're about the strongest bastard I've ever met, and you're a damn good hunter."

"And the boys?"

"They're my sons."

"I know they're your sons," Junior said. "But what do they bring to this plan of yours?"

Harlan smiled, crossed his arms, and leaned back in his chair. "Name me a successful war that didn't have foot soldiers."

# #

When he arrives back at the homestead around mid-day, his knees roar their indignation, and his neck burns like fire. Without a word, he drops the pack at Harlan's feet, hands him the leftover cash, and trudges around the cabin to the tent set behind it. Within minutes, he's prostrate on his sleeping pallet, dead to the world around him.

Sometime later, he wakes to the sound of voices shouting—not his own, for once. He rubs his eyes with the heel of his hands and listens. One voice is Harlan's, another likely Otto's. But there are more.

A man. A woman?

He sits up, grasps his carbine, and sneaks quietly from the tent.

Outside the wind flows briskly through the trees, the shushing sound it makes like an admonition to them all.

TSULA

CHAPTER TWENTY-NINE

Harlan Miles is standing next to the fire with his hands raised, small clouds expelling from his mouth with every word. "Now I guess it's only fair to warn you," he says. "This is not going to go the way you want it to."

"Abbott."

The word is an impulse. Instinct. Something Tsula can't consciously identify clicks in her brain, shoving his name down her synapses and out of her mouth. She swivels her gaze among the three men, anxious for any hint of who will make the first move.

Abbott sidesteps for a better view of Otto behind her and opens his mouth to say something. Then a strange flower blooms beneath his chin, bright and red. The thunderous crack of the rifle comes next, shaking the crimson petals down onto the grass. Abbott's head lolls forward much too far, his eyes wide and darting. Blood blankets his chest and chokes out from his neck in a mist.

Otto kicks Tsula's left leg from behind, knocking her to one knee. His forearm passes over her head, and she lowers her chin to prevent it from reaching her throat. She grips and claws at the forearm with both hands as she's pulled backward and up by her face. A searing pain shoots from her neck to her shoulders. When she's nearly back to her feet, she springs both boots off the ground, draws her knees up to her chest. When her feet land again, she spreads them wide. She squats her knees and flexes her torso forward with all her strength. It feels like her abdomen is tearing in two. Otto, his arms still tight around her, rolls over her back and tumbles to the ground.

Tsula's thick coat is a jumble atop her shoulders and torso. Her hands scrabble for the gun underneath but can't find it. Instead, she unlatches the bear spray canister on her hip.

Otto gets to his feet just as the stream shoots forward. She aims first at him since he is closest, then sweeps back and forth in an arc to force back the other two. Otto stumbles backward toward the campfire, coughing and gagging, and as accelerant meets campfire, Otto is bathed in flame. He collapses, howling. Harlan and Joseph turn to him, eyes and mouths wide.

The smoke is everywhere, thick and caustic, burning Tsula's eyes. It fills the gulf between her and the shooter she still hasn't seen. But given where Abbott stood, she's certain the shot came from the right front corner of the cabin. She casts her eyes in that direction to confirm, but the cabin has disappeared.

Thor and Freya neigh and buck, their heads and manes bobbing above the surface of the haze. She sprints toward Freya, staying low and unholstering her pistol. For an instant the wind blows, dragging the smoke with it, and then she sees him in her peripheral vision—a fourth man stepping out from the cover of the cabin's corner. His torso swivels as she runs, tracking her with the rifle. The wind changes direction, and again the whole world is gone.

A second shot rings out, and Thor crumples with a scream that scrapes at Tsula's skin.

Tsula catches Freya's reins just as the horse spins. It feels as though the force might shear her arm off at the shoulder. She yanks the reins, the horse relents, and she sets her first boot in the stirrup. She lifts quickly, keeping her head low, and squeezes off two rounds as she crests Freya's body.

Tsula kicks the stirrups, but the mare needs little encouragement. She's already galloping, horse and rider fleeing toward the forest at the far end of the glade.

They're nearly to the tree line when a third rifle round cracks the air. Freya rears and begins to fall with an ungodly screech. Tsula contorts her body on the way to the ground, pulling her left boot from the stirrup before she ends up with her leg trapped beneath the horse. Her ribs and shoulder find a long rock concealed in the grass, and her head whips to the ground. Breath leaves her in a violent rush and will not return.

For a moment the world is gone, replaced by a heavy blackness and a high ringing in her ears.

She comes to with another report of the rifle and sucks air in deeply.

A puff of pink erupts from Freya's rib cage inches from Tsula's right leg, which despite her efforts remains stuck in its stirrup. The horse's gut rises and falls. A ragged and shallow panting rattles from its nose.

Tsula tastes blood in her mouth and isn't sure it's all hers. Shreds of tissue dangle inside her mouth behind her molars, and she swishes her tongue around her mouth in search of broken teeth.

At last she wriggles her right foot free of the stirrup and sidles her body up as closely as she can to the horse's. Several more cracks come in quick succession. Freya's body jerks subtly with the impacts, then even the panting stops.

Tsula peers over the horse's haunches and scans from right to left. The fourth man is at the corner, watching her through the rifle scope. Thor and Abbott lie unmoving in the grass. Harlan assists Otto to his feet as smoke rises from the younger man's charred clothing. Farther to the left, Joseph sprints up the clearing in an effort to flank her. Soon he will be somewhere in the trees behind her.

Another crack, this time ripping into the exposed saddlebag sitting on Freya's right haunch. Mist explodes from a spare canteen in the bag and wets her face.

"Goddammit," she hisses. The air is thick with the scents of soil and water and blood.

She takes a deep breath, sits up. Fires several rounds in the direction of the cabin. Turns her attention toward Joseph just as he lunges into the trees.

A mist of pink from Freya's flank sprays her face. She turns back and empties what remains of her magazine toward the shooter. There is only one spare in her pocket. The others lie beneath Freya in a saddlebag that won't budge beneath the motionless mass.

Another crack, and equine skin and muscle splits open next to her ear.

"Fuck." He's getting closer.

She can't stay here. She needs the cover of the trees, but first she must salvage whatever supplies she can manage. Additional rounds in the shooter's direction send him ducking back behind the corner of the cabin and buy her precious seconds. She pulls the knife from her pocket and springs it open. Her hand quakes as she presses the blade to the cantle bag's strap, and she struggles to keep the blade true.

Tsula has the bag halfway freed when she hears the snapping of twigs above the ringing in her ears. Something—a shadow—is creeping at the edge of the forest. She fires in its direction, and footsteps retreat deeper into the woods.

She returns her attention to the bag and finally frees it from the anchoring straps. Fires one more time in the direction of the cabin, then limps toward the tree line.

Within the trees, the world appears more night than day. The boles are dark, indistinct columns leaning and righting themselves. Multiplying, parting, and converging again. She slams into one with her shoulder and grazes another, teetering off at an angle as she struggles to maintain her footing. She scans the pitching forest for signs of Joseph but finds none. She cannot shake the conviction that the next few moments might well be her last, that she won't even see it coming.

Waves of nausea wash over her quickly, each stronger than the last, and soon she can hold it back no longer. She stops behind a wide pine, presses her butt against it to steady herself, and empties her stomach between her boots. Her nostrils burn with frigid air and bile. She heaves again, straining unsuccessfully to hold in her own noise.

Footsteps sound again and grow louder, a rapid crunching of boots on leaves—though from which direction, she can't tell until he's directly behind her. The knife and hand appear first. They swing from behind her in a rapid arc, aimed at her chest. She twists away but feels a brief tugging pull back across her right shoulder. Cold air touches this small sliver of skin, followed by the wet warmth of blood.

She keeps spinning, caroms off another tree, and tips backward onto her ass. The cantle bag drops and slides behind her. Joseph is before her in an instant, eyes hard and unblinking. She trains her pistol on him, her shoulder burning, and claws at the ground behind her with her left hand. The pain in her shoulder has the effect, if only for a moment, of focusing her buzzing senses. Joseph swings the blade down at her when he's close. She raises her left forearm to block its descent.

All of his weight presses down on her left arm. She strains to hold firm, but soon it will give. She aims the pistol hastily with her right hand and fires.

Joseph flops backward to the ground with a yelp which cuts short and gives way to a long, labored inhalation. Tsula scrambles to her feet and trains her pistol on him.

"Don't move!"

The bullet has torn a ragged hole through the right side of his shirt. His breath wheezes and rattles, and a sucking sound escapes the wound when he exhales. He lifts his knife toward her. A thin streak of blood—her blood—paints its edge. It trembles in his hand for a moment, then his grip weakens, and he drops it to the dirt.

She kneels and examines his face. It's browned by sun and dirt. Beaded with sweat. Frightened and angry. The face of a young man whose first brush with mortality will likely be his last. "Goddammit," she whispers. "Hang on." She searches her pockets for something with which she might apply pressure to his wound.

In the distance, more feet pound on the forest floor, drawing closer. She looks up over her right shoulder. An imposing shadow approaches, carbine in its hands. She snatches up the cantle bag in time to see the man stop and take aim. She slips behind a birch trunk and presses her back up against it as papery bark splinters and scatters near her feet.

Ahead, the ground slopes upward before cresting perhaps twenty yards away. If she can reach the downward slope on the other side, she can give herself time out of the rifleman's sight to determine a direction of travel or a place to hide.

She turns and fires as he slides behind a tree. Then she snatches up the bag and sprints up and over the hill.

The downslope is long and descends at a sharp angle. Near the bottom, her feet slip on the loose cover of dead leaves. She slides to a draw at the bottom, her legs folding at the knees as her boots strike the rocks collected there. To her left, the draw terminates at another hill that climbs upward and will expose her to anyone who's behind her. But to the right, it runs perhaps a hundred yards, snaking, descending, and finally disappearing behind a knoll.

An icy gust bellows through the treetops and sends a wave of crumpled leaves skittering across the ground. She turns back, her pistol aimed toward the top of the hill behind her. For the moment, she's alone. She wonders briefly if the man has stopped to help Joseph, or if soon she'll see his rifle cresting the rise. In the next breath, she resolves not to find out.

She finds her footing on the slope, dashes down the length of the draw, and vanishes beyond the knoll.

CHAPTER THIRTY

When she can no longer keep up the sprint, Tsula stops to rest at the rear edge of a dense stand of trees. She doesn't know how long she has run, only that it feels like hours. The frigid air scrapes at her throat and lungs. The exertion has scuttled her nausea, and the world around her has ceased pitching and yawing. But her head screams with pain, and her ears continue to ring. She sinks to the ground against a tree, her knees bent and feet pulled up tight to show no profile beyond the trunk.

Perhaps ten yards past the tree line, a bluff rises forty to fifty feet above the forest floor. The rock face appears nearly white beneath a sky the color of lead.

In time, her pulse and breathing slow, and she begins to focus. She sets down the cantle bag, unzips it, and removes its contents: a folded white gas stove, fuel bottle, flint lighter, metal mug, and waterproof matches. On her body, in sundry pockets, she also carries her map, compass, pistol, GPS locator, small bag of jerky, half-empty water bottle, and knife. She starts to inventory all the items she was forced to leave behind, then thinks better of it. It's done. That knowledge will serve no purpose now.

A cut of cold on her shoulder reminds her of Joseph's blade, and she looks down at the gap in her coat and underclothes. It's long, thin, and precise—the work of a well-sharpened knife. Down feathers peer out from the shell of her winter coat, tinted dark at the edges. Tsula slides the sleeves of her layers up to her elbow. A smear of blood extends down the dorsum of her forearm and disappears into her glove. She flexes her shoulder in every direction, assessing the injury. To her surprise, this movement produces nothing more than a superficial burning.

She picks up the GPS device and locates the SOS button on its side under a plastic casing. She flicks the cover open, presses the button, and waits. A loud tone sounds, and a small red light flashes near the top of the display.

It won't send.

"Shit."

She looks up at a canopy of conifers, the thick needles almost black from this vantage, and at the wall of rock just beyond her. She needs a clearer view of the sky.

The bluff spreads out before her as far as she can see in either direction. Both to her right and left, it appears to bend back around the trees behind her. She stands, her legs already growing stiff in the cold, and trots along the cliff's base fifty yards or more to the left. No end comes into sight as it continues curling ever so slightly back toward where she had come from. She does the same to the right, with the same result. The rock face forms a kind of shallow, broad cul-de-sac which, in the obscuring thicket of trees and the haze of her panic, she'd failed to notice until now.

She considers this situation for a long, breathless moment. She has to assume one or more well-armed men are heading her way. The draw over the hill where she left Joseph and the shooter behind only ran one direction. Even after it ended, she'd followed the easiest route the land's contours allowed her in order to cover as much ground as she could. Chances are good that anyone in pursuit will follow those same contours and find their way here.

Trying to wend her way around the bluff in either direction will mean backtracking an untold distance toward whoever is coming. And there's no guarantee when or if she'll find a feasible route around it. She could just as easily find herself trapped in the same stand of trees as one or more men with heavy firepower.

Looking lengthwise down the rocky face, Tsula can see that it rises in a subtly convex slope. Not entirely vertical, but enough so that vegetation finds no footing until almost the top, where it curves more sharply backward, like a forehead giving way to the crown. Fissures and ledges appear to provide a number of potential handholds and footholds. A skilled climber surely could scale it. She's not at all confident that she can.

She runs through the exchange of fire at the cabin in an effort to determine how many rounds she has left in her last magazine. Three or four? Five, if she's lucky?

"Shit, shit, shit."

She looks back at the looming bluff and feels a pang in her stomach. She has no other choice.

Tsula re-packs the cantle bag. She needs the supplies, but she also needs both hands for what comes next. Using her knife, she punctures a hole through the remaining fragment of the bag's strap. Then she passes her belt through the slit and fastens the belt again so the bag hangs at her hip.

Tsula backs up for a full view of the bluff and begins to plot a route that seems feasible. She knows that, beyond a certain elevation, she cannot safely reverse course back to the ground. When she gets that high, falling or finishing the climb will be the only two potential outcomes. She needs to get this right.

As she maps out her route, her anxiety redoubles. How long is she going to stand here not moving forward? She may have little time before someone finds her, and every minute spent clinging to the rock face is another minute exposed and defenseless, her back toward whoever is coming. When she has gone over the first half of the climb enough times that she thinks she can recall it by sight, she steps up to the base, scree shifting under her boots.

She removes her gloves and stuffs them into her pocket.

The rock is frigid against her fingers.

She sets her first boot.

CHAPTER THIRTY-ONE

Tsula climbs the bluff slowly, deliberately. Her vision is shifting in and out of focus, so she reduces her world to what is within the reach of her arms and feet and concentrates on the tactile details. The subtle, wet scratch of the rock on cold fingertips. The focal pressure of a stone edge and gravity working against a small fraction of her boot sole. The gentle push of wind that picks up. She resists the urge to look beyond where her hands go next. Doing so can only bring about panic and mistakes.

In time, it dawns on her that she has reached the point she fears most: far enough into the climb that she can't change her mind, and high enough that any fall will end in her death. She fends off this realization by digging her fingertips into the rock until her nail beds scream and allowing that sensation to blank her mind.

Near the top, she clutches at thin brush rising up from the rock—the first plant life she has encountered on the climb. Her fingertips ache with a pain both sharp and pulsating, and her nail beds are weeping blood, so she's grateful for something she can wrap her entire hand around for once. In addition, the brush means she's nearing the top, where the bluff rolls back at a gentler slope. Relief washes over her.

But the brush has only shallow roots and gives way as soon as she pulls. Her arm springs back as the tension suddenly releases, and she feels her entire body tilt. All blood seems to drain from her. She flings both hands forward, wraps her fingers around the first edge she can grasp, and pulls herself roughly up against the rock. The side of her face slams against the frigid stone, but she holds it there and doesn't move for several long moments.

Once she has recovered her breath, she continues climbing, sticking to the finger holds that, while excruciating, don't threaten to give way so easily. By the time she reaches the crest, her chest burns. Her thighs ache and twitch, and her hands are drawn into stiffened claws. Her pulse races in her ears.

She stands, keeping her back to the expanse behind her. Something won't allow her to look back at what could have been her death. A coughing fit overcomes her as the gelid air rakes at her throat. She bends double, hacking and spitting.

"Holy shit," she gasps to the rock beneath her feet.

The words are hardly out of her mouth when gravel sprays the backs of her legs with a sound like a sledgehammer striking the rock behind her. Instinctively, she turns. She hears the sound again, and dust and gravel speckle the side of her face. The second round echoes so loudly that she almost misses the buzzing sound that shoots past her shoulder and ear: a third round close but missing. She stumbles backward and lands on her rear with a shock that reverberates up her spine.

Tsula pulls her sidearm and flattens herself prone to the ground. She waits a moment, then shimmies back toward the edge where the rock slopes down gently before dropping off completely. The view above the treetops gives her the sensation of being suspended five stories in the air, and her head feels suddenly light. The trees rock in her vision, and she prays she won't begin to slide down the slope. Flexing her ankles, she presses the toes of her boots into the rock to hold herself in position.

On the rolling canvas below, the same man stands at the threshold of the trees. Tsula pulls the trigger twice, but it feels like firing from a buoy. The man doesn't even move. He raises the carbine, and she pushes back with her hands and curls into a ball on her side. Three more plumes of gravel rise and rain down on her with a *chock-chock-chock*. Dust swirls around her, and all grows quiet again.

She crawls back to the brink and fires twice more. This time, the man melts back into the trees.

Her pistol's slide locks back after the second round. Her ammunition is spent.

Tsula pushes back from the edge and sprints for the large patch of conifers that spreads out behind her, much like the forest floor below. When she grows lightheaded again, she slows to a walk and eventually collapses behind a gnarled fir whose scent surrounds her in the moist air. Her hands quake as she runs them over her face, her arms and legs, her trunk, searching for any new signs of injury. Sweat drenches her and cools as quickly as her pores can release it. Her arms shiver, and her fingers throb with pain.

She takes several deep breaths and blows them out slowly. Her mind is electric, whirring aimlessly through all that just happened and all that might come next.

She has to keep moving, but first she needs a plan. A clear sense of where she's headed and how to get there. Time will work against her in these conditions, and it will not do to move quickly but in the wrong direction. She pulls out her map, spreads it out on the ground, and studies.

Harlan's cabin is situated in a tucked-away bowl maybe ten miles northeast of Twentymile Ranger Station as the crow flies. Taking into account topography, that could mean twice as many miles on foot. But the ranger station is the closest park structure, and they may anticipate she'll head there. That's where they took

Alex's body, so they're familiar with the geography in between those two points. She wouldn't dare take the expected route into territory they're comfortable navigating. She'd be walking into a trap.

Likewise, Fontana Lake lies due south. Given its more populous surroundings—the dam giving the lake its form, the vacation homes dotting the dendritic shoreline, Fontana Village—the men would recognize this, too, as an attractive destination. She can't risk it.

Uncertainty grips her, and she closes her eyes against a torrent of panic. She knows now that at least four men had been present at the cabin, not just the three she had been dealing with. How, then, can she be certain there weren't more? Who else had she not seen? Of the four she knows about, one she safely can count out, given the bullet he took. One will be nursing burns, though she doubts he's incapacitated. A third is distressingly close, plotting his way to her at this very moment. Will Harlan leave his sons to join in the pursuit as well—and if so, where will he go? How many potential routes to safety can they cover?

Tsula returns her focus to the map. The Appalachian Trail runs roughly north and south maybe three miles west of where she sits. The Shuckstack fire tower, situated just off the trail, could provide shelter from the coming storm and the clearest view of the skies for miles. Once there, she could send her distress signal and wait for help to arrive. She considers attempting the SOS again where she sits, but now that the fourth man has spotted her, she can't simply remain where she is. She doesn't know how long it would take for help to reach her, and the odds are great that the man below would find her first. She needs to put space between them, to keep him behind her, and to send the signal in a place where she can hunker down.

She has only one viable choice, then: proceed west for two or three difficult miles—around the mountains where she can, and over them where she can't—until she finds the AT. From there she'll make her way south to the tower, signal for help, and do what she must to survive until help arrives. She consults her compass to confirm her orientation, folds up the map, and returns them both to her pocket.

The last of her water goes down quickly. Just one more problem she'll eventually need to solve. She looks down at the empty bottle as it quavers in her hand.

From overhead comes the rush of thick, wet sleet assaulting the trees before settling all around her.

CHAPTER THIRTY-TWO

The dimming sky tells Tsula she must find the tower soon, or else figure out another means of shelter for the night. Her headlamp rests in a saddlebag below Freya's body, and the clouds will admit no moonlight by which to navigate tonight. The temperature is continuing to drop, and the whipping wind will make it impossible to build, much less sustain, a fire in the open.

A membrane of sleet covers the ground, and her boots slip on icy slopes and rocks. She has not, for some time, seen or heard signs that anyone is near. But her tracks will point the way if someone is truly looking.

She'd found the Appalachian Trail—or, at least, what she *believed* was the trail—about an hour prior, grasping at saplings and branches to pull herself up the slope before turning south. But now, with no shelter to show for her efforts, she has begun to doubt herself. She has neared a decision to turn around and retrace her steps north when the access trail finally comes into view. Tsula squats then, takes several shuddering breaths, and whispers her thanks to the frozen ground.

Shuckstack Tower is a simple, spindly structure built during the Great Depression and situated on a point some four thousand feet above sea level. With views for miles in every direction, it once functioned as a wildfire lookout, though it has not served that purpose in years. Its base consists of a metal frame and a central open staircase leading up sixty feet to a tiny rectangular cab.

Recent budget woes mean the park has not undertaken any maintenance of the defunct structure in at least a couple years. As a consequence, the wooden steps—each a wide, thin plank—are in several places loosened from the frame. Others, though still properly secured, groan sickeningly underfoot. The whole structure creaks and sways subtly with the wind gusts. But adventurous hikers still climb the tower on occasion in search of a minor thrill or a panoramic view.

As she ascends, Tsula grips the railing as tightly as her cold hands can manage. The knowledge that she could have fallen from the bluff lingers in her mind, despite all that came after, and the open-air view just outside the staircase threatens to induce a new wave of panic. To avoid this, she concentrates her gaze on the steps in front of her, thrusting her boot treads forward on each surface to dig away the sleet that has gathered there and to provide sure footing.

When she reaches the final flight of stairs, the cab comes fully into view above her. The sight suddenly reminds her why she'd chosen this destination, and she feels for the GPS locator in her pocket. Dread fills her as she recalls how the device hadn't worked the last time. Surely, she prays, it will work up here. Surely, she's not about to corner herself inside those four tight walls, with only one way in or out, for nothing.

She pauses three-quarters of the way up, unwilling to wait any longer, and pulls the device from her pocket. But as she sets her thumb at the edge of the SOS button's cover and prepares to flip it open, the plank beneath her feet sags with an audible crack. She flings herself forward onto the steps above before the one beneath her can give way. The impact of bone and muscle on wooden edges sends currents of pain through her body. She rolls onto her side, moaning.

Below her, a high ping sounds, and a snapping as something strikes against metal and shatters. She looks down at her hands.

Empty.

She sits up and sweeps her eyes above and below her. The stairs around her hold nothing but her body and the sleet that has blown in and settled on them.

"Shit," she whispers. "No, no, *no*."

Tsula looks over both railings but can see nothing from this height. Stepping carefully over the cracked plank and again gripping the railing, she rushes back down the stairwell. At the landing above the third flight, she comes upon an orange, contoured shard of plastic roughly an inch wide. Another piece lies several steps further below, and she leans over the railing at the edge of the bottom landing to see the remainder of the GPS device in a disordered mess below.

Tsula continues to the ground and scans the base for remnants, gathering up those fragments she can find as though she might be capable of reassembling them into a functional whole. The largest portion still contains the display and SOS button. As soon as it's in hand, she presses and waits.

Nothing.

She presses again. The screen is obscured by a labyrinth of cracks behind which no message or glowing display appears. No tone sounds—not even, as before, to tell her the message has failed.

Tsula stands beneath the looming structure, her head hung limply. Help will not come for her now, she realizes. She's on her own.

In the next instant, she remembers the man with the rifle and knows she has no time to dwell on what is lost. She needs to take cover and devise a new plan. She rushes back up, taking two stairs at a time, her feet spread wide so they fall on either edge of the planks where the brackets provide support.

Once inside the cab, she sags back against the wall and sits. She can hear little above the roar of the wind now. It presses against the siding and the windows.

Tsula no longer has a firearm for protection if anyone finds her. She must improvise her defense. For several minutes, she considers her options.

At length, she removes her knife and springs open the blade. It's almost new and still quite sharp, serrated along nearly its entire length. A gift to herself on her last birthday that she's not had much occasion to use. On the top landing, she lies down on her belly to disperse her weight and slowly descends, head-first, back down the last full flight of stairs. She stops just above the step which had nearly given way under her and digs her boots into the edge of the landing to hold her body in place.

She presses her hand lightly on the weakened step, testing its remaining strength but taking care not to crack its surface. Tsula feels confident it can no longer hold a man's weight. She also doubts, thanks to the layer of sleet accumulated on its surface, that anyone would note the defect from above. Still, the steps overlap each other slightly, and any man would be too large for the gap created by just one stair giving way.

She needs more.

She slides back up the flight and hooks her arm around and under the step just above. Pressing the blade to the underbelly of the wood, she works in haste, scoring a deep line through its center. She cuts deeply, sawing back and forth for several minutes, careful to ensure the defect cannot be seen from above. She repeats the same procedure for the next two steps above that as well. When she's satisfied she has four consecutive steps ready to give way, she removes her boots and carefully reshapes the thin layer of sleet that tops them, until they bear what appears to be only one footprint apiece. Left, then right, then left again, before they reach the cab at the top.

This task now complete, Tsula clambers up into the cab and sits, pulling her knees up tight. There she remains, panting and waiting, massaging her elbow and wrist.

Nightfall is all but complete now, and as darkness envelops her, the air grows noticeably colder. Her core temperature, which had remained high from exertion almost all day, is starting to drop as well. Her accumulated sweat is cooling rapidly, and soon the moisture on her skin will work against her. It's a pernicious formula, Tsula knows.

Excessive cold brings death.

Exertion brings warmth, but it also brings sweat.

Sweat turns cold.

And cold brings death.

Tsula rips off her toboggan, coat, and underlayers as quickly as she can. The icy air steals her breath when her skin meets it. Her long-johns undershirt is now thoroughly damp with sweat and, down the right arm, blood. She spreads it out on the floor of the cab, where it will hopefully dry but, more likely, will freeze overnight.

Briefly, she raises her arm and crooks her head to inspect the wound on her shoulder. It's long, thin, and seemingly superficial, though she's reluctant to probe its depth. It has crusted over by now, and she'd prefer that it not start bleeding again.

Once finished, Tsula dons her remaining layers just as rapidly as she took them off. She places her underlayers on backward in order to provide her shoulder some coverage from the cold where Joseph's knife sliced through her coat and clothing. Her muscles quake with the cold and the exertion, and even after she's fully clothed again, she continues to shiver.

From the cantle bag she removes the white gas canister, small collapsible stove, and waterproof matches. She connects the fuel line to the canister and opens the valve. The gas hisses, then pops as a lit match contacts it, giving birth to a luminescent ring. She hunches over the flame, unzipping and tenting her jacket to contain as much of the heat against her chest and face as possible.

As she warms, the whole of her body relaxes. But in the relative peace and comfort of the moment, her eyelids grow heavy. She repositions herself several times until she finds the least comfortable posture—legs bent under her, knees and toes pressing into the wooden planks. She slaps her face, pinches her skin, holds her fingers too close to the flame.

None of it works. In time, exhaustion and the dissipation of adrenaline overtake her. Her torso slackens. Her shoulders slump. Her eyelids flutter and close.

JUNIOR

CHAPTER THIRTY-THREE

By the time his headlamp illuminates the first leg of the fire tower's base, Junior has had plenty of time to think. Hours in the dark and the cold might induce panic in some, but they had bestowed him with a kind of focus. He had, over the intervening miles, whittled his myriad concerns down to two: Where is she headed, and how will he kill her?

The answer to the first question came readily enough. After making his way to the top of the bluff where they'd last exchanged pleasantries, he tracked her west. West in this situation could only mean one thing: the Appalachian Trail. She would know that an established trail is the most efficient route out of the park. She likely would also need to find shelter at some point, and the AT offered it in both directions. From where he came upon the trail, the Mollie's Ridge shelter lay probably five miles in one direction, Shuckstack Fire Tower three or four in the other. He'd chosen to check the tower first, figuring the cab's four walls might hold more attraction in this wind than an open-air shelter. In short order, he'd come upon faint tracks that the latest waves of snow and sleet had not yet fully filled in. He followed them until they turned off at the tower access tail.

The first problem solved, Junior turns his attention to the second: how is he going to kill her? The first option involves patience and is, for that reason, unattractive to him. She'll have to leave eventually, he figures. She can't simply ensconce herself in the tower's cab for days on end. But he doesn't have the time or the inclination to wait her out in these conditions. Who knows how long that might take?

Alternatively, he could spray rounds from his carbine into the cab until it and anyone inside is good and shredded. That would achieve the desired result. But the tower is the only shelter for miles, and he'll need to rest once he has disposed of her body. There's no sense in creating new problems while solving the one at hand.

That leaves only hand-to-hand in close quarters. He nods to himself as he climbs. So be it. He figures he could fire one or two rounds straight up through the floorboard to stun her, move her back to one wall, before pulling himself inside. And if one or both of those rounds just happened to strike her, well, all the better.

The cab has come fully into view above him, only two short flights of stairs left and a small landing in between. He pauses, cranes his neck, and aims his headlamp up into the dark, square opening in the floor. The beam catches in the cab's windows above him and reflects back. He isn't certain, but he believes he spots a brief movement at the edge of the entrance, a figure pulling out of sight.

He smiles. *After this shit right here*, he thinks, *we're starting on my cabin next week. The savior of the settlement doesn't live in a goddamn tent.*

He grasps the gun in both hands and takes aim, but the angle isn't right. Just a few more steps. His pulse picks up.

He visualizes his return home, holding high some memento he removed from his quarry.

He steps, he breathes in, and—

TSULA

CHAPTER THIRTY-FOUR

Tsula wakes to a blinding light, the glass of the windows a dizzying white. She blinks, puts her hand up to shield her eyes. She pulls her legs up to her chest and flattens her back against the wall. She takes her knife in one hand, the pistol in her other, prepared to strike at anything that peers in. The pulse in her ears overlays the rush of wind pressing against the cab's walls and windows.

The first crack of wood comes a moment later, followed by an audible huff of breath and then a second crack and a third. The flashlight beam hits the ceiling and disappears. A rifle report fills the cab with a deafening punch, and her body jumps. A deep voice cries out and fades. Metal clangs. The whole structure shakes with an impact, the sound like a collision.

Another cry, then the bumping rustle of this same weight sliding or rolling down stairs until it comes to rest.

Tsula runs her bare hands over her arms, legs, neck, and torso, feeling for any warmth or wetness. Any new points of pain. Nothing. But the gusting wind whistles through a new gap in the ceiling above her head. Her portable stove, still on, hisses along. She curses, wondering how long she was asleep, how much fuel she has wasted, and turns the stove off.

In time, the wind settles, and she can hear the man faintly as he grunts and gasps in the darkness below. That she could hear him at all tells her he didn't fall all the way to the ground. He must have ended up somewhere on the stairs.

Death comes slowly for the man. At times, he falls quiet, only to awaken again with a heavy groan and begin his labored breathing anew. Once, she believes he shouts a word, though she can't make it out. Something short and pleading—a name, perhaps.

Finally, the sound fades and doesn't return.

Tsula sits alone in the quiet and the dark, shivering with such force that she fears her teeth might crack.

HARLAN

CHAPTER THIRTY-FIVE

The sun sets on the ranger's body lying in the grass, a spray of blood now frozen on his cheeks like a beard. By the time Harlan searches that body for valuables, it has grown stiff and all but merged with the shadowy ground below it. He collects what he can. Semi-automatic pistol. Satellite phone. Bottled water. Uneaten snack bar. Harlan pockets it all except for the pistol, which he holsters in the rear waist of his pants.

In the morning, the body will be capped in a crusted layer of white. Already the sleet has been falling for a couple of hours.

The glow of a small kerosene lamp shines dimly through the cabin's front door and keeps vigil over a second body inside. Joseph lies on his flank, motionless and pale. His breaths are slow and shallow.

Earlier they had applied a makeshift seal of plastic bag and duct tape over the sucking hole in his chest, but the seeping blood had, over the course of several hours, crept beneath the tape and weakened the adhesive. Half of his chest had expanded alarmingly when they covered the hole, and the strain eventually pulled most of the loosened tape from his skin. With the release of the seal had come a sound like a valve opening, and the chest contracted. The sucking did not return, but neither did Joseph's breath, except in thin, raspy draws. The bag and tape hung loose, stuck only to his body at the sternum.

The one small lamp casts long shadows across the room. Otto sits next to Joseph, his clothes charred and stinking of smoke and chemical fire. He rests one blistered hand on his brother's shoulder.

"We should take him, Pop. He needs help."

"That simple, huh?" Harlan says. "Just throw him in the back of the truck and get him to the hospital? Maybe we call 911, see if they can swing by and pick him up? You think that'll work?"

Otto averts his gaze.

"We're tomorrow away from a hospital, even if he could walk. He won't make it."

"But what if he did?"

"You tell me, Otto. What if he did? If by some miracle he survives, you think they're just going to treat the guy with the gunshot wound, no questions asked? You think the police won't be on him from the start? They figure this out, they'll be coming for us all. And Joseph will be in jail for attempted murder of a cop, spend most of his goddamned life behind bars. You want that for him?"

"I want him to have a chance."

Harlan sees the look on Otto's face, at once pleading and indignant. "There isn't one to be had," he says. "He's been shot through the lung, son. He won't make it the night."

The light from the lamp sways against the walls and flickers at its edges. Harlan's eyes ache and blur. He turns his face away from Otto and kneels to stroke Joseph's matted hair.

"My boy," he says, his lips suddenly thick and sluggish. "My brave, brave boy."

He tells himself this is a risk they all accepted, freely and with eyes open. That these are the costs of the freedom they've chosen. That a father's job is not to keep his sons safe at all cost, but to show them how to live and to give them a fair shot at it. He tells himself these things, but they bring him no comfort as he caresses the blank face of his dying boy. For the first time, he wonders if they are even true.

The temperature inside the cabin is dropping as night comes on. Harlan gathers up Joseph's sleeping bag, unzips it, and lays it gently over him. He has not yet gotten around to repairing the chimney, as the walls, flooring, and roofing have proven to be larger jobs than he'd initially estimated—especially with their tools. But it wouldn't hurt to light a log or two in the hearth, to provide his son a little warmth. They have a full cord stacked in the tent out back, and it's been curing for months.

Harlan stands, pulls on his coat, and steps out into the descending dark. In the privacy of the tent, the wind slapping at the walls, the patter of snow and sleet on the roof, Harlan leans against the stack of wood and weeps.

CHAPTER THIRTY-SIX

The problem with Harlan's father was that everyone saw him coming. It wasn't that Carl Miles had spent most of his early life a petty criminal, stealing bikes from the time he could ride one and gas from the time he'd learned how to drive. It wasn't even that he later supplemented his meager income as an on-again-off-again carpenter with drug distribution, or that he was capable of grave violence in furtherance of his goals. All that may have been true but was beside the point. He'd never been convicted of anything.

But even if people did not know of his misdeeds, still they had a solid suspicion from the first moment he came into view. They saw it in his slinking, feral gait. His hunched, perpetually naked and sunburned shoulders. The smile he gave as he passed the townsfolk, as though inventorying the many ways he'd wronged them.

It might not have been so bad if he hadn't reveled in the suspicion he inspired in people, as though he wanted their image of him to be all the criminal he was, and then some. He wore his dishonor like a freshly pressed Easter suit, a sociopath's grin on his face anytime someone accused him of malfeasance—which, it turns out, was often. The neighbor's pit bull went missing? Carl Miles probably killed it. The outboard engine on some rich dude's pontoon boat disappeared? Be sure to question Carl. Did someone steal crops from a marijuana grower down in the gap? Bet me Carl's wife will be buying steak at the grocery store next week.

As he grew, Harlan registered the looks people gave his father. The neighbors eyed his pickup as he drove by and did not stop looking until he was well out of sight. The teachers pursed their lips, inhaled deeply, and shot Harlan pitying looks on the rare occasion he missed the bus and Carl picked him up from school. The church folk sidled closer to each other as his father passed them on the sidewalk. The law, of course, had no compunction about showing up unannounced to question him about the most recent local crimes. Never once did Harlan hear his father deny having committed a crime of which he was accused. He'd simply look the accuser in the eye, stretch his stringy mustache and chin patch into a grin, and dare them to prove it.

Only in private did his father let on that the constant suspicion bothered him. "I can't go anywhere without getting the eyeball from people," he would say. "Cops always stopping me to ask me about some bullshit I had nothing to do with. I can't even go into the pharmacy without someone following me around."

It was his father who first began scouting for his granddaddy Lowell's land. He first took Harlan with him when the boy turned thirteen. "My Pop gave me a bunch of letters and drawings that were passed down to him," he explained. "There's lots of descriptions and drawings about where it is and what was around it. I bet if we keep at it, we could find it, fix it up. And then we could get away from all this bullshit. You eat what you gather. You enjoy only what you make yourself. You don't owe no one else nothin', and nobody can say shit to you about it. The way it was all supposed to be before people started getting so damned scared and soft."

As a teenager, Harlan pored over maps of the park like sacred texts and skipped school to follow his father deep into its interior.

They must have taken at least a dozen such trips before they finally found it. And when they returned that last time, giddy with their success and the possibilities that now seemed open to them, they spent hours planning what would be required to render the cabin habitable again.

And then, just like that, his father was in custody, arrested on charges of holding up a pharmacy with two friends. All the suspicion he had engendered in people, all the ill will he had given the police cause to bear, all the prosecutors he had told to fuck off—it all came back on him in that one episode with a force even he could not evade. Innocent or not, by God, he was going away this time. Within a year, he had been convicted and sentenced to fifteen years in prison. He would die there a decade later.

It was a crippling setback to the dream that now functioned as Harlan's north star. Restoring a homestead that deep into the backcountry would have been difficult for two men. It would be impossible for a seventeen-year-old who didn't yet know the first thing about carpentry. Harlan packed away the maps and plans they'd written out together, vowing to return to them when he'd amassed the required skills and surrounded himself with like-minded individuals. Perhaps one day he'd have his own sons.

The lessons Harlan took from his father's fate could have been many. He could have railed at the perceived injustice—at the inability, as his father lamented, to get a moment's peace. He could have declared the law his enemy and defied it, openly and at every turn. But what, in fact, he learned was to draw no attention to himself. Little could be accomplished under the watchful eyes of those who mistrusted him and who would enforce the limitations he intended to breach. If he gave the authorities a reason to target him, they happily would oblige. They needed a nemesis, after all. Better to be a stranger they had no reason to suspect or surveil.

Harlan therefore composed an external life distinct from

his father's: free of controversy, unworthy of comment, entirely forgettable. In his remaining year of high school, he turned respectful and hardworking, if not scholarly. He trimmed his shoulder-length hair, opting instead for a cut of moderate length with a standard part. With great effort, he molded his diction and patterns of speech, modeling them after the newscasters he saw on television and heard on the radio—the men everyone trusted back then.

After graduation, he took odd jobs with carpenters from whom he could learn the craft, eventually securing an apprenticeship with a gentleman named Wilson whose deep knowledge of historical construction methods and passion for old wood invigorated him. He stayed in Wilson's employ for over a decade, ascending to the old man's right hand while mastering the craft of restoration.

Harlan later assumed the business when Wilson dropped dead from a heart attack—though with some changes to operations necessitated by Harlan's desire to avoid official scrutiny. He took payment for work only in cash and opened no bank accounts in his name. He maintained no corporate entity or business address, and he required property owners to hire his crew directly for the duration of their projects rather than employing them himself. As his reputation among log home restoration enthusiasts grew by word of mouth, he took at least as many jobs out of state as he did in the surrounding mountains. This ensured that he did not develop such a local presence that his eventual disappearance would be noted with more than a shrug and a shaken head.

To this professional life he trussed a private one sculpted in much the same fashion. He courted and married a woman whose ambitions for a quiet and humble existence matched his own. He eschewed organizations of all stripes, including church, and was on the barest of first name bases with his neighbors. He drank minimally, when at all, consumed no recreational drugs, and avoided places and situations which might result in interactions with law enforcement. They rented, rather than owned, their home, to avoid any public records of their residential address.

Still, despite the careful and unremarkable façade he erected, Harlan could not deny he was his father's son. He felt it in his bones sometimes, the same rage and capacity for harm. It flared at indignities suffered, at injustices witnessed, a signal pulsing faintly at first but growing fulminant over time. He feared it initially, feared what might happen if he removed the straps of the studied civility that bound it in place. Eventually, he came to realize that what he needed was not to reject this inheritance, but to quietly embrace its potency. To hold these two opposing qualities in balance—the carrot paired with a thick and well-concealed stick.

About two weeks before Janie's passing, the air in the Miles home by then thick with stale frustrations and unripe grief, the hospice nurse pulled Harlan aside and announced that too many of her pain pills were missing. "I'm very careful, Mr. Miles, and I need you to be as well," she explained. "We can't just give her however many we feel like. We're not at that stage yet."

Harlan knew full well it had not been his doing, but he apologized nonetheless for his carelessness and assured her he would do better. He begged her pardon then, telling her he had an errand he needed to run and he'd be back soon. He climbed in his truck and raced down the single-track access road and onto the blacktop.

When Harlan had returned from work the prior evening, Janie told him Billy had stopped by to visit with her that afternoon. Billy, her younger brother and three-time rehab dropout with a hunger for opiates to rival any in the region. Billy, who only came around when he wanted money or called when he needed bailing out. Billy, whom Harlan had told never to show up when he wasn't around.

If the washed-out road to Billy's trailer had ever been covered in gravel, it was now buried under several layers of loose clay. Harlan could barely see out the windows for all the dust his truck kicked up. Billy was out the door of the trailer before the truck skidded to a halt, his hands up in a supplicative gesture. "I didn't do it." His words slurred, and he nearly stumbled forward down the three concrete steps that led from his front door to the grass.

"Didn't do what, Billy?" Harlan said.

Billy opened his mouth to respond, but Harlan stopped the words with his fist. The man's teeth scraped against Harlan's knuckles, and electricity shot the length of Harlan's arm. Billy stumbled backward onto his ass, his face smeared red. He clasped his nose with one hand, whimpering, and held the other out in a plea.

"The doctor'll give her all she needs, Harlan. She runs low, he'll write her another prescription. It ain't hurting nobody."

"You no longer have a sister, do you hear?" Harlan said. "You even think about coming by anymore, and I'll kill you."

Billy rolled on his side in the weeds and sobbed in the pitiful way of someone who'd lost control of his own person. When he could form words, he told Harlan he understood and would stay away.

But a week later, the hospice nurse repeated her prior lecture, this time with more force. "She's running out way ahead of schedule, Mr. Miles. It's a wonder you haven't killed her giving her that much. The doctor is going to ask questions."

This time, Harlan found the front door to the trailer ajar and Billy passed out half on and half off the couch. A small, clear sandwich bag sat next to his head, the few remaining Vicodin tablets now spilled onto the floor. A plastic fifth of gin lay tipped onto its side in a puddle.

Harlan knelt and placed his ear just above Billy's face, listening. Foul breath seeped from his open mouth, faint and slow. Harlan glanced around the room slowly. Dust motes danced in the evening light slanting through the windows, the day's last gasp.

He lifted a pillow from the couch and pressed it down on Billy's face, lending his weight to the effort, until the man's arms and legs twitched and kicked. When the rest of him fell off the couch, Harlan straddled the body to keep it still until it ceased spasming. He was surprised how much effort it required, how winded it made him. Harlan bent down again in search of breath that no longer came. He left the pills and bottle where they were. As he left, he wiped over his dusty boot prints with the pillow, then tossed it into a thick stand of hardwoods a quarter mile from the trailer.

The air washing through his truck's open windows felt crisper on the drive home, the sun somehow softer as it dipped behind the hills. The sharp curves in the road appeared to straighten as he approached. He rarely listened to the radio, but that evening Harlan stopped on a classic country program and hummed along as a woman sang of a killer down in Georgia who would never be suspected and a body that would never be found.

Janie was awake when he returned to the house. He sat on the bed next to her and kissed her forehead.

"Where you been, Mystery Man? Nurse Glenda was worried."

"Sorry," he said. "I had to take care of something."

"Help me sit up," she said, and Harlan did. "Billy came by again this morning. I know you don't like him, Harlan, but I think he's doing better. Trying, anyway."

Harlan smiled and kissed her. "I hope so."

"I know you're just trying to protect me." She coughed and stretched a hand to touch his face. "When I'm gone, I want you to look after Otto and Joseph the same way. They're sweet boys."

"They are," he said. Perhaps too sweet. But they were grade-school boys and had not yet been given the opportunity or reason to harden into men. He would see to that in due time.

"Your family's place," she said.

The words took Harlan by surprise, and he paused before answering. "I'm not worried about that now, baby."

"But you will be, one day. We both know it."

"Janie—"

"Tell me I'm wrong, and I'll know you're lying."

He said nothing.

"I know you set it aside for us," she went on. "Just us and two little boys out there, could you imagine?" She chuckled softly. "But one day, when the time was right, I would've gone with you."

Harlan hung his head, an ache building at the top of his throat.

"Just promise me you'll give our boys a choice, Harlan. Wait until they're old enough and know what they're signing up for. Don't just drag them out there because it's what you want. And don't give them a hard time if they want something different for their lives. Promise me that."

Harlan nodded but didn't look up. "I promise."

CHAPTER THIRTY-SEVEN

By the time the dead ranger's satellite phone rings, Joseph has ceased breathing entirely. The tone pierces the grim stillness with all the force of a tornado siren and brings a sudden end to Otto's sniffling. Harlan removes the phone from his pocket and studies the bright green display. Otto glances at Harlan, then at the device, and back again, as though his father might be holding a moccasin.

"Pop."

"Hush. I'm thinking."

In a moment, the phone is quiet and dark again. Otto begins to pace, wringing hands that glow dimly yellow in the light of the lamp and the dying fire. "They know we're here," he says.

"They don't know anything about us."

"Then why are they calling us?"

"They're not calling us," Harlan growls, pointing outside. "They're calling him."

"What happens when they don't get him?"

"Hush, damn it, and let me think."

It's night now, and snowing. Harlan suspects his two unwelcome guests were due back before nightfall, or at least before the weather came in. On horseback that would be feasible. If whoever is calling doesn't reach him, how long will it be before others come in search?

The phone sounds again, and Harlan holds his finger to his mouth to shush Otto's fretting before it can begin. He thinks back to what little the ranger said before he died, to the baritone in which he'd said it, and answers in his best impersonation. "Hello?"

"Abbott," a woman's voice says. "Oh, thank Christ. Do you know what time it is? Where the hell are you?"

Harlan registers the question. They're not tracking the ranger's location with the phone. "I'm . . . here," he says.

"Where the hell is here?" the woman says. "And where's Special Agent Walker?"

"With me."

"She was at Shuckstack, but we lost her signal. Is that where y'all are?"

Harlan's mind whirs through his options and the likely outcomes of each.

At length, the voice speaks again: "Abbott, are you there?"

"Sure am." Harlan keeps his words few and clipped. The more he speaks, the more likely the caller will recognize she's not actually speaking to Abbott. "We're at the tower. For the night."

"What the hell happened?" Concern has left the voice now, supplanted by anger. "You were supposed to be back before the weather."

"Sorry. We saw some stuff. Explain tomorrow."

"Abbott, are you okay?"

"Gotta go. Gotta build a fire."

Harlan hangs up just as the woman is shouting something else into the phone. Before she can call back, he smashes the device with a roofing hammer he'd left sitting on the front porch. He can't continue to speak with her for fear of giving himself away, and he can't risk them deciding to track the phone's location now.

Otto stares at him, mouth agape.

"She's at Shuckstack," Harlan says.

"You think Junior's still on her?"

"I don't know. But we can't take any chances."

"We going, then?"

"Not we," Harlan says. "Me. You'll stay and prepare a grave for Joseph out there." He points to the side yard. "We'll bury him when I return."

"When will you be back?" Otto asks.

"When it's done."

"When's that?"

"When she's dead."

Otto places a thin sliver of new wood on the embers. "What if she gets away?"

"Then we run. Find a new place. Regroup."

"Run where?"

"Stop," Harlan says. "Enough questions, son. I need to focus." But he can see in Otto's face that the questions won't cease even if his son stops asking them. Otto, the family's Worrier in Chief, afflicted with the burdens of the firstborn. Harlan sighs and places his hand on his son's shoulder. "If we have to run, we'll find a new place. You need to trust me."

Otto hangs his head and nods.

Harlan lifts his chin with his hand. "And if you see or hear anything while I'm gone, if it looks like anyone's getting close, you need to leave. Head down to the lake and hunker down somewhere."

"Without you?"

"I'll find you."

Otto's widened eyes reflect the glow of the fire, and Harlan wonders if his son is actually capable of what may be required. But he dismisses the thought quickly. Speculation will accomplish nothing now.

They carry Joseph's body to the porch and remove his clothing. Otto draws frigid water from the catchment basin outside, and with it they clean Joseph's body of blood and stench. Then they bear him back inside and dress him in his spare pants and shirt.

Harlan lies down on the floor, sidles up to Joseph's still form, and pulls his unzipped sleeping bag over them both.

There he remains, next to his youngest boy, until first light.

TSULA

CHAPTER THIRTY-EIGHT

December 17

Morning comes with an icy grip, and Tsula's first thought is one of surprise that she has survived the night. She blinks hard at the eastern light flooding the fire tower's cab and wipes crusts from the corners of her eyes. She rises, shivering, and lifts her hands to meet the sun's beams. They provide her little relief.

As her mind emerges from the night's irregular sleep, she flaps her arms across her torso and sprints in place to warm her body. Then she takes inventory of the facts confronting her. She currently shelters inside the cab of a lookout tower west-southwest of Harlan's cabin, on the spine of a high ridge just off the Appalachian Trail. She has a knife and pistol but no bullets. No water and no food aside from deer jerky now frozen hard. A small amount of white gas for the stove, a flint lighter, and waterproof matches. One less clothing layer now that her undershirt lies frozen stiff on the floor. A map and a compass, but no means of communication with the outside world.

A mother who will die with no daughter by her side if Tsula does not make it home.

The groggy headache and acerbic film in her mouth tells her

she's dehydrated. Frozen precipitation is all around her, but eating snow and ice will only speed the onset of hypothermia. She needs to melt and warm it.

Tsula proceeds back down the stairs, hewing primarily to the inside edge where the steps rest on the metal brackets and are unlikely to give way. When she reaches the chasm where the steps have fallen away, she mounts the inner handrail and shimmies down the metal feet first, her hands and thighs clamped so tightly they burn. Once past the gap, she returns her feet gingerly to the stairs and proceeds down the remainder of the stairwell.

Tsula finds the man on one of the lower landings surrounded by a halo of frozen black. He lies on the small wooden platform, recumbent except for his legs, which still extend up the flight of stairs. One is folded beneath him mid-thigh. A spear of femur juts through his torn pant leg, a sculpture of rime ice adorning its scalloped edge. Frozen beads of purple and black splotch the surrounding wood and metal. The scents of iron and bowels hover in the frigid air.

A shroud of blown snow and frost overlays the body. Tsula brushes it from the man's face and torso. His hand still clutches a post as though he had tried to pull himself up at the end. His mouth gapes open still, a final request or protest choked by a slurry of blood and ice.

Tsula searches the man's coat and the layers underneath but finds nothing in his pockets but a half-empty pack of cigarettes and a lighter. She reaches across the torso and legs to roll the corpse over, but he's mounted to the wood beneath.

She proceeds to the ground, scanning as she does in all directions for any indication that she's not alone. At the bottom, she squats on the hardened snow in a patch of morning sun, vaporous whirls rising around her from the white crust. The snowpack is capped with hoar frost, except in patches where platy flakes rise from the crust like windswept feathers. Now and then a gust lifts a dusting of ice, and it glitters crystalline in the sun.

She removes the stove, white gas canister, and a metal mug from the cantle bag. Then she pounds the hoar with the heel of her fist and shovels the shattered crust into her mug. A match ignites the stove with a soft *whoosh*, and in minutes the frost is melted and near boiling. She cups her gloved, numb hands around the mug to warm them. As she drinks, the heat traces the length of her gullet before radiating out to her core. Her fingers come alive with a burning tingle. She melts and drinks greedily, downing several additional mugs in preparation for the long journey ahead.

When she's full of water and fairly thawed, Tsula stands and scouts the ground around the tower for the dead man's rifle or anything else which might be scavenged. But all is flat, unbroken white save for higher berms of freshly banked snow. Tsula knows the danger to her hands posed by digging aimlessly in the wet and cold. What is lost must now wait until the next thaw to be found.

As she trundles around the tower's supports, the full weight of her body collapses the crust, and she sinks in the snow nearly to her knees. Droplets of cold seep through her wool socks and wet her ankles. Tsula envisions the hike ahead of her and knows this won't do, that she can't make it as many miles as she needs to if every footfall drops her that deeply into the snowpack. She'll exhaust herself in only a fraction of the distance she must cover, and she'll lose her toes, if not her feet, to frostbite.

Tsula ventures into the neighboring trees and, after several minutes, finds a clutch of young pines still thick with needles and heavy with white. She identifies a half-dozen boughs the diameter of a dowel rod and twelve to eighteen inches long, and she shakes the snow from them. With her serrated blade, she saws the branches free from their trunks. Her frozen undershirt cuts easily into long strips, and she uses them to knot the branches together in groups of three. She steps each boot sole onto a cluster of branches, the thickest ends jutting out beneath her toes, and brings the strips of cloth up and over the tops of the boots, where she weaves them among her laces and ties the ends tightly together. Tsula takes several test steps in a wide circle and, satisfied with this improvisation, sets out back down the access trail toward the AT.

That one of the men found her is a reminder of their skills in this environment and the danger of heading south into territory she knows they're likely familiar with. North will be hard. It will take much longer. But if she moves quickly, it hopefully will keep them behind her.

To the west, clouds gather again, dumping snow like a curtain over the mountains and the passes below. She prays she can stay ahead of it. Overhead, a jet streaks east as though to outrun the coming weather.

"Take me with you," she says, but there's not a soul around to hear.

HARLAN

CHAPTER THIRTY-NINE

s Harlan approaches the tower, his breaths scald his chest and throat. Moments before, he had noted shallow, indistinct footprints leaving the access trail and turning north on the AT. Still, he presses on to the structure first, to see who or what might remain. He makes his way up the stairs, pausing when he reaches Junior's body.

The strenuous work of reaching this place had buried his rage, like sand thrown over a fire. But now the flames revive and grow, melting that sand into shards of glass. Images of what must have been his friend's last moments drown out all other thoughts.

Harlan forces himself to climb on but stops when he reaches the gap in the stairs near the top. Half a plank still clings to the edge of its bolt. The wood fibers are jagged at the break, but it appears to have split through the center vertically. These boards, he knows, were weakened on purpose.

Though he hates this woman—though he wishes to take her life in a manner that will allow them both to linger over its agonizing ending—still he cannot help but admire the ingenuity. Tsula Walker is smart, and he would do well to keep that in mind.

Harlan won't leap the gap for fear that the stairs above it are similarly weakened. And now that he knows the footprints leading away from the tower are hers, there's no reason to risk it. She has fled north, and he will follow.

He returns down the stairs and kneels over his friend. Harlan opens his mouth to tell Junior he's sorry, that he'll return to bury him if he can, but stops short when he hears the light crunch of approaching boots on the frost. A figure ambles into view—a man wearing a toboggan and a Park Service coat, a day pack slung over his shoulders.

Harlan's stomach lurches. They'd not bought his impersonation of Abbott last night after all—at least, not entirely. Perhaps they'd attempted to call him back after he destroyed the satellite phone.

What now? Harlan feels a heaviness at his shoulders, as though a thick noose has been tossed around his neck. Everything he holds dear is slipping away from him. He clenches his eyes and breathes in deeply to quiet the noise in his mind. It's not all gone, he tells himself. He can still salvage what remains.

He rises to his feet and opens his eyes wide. "Help!" he shouts, running down the remaining stairs and toward the man. "Thank God you're here! This guy up here, he needs help!"

The ranger freezes, his mouth gaping at the unexpected sight. "What the—what's going on?"

"This guy up here is hurt bad. Is it just you?"

"It's just me. What's wrong with him?"

Before the man can reach for his radio, Harlan maneuvers himself behind and pushes him toward the stairwell. "Hurry! He needs help!" They ascend the stairs, the first man clomping up as fast as he can, the latter reaching behind his waist for the pistol holstered there.

As Junior's body comes into view, the ranger stops abruptly. His shoulders droop, his body sways, and his hand shoots out to grasp a support post.

"My God," he says. "What—"

The mountains echo back the report as the ranger slumps to the planks.

Harlan drags the ranger off of Junior and midway down the flight below, then removes the man's radio and clips it to himself. He can't spare the time to hide the bodies now, and eventually someone will come looking for this man. But if someone were to reach out by radio, he perhaps could answer and delay the search a bit longer.

At the base of the tower, Harlan hits the trail at full stride. She has a generous head start on him, and she's capable. But she's headed north, deeper into the park—likely with the intention of emerging near one of the ranger stations or public areas at the border. It's a difficult trek even in favorable circumstances, and much more so in the conditions they both face now. It should take at least until tomorrow for her to reach her destination, which means he has plenty of time to catch up. She has left him a trail to follow, and he knows these mountains like he knows his own skin.

He tucks the pistol away, drinks from his bottle of water, and heads north when he reaches the AT.

TSULA

CHAPTER FORTY

The snow returns mid-day and falls in dense, obscuring sheets. The wind gusts constantly, stealing Tsula's breath and banking drifts that grow to waist-high. The wind's scrape and howl obscure the post-concussive whine that has returned to her ears and the crunch and occasional slip of her boots.

This is why she nearly misses it when the first tree gives way. She catches only the last of the crescendo as it falls beneath its burden of snow and ice. Turning, she sees, not the tree itself, but the disturbance it makes: other treetops jostled and shifting, crystalline powder erupting into the air around them like billowing smoke. She shakes her head and keeps moving.

As if to reinforce the message, a large pine goes next—this one only twenty yards ahead of her. It whips down onto the slope to her right, slides down the hill, and settles on the trail in a violent flourish of white and green. The sound is like a thunderclap overhead. The impact shakes the ground beneath her feet.

Tsula pauses, her heart racing and her stomach suddenly sour. If she'd only hiked that much faster over the last stretch, or ended her last water break that much sooner, she'd have been directly in its path. And then what? Her knees and ankles are struggling to flex now, and her feet are growing numb. Could she leap out of the way if it meant her life? Or would rangers or volunteers find her remains beneath some trunk they came out to clear from the trail when the weather turned more favorable?

Wouldn't that be some shit? she thinks. *After all this.*

She looks up at the dozens of other trees well within reach, as though she might by examining them discern which will be the next to go. They stand impassive and give nothing away—all of them thick with glaze ice and glinting like jeweled weapons. Tsula can do nothing but stay alert. She descends the slope to her left to skirt the felled tree's crown and, once around it, struggles back up to the trail. The air smells of dirt and sap.

Tsula hikes the rest of the afternoon, stopping only when the wind abates to melt and warm water over her burner. Despite the fluid she's taking in, her urine is growing darker. She's dehydrating and hungry. She places a slice of the frozen jerky in her mouth and attempts to soften it with what warmth and saliva she can manage. The meat simply adheres to her bottom lip and tears the skin when she pulls it away.

The mountains she'd viewed in childhood as nurturing have now taken on a menacing quality. Their stippled surfaces—the dark of trees rising from a background of white—give the impression of something more mythic than geological. Leviathans hibernating in the open, ready to stir at any moment and swallow her whole.

Waves of panic lap at her. In the gaps between trail markers, she stops, worried she has lost the path, and scans for clues of its whereabouts. A slightly wider gap in the trees. A natural break between harsher topographical features. Contours more suited to foot travel. But poor visibility makes the task difficult.

To stave off her anxiety, she resolves to keep her mind occupied. She counts her footsteps in intervals from peak to peak or down a slope. In this manner, she keeps a rough tally of distance covered and how much she must yet travel. She hums tunes in rhythm with her feet, as well. "Skip to the Loo" seems to work best, the downbeats timed to her footfalls. But the song grows slower and more dirge-like as the day progresses and her energy wanes.

When she tires of counting, she instead repeats out loud the plan she has devised for herself, attempting by repetition to etch it into her brain. To preserve it like a conditioned response that can still govern her actions even after her conscious mind becomes addled by the cold. *Head north on the Appalachian Trail. When it hooks east, turn north again on a tributary trail. Keep heading north until you reach Laurel Creek Road. Follow the roads to the Townsend Visitor Center.*

Tsula notices the coyotes for the first time at what must be three or four o'clock. Two rust and charcoal-fringed faces lurk behind a curled rhododendron no more than ten yards off the trail. They keep pace with her as she walks, feet so sure and careful that they make no sound. Tsula stands up straight to render herself more imposing but does not turn to face them. Instead, she keeps walking, concentrating on her movements to ensure they give no indication of weakness or distress.

In time the sun slumps low, and all but the surrounding peaks is robed in shadow. The coyotes surface from this seeping darkness on a high snow drift, staring down at her and the slope beyond. Without warning, the larger of the two—a male, she figures— pricks its ears and descends the drift toward her at full speed.

Tsula's mind registers an urge to run or to fight, but her body can put neither into action that quickly. She is theirs if they want her.

Instead, the male crosses in front of her so close that his paws toss snow on the toes of her boots. In the next instant, he disappears down the hill, his companion following close behind.

Tsula stares after them, unable for several long moments to breathe or move.

CHAPTER FORTY-ONE

The storm has passed, and the night is cloudless. Stars glint sharply against the black canopy like diamonds carelessly scattered. The moon hovers over the trail, a bright and gleaming scythe. The white blanket of snow catches the light and returns its own spectral glow. In this way, Tsula is able to hike—slowly, cautiously—for some time even after the sun has fully set. She passed up a shelter several hours back, concluding she had not covered enough ground and could not yet stop for the night. Her map told her another shelter was situated just off the trail some five additional miles ahead. And near that structure, a smaller trail would break north toward Laurel Creek Road. She'd decided to try for that second shelter.

But trudging now in the low light with the temperature dropping into what must be the low twenties, Tsula fears she's made a grievous mistake. Shouldn't she have come across that trail junction by now?

Her whole body shakes from ankles to shoulders even while in motion. Her empty stomach has rebelled, and she keeps vomiting bile. If she doesn't find the shelter soon, she'll have to stop where she is, improvise a shelter in a snowbank, and do her best to build a fire from dampened wood.

Finally, she comes upon a level expanse with scant trees and then a post holding two wooden placards, each oriented in different directions. She removes a match from its case, wills her numbed fingers to hold on, and manages to light it against the sign post.

In the quavering orange glow, the lower of the two signs tells her the shelter she seeks lies a short distance down a trail that cuts sharply to the right. She doubles over, hands on her knees, and whispers, "Thank you, thank you, thank you."

The snow-capped roof comes into view first, glowing dimly above a shadowy rectangle. Soon that rectangle reveals itself to be a squat, open-air wooden structure with a stone fireplace on one end. Tsula lights another match against a support post, and its glow allows her to survey the shelter quickly. A waist-high drift has collected at the threshold, and she kicks through it with her boots. Inside, two layers of wooden sleeping platform lie beneath the ceiling, which slants rearward. Snow has also gathered on the lip of the lower platform, and she sweeps some of it off with her free hand. To her right, a fireplace sits cold and empty but for charred scraps of half-burned logs which had avoided the snow. On the ground below the fireplace, some kind soul has stacked additional tinder.

Tsula shakes out the match, sets the cantle bag on the sleeping platform, and removes its contents in the dark. She identifies each item by examining it with her bare hands, focusing on what sensations her numb fingers can still register. The relative weight and shape of things. The slight sense of concentrated pressure at an edge. The sound an object makes when shaken or struck lightly against the wooden pallet.

The gas canister sloshes noisily, only a little liquid left. Tsula is tempted to save it for the next day but also knows she likely won't live to use it if she doesn't warm herself tonight. She shakes snow off the tinder and stacks it in a crosshatch pattern as best she can. The cap of the gas canister twists off with an effort that leaves her nearly breathless and her fingertips throbbing. She dribbles the fluid over everything, squeezes her flint lighter several times, and watches as a bright yellow spark gives birth to blue and yellow flame.

With the aid of two more matches, she searches outside the shelter for low, thin tree branches sheltered from the snow by the larger ones above them. She breaks them from their trunks, using her knife when necessary to finish the task. Between two of the trees, her boot steps on a flat stone. It's almost as wide as her sole and rocks loosely when she flexes her ankle. She scoops the rock up and places it in a coat pocket.

The new branches smoke furiously when placed on the fire, hissing and bubbling at their shorn edges, but eventually succumb to the flames. Tsula places the flat stone within inches of the fire and sits huddled as close to the hearth as she can, hands extended toward it. When the bitter smoke billows out into her face, she coughs and clamps her stinging eyes shut. Still, she's grateful for the warmth.

Something moves outside, footsteps in the blackness. She turns slowly, willing whatever or whoever it is to move on. But they don't. Ravening eyes stare back at her, gleaming through the opening she'd cleared through the snow at the shelter's threshold. No growl or bark ushers from the darkness. Only the eyes give the coyotes' presence away—steady, calculating, intent.

She pats her coat and pants for her knife but finds instead the bag of deer jerky in her pocket. She pulls it out, slides the bag open, and tosses two brown disks onto the ground outside. The eyes dip and disappear. A sound like the snapping of twigs pierces the silence, and the eyes rise to look at her again.

Still hungry.

"Fine. Here," she mumbles. She throws out the rest of the bag's contents and waits. When the eyes again return to her, Tsula stands on quivering legs and spreads her arms out wide.

"That's all you get. Now go on!"

It's more a hoarse whisper than full-throated cry, but they jump at the command and disappear with a hurried rustle. Their yips recede into the night and give way to a ghastly keening that floats above the trees. The sound fills her with unease. She continues to search her pockets and eventually finds her knife.

Tsula returns to the fire, lifts the stone she's placed there with her sleeve, and inserts it into a front pocket of her coat. She sits back against the wall near the fire, her legs pulled to her chest and her forehead resting on her knees. She closes her eyes and concentrates, listening for any hints of motion above the fire's soft crackle. The stone's heat radiates to her trunk and her thighs and even brushes her cheeks with a faint warmth. At last, her body slackens, and sleep erases her fears.

CHAPTER FORTY-TWO

December 18

The first thing Tsula notices when she awakens are slices of deer jerky lying scattered on the snow outside the shelter, the empty plastic bag nearby. For the life of her, she doesn't understand why they're there. She rubs the crusts from her eyes, yawns out her foul breath, and looks around her. Nothing but snow, shelter, and cold ash.

Tsula uses the last few drops of fuel. She dribbles them over wet twigs tented atop crumpled leaves she has found deep in the shelter's dusty corners. The tinder hisses and pops and eventually gives life to a small flame she feeds with pine needles, sticks, and more leaves carelessly scooped from beneath the trees outside. The snow she melts in her mug becomes a lukewarm puddle that tastes of smoke and dirt.

As she sips, Tsula inventories her condition. Her stomach growls and aches with pangs so fulsome they resemble nausea. She can't recall the last time she's eaten. Her bowels have been halted since the prior morning, and this morning she feels no urge to urinate. Her mind is slipping. Her fingers, though gloved, can sense only the heaviest pressure. Even that registers simply as a dull ache. Her feet, despite being covered by two layers of socks and boots, are numb from toe to heel. The muscles of her core, arms, and thighs shiver unrelentingly, though she's at least grateful to feel this anatomic response. She knows what it will mean if she stops shaking.

In her clear moments, she knows these observations add up to one objective fact: If she doesn't find her way to warmth and safety today, she won't wake up tomorrow. She's in the process of dying.

The sun shines brightly over the easterly tree line, and she turns away, blinking, from the sharp light. To the west, the sky is crisp and clear blue—except for a thin column of smoke rising just above the trees in the distance and dispersing like low-lying cloud. She turns back to the shelter and sees the thin wisps ascending from its chimney as well.

"Shit," she whispers to no one. How far away is that smoke? One mile, maybe two?

Who would be out here in these conditions other than Harlan or Otto or some other member of their settlement she hasn't yet encountered? Someone is closing in on her, and the smoke from her own small fire will lead the way.

She dashes back into the shelter, scooping up snow with her gloves and burying the fire with it. She hastily packs her bag, attaches it to her belt, and leaves for the trail in as close to a run as her legs and the crusted snow will permit.

She looks toward the sky again as she flees. The distant column of smoke has disappeared, the thinning haze hovering against a background of electric blue.

CHAPTER FORTY-THREE

Amid waist-high banks of snow, Tsula's thighs give out. It's only mid-day, and already her knees are refusing to work. She crumples to the ground and attempts without success to rise again. Seated on her rear with her ineffectual legs folded beneath her, she feels an uprush of fear and anger. She punches her thighs with loosely clenched fists and curses, as though such punishment might enforce some duty to cooperate. Blow after blow lands, but she feels nothing—not in her hands, not in her legs. She gives out quickly and sits there panting.

When clarity returns, she realizes how she must have appeared in her frenzied state, wailing away at her own body. Growling like a hackled dog. The noise she made surely would draw the attention of anyone who is close. She turns her head in both directions but sees nothing. She listens for the sounds of feet on crunching snow or of ice-brittled branches snapping. Instead, she hears only the murmur of wind in the trees and breathes out slowly in relief.

Tsula reaches for the snowbank rising to her right, cupping her hand to grip the top as best she can and pull herself upright again. By the time she's on her feet, her legs have agreed to rejoin the mission, though only halfheartedly. She begins to move again with caution.

At a crest on the trail she halts, uncertain of what she sees before her some fifty yards ahead. A gray and rust-colored welter, bright crimson beneath. Tsula walks on, and as she nears, she recognizes the two coyotes, her steady cohorts, now roiling at some larger prey. Had they come upon an elk calf or a fawn out searching for food beneath the icy crust? The bright red spreads like an opening mouth in the ground beneath them. Where the blood spills onto the snow, steam rises and the white melts. The beasts feed hungrily and fight over morsels as though they know this will be their last meal for a long while. Their muzzles, slick with blood, shake splotches onto more distant snow.

Something tells her to turn back, to find another way. But here the narrow trail cuts between a steeply rising slope on one side and an equally steep slope falling away on the other. There is no feasible path forward but through the scrum. Tsula removes her pistol and prepares to strike them with it if necessary—if her arm will do as it's told.

When she's so close she can smell the coppery tang, the large gray male turns to her with something long and fleshy in its mouth. She squints, straining to discern the object, then gasps. A hand hangs limply from the stump clenched in his teeth. He steps forward and lifts his muzzle as though to offer it to her.

She clamps her eyes shut, her breaths coming in quick, shallow bursts.

"Here."

A chill shoots through Tsula. She opens her eyes and strains to focus.

"You gotta eat."

Before her stands Eddie. Dingy south Florida sand and pine needles still cling to his naked chest and arms, but his face is now painted with blood to the gaunt cheekbones, tinting his beard. He holds the limb out to her, his mouth working noisily on a morsel.

She looks down at the body behind him and sees the same crumple she came upon in the field that day in the Everglades, tanned and bruised except where teeth have now removed flesh.

"Red's your friend," she says.

Eddie shrugs. "Man's gotta eat."

"Aren't you cold?"

He laughs and picks sinew from between his teeth.

Tsula shakes her head, blinks heavily, and looks around again. In that instant, Eddie is gone, though his smoker's cackle lingers in the air like an echo. Gone, too, are the coyotes, the body, the gore. All has disappeared but the blank, undisturbed white and the trees laid out endlessly before her.

Tsula is alone again and deeply fearful now. Frightened even of her own thoughts.

CHAPTER FORTY-FOUR

S he's been following the water for some time. Her sopping boots and soaked pant legs mean she must have crossed a stream at some point. But she can't recall when or fathom how she hadn't fallen in.

The tips of several fingers are dark. She notices this when she reaches up to steady herself against a tree. Where are her gloves? She can't remember removing them.

The trail climbs high above the river to her left. The rush of whitewater, still some distance away, grows ever louder. She trudges on without will or thought until she's standing atop a precipice presiding over a bend in the stream. It feels familiar to her, this place with the river below and the waterfall in the distance off to the right, though the stream is fat with snowmelt, and the cataract roars louder than she recalls.

The Sinks. Where Jamie had brought her so many years ago.

It's farther east than she had intended to go—probably by several miles, isn't it? Somewhere earlier in the day she must have missed—what? An earlier trail junction? Perhaps two? Tsula feels for her map but can't find it anywhere on her.

Even so, she finds comfort in something familiar, something imbued with such a pleasant association. The deep hole below, the water in which she's previously swum. The road on the other side, the bridge upstream.

Wait—yes, the bridge. The road! It's so close she can see it, just on the other side of the river.

Then she sees him, too. Or her—she can't tell from this distance. A head—no, two—hovering above the parking lot's guardrail, slowly floating up the road as though a second stream she can't see flows the opposite direction. She tries calling out to them but can manage no more than a squeak. The heads don't hear her and keep floating away. She turns unsteadily, intent on returning to the trail and making it down the trail to the road. She must catch up with whoever's over there.

Harlan Miles stands before her then, a pale, bedraggled figure positioned between her and the trail. He removes his pack and sets it down.

"Hello, Tsula Walker."

She pauses, swaying on her feet and squinting at this apparition. "You're not real," she declares at length. "I'm seeing things again."

She steps forward to pass around the figment.

A fist swings into view, wide and eclipsing, just before it strikes her face. But she feels little other than the halt of her progress forward, a backward thrust of her body. She can't summon her feet to her aid and lands on her rear. She tastes blood in her mouth, smells it in her nose.

"That real enough for you?"

She scrambles backward, looking behind her for the edge. She has only a few feet before she reaches the drop-off. Her hand slips on the ice, and she falls flat onto her back. Before she can sit up, Harlan is on top of her, his hands wrapped around her neck, his thumbs pressing against her larynx.

"You took Joseph's breath," he grunts. "Time to return the favor."

But the pressure at her throat is familiar, and it has the effect of waking her, summoning mind and memory and practiced action. His face grows red when she does not thrash or attempt to shout, and he adjusts his body forward so more of his weight presses down through his arms and hands. This shift of his heft up her body affords her legs more freedom. She bends her knees, pulls her feet to her buttocks, and presses her hips up off the rock. It's only a subtle rise, but Harlan lists unsteadily to his right. He removes a hand from her neck to catch himself on the rock.

In the next instant, he howls and falls off Tsula entirely. She sucks in air, deep and hoarse, and rolls onto her side, coughing. Her hand is warm and wet, and she holds it up to look. Blood smears the palm and the webbing between her thumb and forefinger. She glances at Harlan, his face a shocking mixture of confusion and pain. They both look down to his left thigh, where her knife is buried to the handle.

"Tsul," a voice says behind her.

She knows this voice, and her heart thrills.

"Tsul, do you trust me?"

She doesn't turn toward him. She knows where he is and what he wants. Instead, she keeps her eyes on Harlan. His hands hover over the knife as though he might remove it. He falls back and pounds his fist on the stone beneath him.

She scrambles onto her knees and then to her uncertain feet.

Harlan sits up again and reaches behind to his waistband.

"We'll go together. You jump where I jump."

Harlan's arm is swinging forward.

She turns, takes two strides, and then they are airborne and falling, she and Jamie, side by side in the warmth of the late summer afternoon.

The pistol cracks, and the water swallows her.

PART III: REMAINS

HARLAN

CHAPTER FORTY-FIVE

Harlan's leg howls as he crawls to the rock ledge and looks down at the river below. He grunts and squeaks and whines and lets all the breath in his body out at once when he sees her down there fighting the current, moving farther and farther away from him. He rests his forehead on the cold rock and laughs. She'll die for sure now, though he won't be there to see it happen. *So be it*, he thinks. *Let the river claim her, bury her beneath a rock.*

Warmth comes in pulses from around the knife blade, sliding down his skin and pants before pooling beneath him and cooling. His leg is aflame, but still he feels faint. The world has covered itself in a delicate gauze that grows thicker and more obscuring with each passing moment.

He tries to roll onto his back, but the knife handle strikes the rock. The blade flexes in the meat of his thigh, and it feels in that moment like this might be the end of his leg. He screams, tears welling in his eyes, and curses himself for his carelessness. *Pay attention, goddammit.*

He needs to move, to take cover, but to do that he needs the knife out. He searches for a suitable tourniquet and settles on the belt of his pants, which is made of some synthetic material, both tough and flexible. He removes the belt clasp with his own knife, slides the fabric under his leg, and ties a simple overhand knot above his thigh. His breath leaves him in ragged moans as he pulls both ends of the knot tight and fastens a slip knot on top.

The handle of Tsula Walker's blade is cold as he grips it firmly. Before the fear can make him think twice, he removes it with a swift pull. Another groan finds its way through his clamped lips. As the metal rattles onto the rock, he stares down at his leg. The seeping appears to have reduced to a light ooze thanks to the tourniquet, but it has not stopped entirely. He removes his toboggan, folds it in half, and presses down on the wound with his hand. Lightning flashes in his thigh, from skin to bone. Lightning in his vision, too, and thunder rolling in his chest and throat. Still he keeps pressing even after the fabric is sopping wet, until his body finally gives out and he collapses on his back.

He rests for a long while, staring up at the sky until his mind is still, the trees come back into focus, and he feels his strength returning. He rolls onto his belly and pushes up with his hands and his knees. En route to his feet, he swipes his pistol from the rock, flips on the safety, and places it again in his waistband. A shooting pain tells him his left leg can bear little weight, and it takes him several moments to figure out a new posture that will shift the weight but keep him upright. He hobbles, then, slowly, back to the trail, stopping only to grab the loop at the top of his pack and drag the mass behind him. He dares not attempt to shoulder it, as that would send him back to the ground.

He limps up the trail in this manner for a quarter mile or more, until he has rounded a bend and is well out of sight of the road and the bridge. By then, he is exhausted, and bright spots are darting through his field of vision. A clammy sweat covers his face and neck. A cold stickiness paints his left leg and extends down into his socks and boot.

He has lost a significant amount of blood.

Night will be upon him soon, and he needs to find a place to hide away. To his right rises a high snow drift. He claws his fingers in and confirms it's solidly packed. It will do.

He digs carefully, shoveling and panting, until he has fashioned a shallow cave just high, wide, and deep enough for him to lie down inside. On the ground nearby, he builds a tiny fire that smokes more than flames and is good only for warming his numbed hands before it dies.

He knows he'll likely lose his leg if he sleeps the night with the tourniquet on, so he releases the slip knot and watches for several minutes for signs of renewed bleeding. Seeing none, he removes his sleeping bag from his backpack, pulls it over his body and around his head, and slides into the dugout.

There he lies in the dark and the silence, unspeakably tired but unable to sleep. Trying to decide what he'll do when morning comes. For the first time, some small part of him hopes that he will not wake to see it.

TSULA

CHAPTER FORTY-SIX

Did she swim? She must have. Water drips from her clothes and hair. And didn't she climb as well, over rocks and through brambles and brittle ground cover? Her hands are scrubbed raw and gashed in thin, weeping lines. She can remember none of it clearly. But there she is, no longer in the river, walking up the road toward those specks in the distance. She can't remember why, but she knows she needs to reach them.

She notes with amazement how warm it is. Warm like the days in early May or mid-September when she wears a flannel shirt and coat in the morning, only to find by noon that she's sweating beneath those thick layers. In fact, she's sweating now. Why is she wearing this coat when the weather is this pleasant?

She lets it fall off her shoulders and keeps walking.

Before her face, a firefly flickers and floats. Strange, she thinks. It's still daylight. Two fireflies, then ten. Then thousands, like those her mother once took her to see in Elkmont, strobing in a rapturous call and response, swirling in more intricate patterns than she could have imagined or described, coalescing finally into one luminescence that covers everything. A light and a heat like a blanket laid over her and all that surrounds her.

She unbuttons her lined flannel shirt and tosses it aside. She has no need for it now.

She glances down at the grass below her boots—verdant, fulsome, soft as down—and imagines its touch on her bare feet, brushing between her toes. When she stoops to remove her boots, she loses her balance and totters onto her hands and knees.

She's so very tired. How long has she been walking? But she has reached warmth at last. She has made it, and now she can rest. She rolls over onto her back, blinking at the looming sun.

A voice speaks to her, as indistinct and hollow as an echo. And then a face hovers over her, shadowy and limned in backlight, its margins spreading and dissolving until it blots out the light completely.

CHAPTER FORTY-SEVEN

Tsula wakes in a chamber whose depths her eyes cannot plumb, but which she gathers from the distant sound of water purling in the blackness must be impossibly wide. A small fire on the rock and dirt floor beside her casts a capering glow on the ground and the near limestone wall, but not on any ceiling that she can see, and not beyond the archway which seems to lead from this small chamber into utter darkness. Out of the void above them peers a stalactite, water dripping from its tip. It gives the impression that the room is slowly melting around her.

She's not warm, but she's warming. The fire provides a nucleus of heat beside her, but when she stretches her hand out in the other direction, it's met with frigid dank. Her mind is sharpening, though her body still feels thick and stiff. She smells blood in her nose still, tastes it in her mouth.

A shuffling sound in the periphery draws her attention. She turns to find a hunched form facing the wall just beyond her head. Unruly silver hair peeks out beneath a toboggan, and one bony hand trains a flashlight beam on a section of the wall. The other hand hovers next to the limestone, tracing something she can't at first make out until the old man turns, catches her eye, and steps aside.

Then she sees them, written in some form of ash or perhaps charcoal. The same symbols her grandparents tried to teach her as a child. The same ones she sees on signs erected all over the Qualla Boundary. They're here, inscribed on a stone canvas. A messenger reaching out over two centuries.

And then she knows where she is.

"I finally got through," a faint voice calls behind her. "They're coming."

Boots approach hastily. A hand places additional sticks on the fire. This second man kneels beside her, and Tsula looks up into the puzzled face of Tommy Weathers.

When she tries to rise, she feels fabric slide against her bare skin. She looks down at a long coat draped over her. The coat is not hers. Alarmed, she lifts it to look beneath and finds she's stripped to her undergarments. Another coat is laid out under her as a makeshift pallet. Her eyes widen, and her breath quickens. She opens her mouth, but no words will come.

"Whoa, it's okay." Weathers raises his hands to assure her he means no harm. "We're just trying to get you warm. Your clothes were soaked and nearly frozen. Look, they're right here next to the fire."

Soaked? The memories swell, flooding her mind with all that has occurred and carrying her panic along with it.

Where is Harlan?

"Man," she whispers, but her lips are heavy and dense, like drying concrete.

"Just lie back," Weathers says. "You need to stay covered up."

She shakes her head, tries again. "A . . . man."

"Who? We haven't seen anyone but you." His eyes move as he scans her, his expression grim. "What the hell happened to you?"

She lifts her hand toward the old man. "Leave."

"We can't leave now," Weathers says. "Paramedics are on their way. We need to stay here and keep you by the fire until they arrive."

She reaches up with her black-tipped fingers to grab him by his coat. She needs him to listen. But she's exhausted, and the few words she has managed already have sapped her reserves. She closes her eyes and lies back. Whatever happens next is utterly beyond her control.

Several minutes later, voices call out from the darkness. Weathers shuffles away and leads those voices back to where she's lying.

When they arrive, the paramedics speak to her directly, asking her a battery of questions she cannot find the strength to answer. There's a stinging prick to her left arm, a light shined briefly into her pried-open eyes, a cuff inflating on her other arm and loosening with a hiss. Then hands lift her onto a softer surface and wrap her in a blanket.

As she rises and begins to float, she opens her eyes upon the craggy face of the old man hovering over her. He looks down, smiles, and places a withered hand on top of hers. Then she drifts into the dark, beyond the reach of the fire, before emerging into a frozen night awash in pulsing color.

HARLAN

CHAPTER FORTY-EIGHT

December 19

When morning comes, Harlan knows he won't make it back to the homestead. Not today, not in this condition. The toes of his left foot don't move when he tries to wiggle them, and the rest of his body quivers uncontrollably. Everything hurts except the parts that are numb. His mouth is caked dry, his eyes are slow to focus, and he's colder than he can ever remember being.

The only option Harlan sees is to head toward the bridge and the roads beyond. If he leaves soon, he might be able to make his way out of the park before sundown and either steal a car or hitchhike his way back across the North Carolina state line. He knows of a former client, now retired and living in an aged log cabin deep in the hills near Fontana, who would allow him to hide out and recover for a day or two before returning in search of Otto.

Sluggish hands and arms make packing difficult, and it takes him three tries before he can stand without falling. Even then, he can't lift his foot at the ankle. He has to modify his gait, drawing the leg up in an exaggerated motion, to keep from catching his boot on the ground and toppling over.

He stops frequently as he walks, leaning against high snow

drifts and tree trunks bordering the trail when he gets winded. He slips on a downslope when his one firmly planted boot steps on a patch of ice. But by the time the sun has risen fully, he has nearly made it back to the Sinks.

As he draws nearer, other sounds float above the rushing water. The choppy whir of a helicopter. The occasional quick burst of a distant siren.

Ranger vehicles are parked on the bridge, their lights flashing, the rangers themselves arrayed on the bridge and the road beyond. They're occupied with their individual tasks and don't appear to have spotted him yet. But their presence tells him that what remains of the life he'd planned for himself is over.

Only two paths lie before him. He could approach and open fire on them with the pistol still hidden in his waistband. But he doesn't have enough ammunition to sustain the fight, and in his condition, he'd be an easy target. There would be honor in that end, at least. A warrior's death.

But what, then, once he's dead? In the absence of a living suspect, the investigation into the deaths of three park employees no doubt will continue in earnest. And what if they find the homestead and Otto? As the last of the settlement alive, what would be his fate then? The public will require a villain to vanquish, and his eldest son would be the only option left.

Or Harlan could surrender himself and confess to it all. Be the evildoer the story requires. Unless the woman survives to tell them, the authorities would have no reason to know of Otto's presence at the settlement. Harlan could deny his son's involvement, tell them he'd moved away when he turned eighteen, declaring his father unwell and wanting nothing more to do with him. In this manner he could, at the very least, buy Otto time to disappear, and perhaps shield him from suspicion altogether.

All Harlan has ever wanted for himself and his boys is the

prospect of a truly free life. What remained of his own prospect has now vanished in its entirety, and this realization rests on his shoulders like grief, heavy and oppressive. Otto's odds might be slim, but they'll be greater if Harlan remains alive to confess the blame and endure the punishment the authorities would insist on placing somewhere.

The trail to the bridge seems to stretch for miles as he hobbles on. When he nears the bridge, the first rangers catch sight of him and stare, gap-mouthed, at the strange beast limping in their direction. They look at each other, then two of the rangers begin trotting toward him. He removes his pistol from his waistband and holds it high by the barrel. The men, having spotted the weapon, halt in their tracks and reach for their sidearms. Slowly, with all his remaining strength, Harlan sets the pistol on the ground and lowers himself prone.

As they search him for more weapons, one of the rangers asks him his name. Harlan laughs quietly to himself at the question.

"Tell me your name, sir!" the man barks a second time.

"My name," Harlan says. The side of his face is pressed roughly against the freezing ground, and the words come slow and awkward. A warm tear escapes his eye and rolls over the bridge of his nose. "My name is Harlan Miles. You assholes stole my family's property."

TSULA

CHAPTER FORTY-NINE

Tsula opens her eyes to a hospital room bathed in a warm, yellow radiance and to Clara Walker's head lying next to her on the bed. She strokes her mother's hair with a bandaged hand, and in a moment the woman looks up with a start. Clara begins to weep. Tsula joins her.

In the safety and warmth of this room—with guards no doubt posted outside—she has no pressing tasks or future needs to occupy her mind, so the events of the past three days rush into that void with irrepressible force. She hasn't had—or, at least, hasn't allowed herself—time to reflect on Abbott's death, and now the memory returns to her laden with a shame she knows she'll never relieve herself of. She had insisted on going deep into the park to satisfy her curiosity. But for her decision, he would have had no reason to be out there. She could have made the call not to engage with Harlan when they spotted each other. She should have sensed the full scope of the danger he posed. How had she not? And yet, despite her failings, he's dead while she lies in this bed recovering.

And wasn't the blood of at least two others on her hands as well? Had they simply withdrawn to report what they'd seen and returned with a more robust force later, might they have avoided the encounter that prompted their deaths? She's wracked by a conviction that she is to blame for it all. That she tipped the first domino.

Tsula can share none of this with her mother, of course. Clara Walker can rest easy that her daughter is safe now. She doesn't need to know at what cost.

Batchelder visits later that morning. His haggard face—all sagging lines and baggy, bloodshot eyes—tells her he has slept little, if at all.

"What did I tell you when you pitched this half-baked plan to me?" he says. "Do you remember?"

"You said, 'If I have to send a search party after your frozen ass, I'm going to be pissed.' Or something like that."

"You do listen," he says. "You're not deaf, just insubordinate."

"Maybe a little of both."

Batchelder smiles, and the sight reminds her that he also had been present in the Emergency Room the night before. Chief Ranger Brannon was there, too, she thinks. She faintly recalls speaking with them while rolling into an examination room, though she can't recall what she told them. The process of rewarming her body had resulted in a sensation like a blowtorch being applied to her hands and feet, and the hospital staff had been generous with the IV narcotics. As a consequence, much of the prior night is a blur.

He pulls a visitor's chair up beside her bed, sits down, and leans toward her. She knows the look on his face. They have much to discuss, and it can't wait much longer.

Tsula turns to her mother. "Hey, Mom, could you do me a big favor?"

"Name it, my sweet."

"I would kill for a good cup of coffee. Is there a cafe downstairs or something?"

Her mother pauses, looks at them both, then nods. "I'll see what I can find."

"Thanks, Mom."

Clara Walker kisses Tsula on the forehead and shuffles slowly from the room. Batchelder waits for the door to close before speaking again.

"Tsula, you know there are going to be a lot of questions we'll need your help answering. This whole. . . incident has got a lot of people interested. Bureau, Interior, Park leadership. I can try to limit how much you get bombarded, but I can only do so much."

"I understand," she says. "How much do you know so far?"

"We know Abbott's dead. You told us last night. There are two bodies at the fire tower. One of them, we don't know much about. Looks like maybe he took a tumble."

"That's the one who shot Abbott. He came after me, too. But who's the other one?"

"He was a park ranger who got sent out looking for you two."

Her breath catches sharply. "I didn't know about any ranger. How'd he die?"

"Shot from behind, looks like. Our guess is he got ambushed. You said one of the men out there followed you to the Sinks?"

She nods. "His name is Harlan Miles."

"Probably it was him. My guess is he came there looking for you."

She hangs her head when her eyes start to ache. "So at least three people are dead because of me."

"I'm not sure I'd look at it that way."

"How would you look at it?"

"I haven't heard the whole story yet," he says. "But I feel certain there's a lot more to it. So how about it?"

She looks down at her hands in her lap. "How about what?"

"You wanna tell me what happened out there? The whole story, I mean?"

The honest answer is no, she has no desire to tell anyone what happened out there. She wants to bind the memory up in razor wire, lock it in a box, and bury it deep in the ocean where it will never be found again. But she knows that's not an option. In the hours and days to come, she'll have to give her account a dozen times to scores of people. It's right that he should hear it from her first.

She tells him everything she can remember, from finding the cabin to the man with the rifle they didn't know was there. From two days out in the frozen wilderness to the Sinks and waking up in the cavern. Batchelder asks no questions and makes no notes. He simply listens. When she finishes, he studies his balled fists for a long moment and exhales noisily through his lips. "On the bright side, I guess I don't get to say I told you so."

"I really wish you did."

"I know." He smiles weakly. "But this isn't something you could have seen coming."

Tsula runs a finger over the tape holding her IV in place. "Abbott had a fiancée," she says. "Amy something. Does she know?"

"I don't know," he says. "I'm leaving notifications up to the park."

"Is his body back?"

Batchelder shakes his head. "Not that I've heard. I don't know if they've even found him yet."

"He was shot right out in front of the cabin. Unless they moved him, he should still be there."

"Well," Batchelder says, "that's the problem."

"What do you mean?"

"Where's your TV remote?"

She looks around, then motions with one clubbed hand to the bedside table. "What is it?"

Batchelder turns the television to a local news channel. Tsula raises her bed to a sitting posture so she can see. On the screen, an aerial image filmed from a helicopter shows a structure fire in a small clearing. It must have been filmed last night, because the screen is dark except for the inferno at the center and a liminal area bathed in a splendid orange glow. The caption below the image reads "STRUCTURE FIRE IN GREAT SMKY MT NAT PARK."

"Jesus," she says. "Is that—"

"Yep."

"How?"

He clicks the TV back off. "No idea, yet. That was early this morning. Fire's finally burned itself out, and they've only recently been able to get into it. All I know is they think they found two bodies inside. Nothing outside but some medium-rare horses."

"So either they brought Abbott into the cabin and he's one of the two bodies there, or they hid him somewhere else."

Batchelder shrugs. "It'll take the lab a while to figure out what's what and who's who. In the meantime, we'll keep searching the area."

"And Harlan?"

"Picked him up this morning coming off the trail. They called me just before I got here. If it makes you feel any better, it sounds like he looks worse than you."

Tsula's mind whirs for a moment before she says, "They might need to be looking for one more suspect."

"Explain."

"Two bodies were found in the cabin, right? So who are they? All we know for sure is we can count out Harlan and the guy at the tower."

Batchelder leans forward in his chair, counting on his fingers as she speaks. "Go on."

"That leaves three others unaccounted for: the two brothers, Otto and Joseph, and Abbott. As far as I could tell, only Joseph was really wounded. So he's probably one of the two bodies. But if the other body is Abbott—say someone drug him inside before setting the place on fire—"

"Then the other son's still out there."

She nods. "Otto."

"Shit," Batchelder mutters. He's on the phone before he has fully stood up from the chair.

OTTO

CHAPTER FIFTY

December 18

When the sun sets on the second day of Harlan's absence, Otto concludes that his father isn't going to return. The tower isn't that far, and he knows these mountains too well. He should have been back by now. Otto's back has begun to ache, and he rolls onto his side to face Joseph's body.

Then he hears it. A buzzing roar, distant but slowly drawing nearer. This new addition to the nighttime soundtrack fills him with dread. He steps onto the porch and looks in each direction but sees nothing. Nothing yet, he tells himself. But they're coming.

They're coming, and he has to leave.

He paces the porch in the dark, his hands pressed to the sides of his head, puzzling on what to do next. He remembers his father's words. *If you see or hear anything while I'm gone, if it looks like people are getting close, you need to get out. Head down to the lake and hunker down somewhere.*

But how does he know they won't follow him?

He feels his way in the darkness to the ranger's body in the yard. He dares not use a flashlight or lamp for fear of attracting attention. His foot strikes the mound first, and he has to sweep away a blanket of snow with his hands. Once cleared, he feels along the body until he finds the man's boots. Rigor mortis has come and gone by now, and the hips flex when he lifts the ranger's legs. He drags the body back toward the cabin, up the stairs onto the front porch, and finally through the front door. It's hard work, and several times he has to stop and catch his breath. Once back inside, he slams the door shut and leans against the wall, panting.

He has no time to waste, though, and gives himself only a moment before sprinting back outside and around the cabin to the tent. He throws open the flap and feels again in the dark. He'd placed the new can of linseed oil Junior brought back on the ground in the near right corner. The contents slosh dully as he lifts the can by its thin metal handle and runs back toward the cabin.

In the clearing, he pauses. A distant white glint hovers low in the sky like a too-near star, its light falling at an oblique angle toward the bordering ridgeline. They're getting closer.

Inside once more, he lights the oil lamp and dims it to the lowest useful light. He empties the cash jar resting on the fireplace mantel, stuffing the contents into his charred pockets. He packs his sleeping bag, flashlight, and spare clothes into the park biologist's backpack and dons his coat, toboggan, and gloves. He kneels then beside his brother, lays a hand on his cold shoulder, and allows himself a moment to weep.

"I'm sorry, Joseph," he said. "I'm so sorry I couldn't protect you. I'm sorry I can't bury you. I have to go now."

The helicopter chuffs louder now, a rumble like ceaseless thunder.

Otto dribbles out the linseed oil in a long arc near the walls and shakes the dregs over the bodies. He takes a long, final look around the cabin before dropping the kerosene lamp on the floor near the front door. The shatter of glass echoes in the spare interior, and in moments flames roar and lick the walls along the length of the room.

Outside, the glassless windows and open door flash and flicker amber in the surrounding black. By the time Otto reaches the tree line at the far end of the clearing, fire and smoke billow out of those apertures and lap at the roofline. The blaze casts a dim orange pallor over the trees on the periphery and allows enough light to move quickly into the forest. The too-near star has adjusted its course by then and is heading for the cabin, flying straight and low. Otto keeps his eye on the spotlight and takes cover behind a wide trunk as it passes.

The helicopter comes to a halt, hovering above the fire with the spotlight trained on it, as though it has treed some prey. Otto looks back briefly to watch, mesmerized by the sight. This costly machine, one of the world's great contrivances, capable only of illuminating the destruction and calling for help that will come too late.

CHAPTER FIFTY-ONE

December 19 and 20

For two days, Otto skulks around the western shore of Fontana Lake. The lake has countless tendrils stretching out from a body that is miles and miles wide, oriented primarily east to west. Otto assumes his father meant for him to stay on the western edge, which abuts the Appalachian Trail and is not too distant from Shuckstack. This would be the most natural meeting place along the lake. But the western shore alone is a vast and serpentine area, and he wonders how exactly his father will find him. Doubt gnaws at him, just as doggedly as the cold and his growing hunger. Otto remembers how his father had grown impatient with his questions while preparing to leave, but he wishes he had insisted upon just one more for clarification—"*Where* on the lake, Pop?"—even if it had incurred the man's wrath.

Otto spends the daylight hours of the first day hidden near the trail, watching for any sign of Harlan. He sees only people with badges affixed to their jackets marching the trail in both directions. Later, as the sunlight wanes and he prepares to seek shelter, more men proceed down the trail toward the dam. But these men are carrying body bags in a grim and careful procession.

The sight catches his breath.

He returns to the lakeshore, a swell of despondency threatening to drown him, and erects a small shelter. He waits until night to build a fire so its smoke won't be seen so easily, and tries without success to sleep.

By the second morning, his meager supply of food is long gone. It feels as though his stomach might tear itself open. While slinking through the grass and trees of the shoreline, searching for anything he might forage, he comes across a burrow dug into a hillside. It sits beneath the exposed roots of a magnolia, which have largely sheltered the entrance from the snow and ice. Otto wonders what is hibernating in that hole and what it would take to roust and trap it. Perhaps he could whittle a stick long and sharp enough to spear it. When he reaches into his pocket for his utility knife, he feels the crumpled money at the bottom brushing against his fingers.

Otto bathes furtively in a small stream hidden behind a withered thicket of mountain laurel. His chest convulses as he splashes the water on his skin and as he scrubs with his hands, removing a slurry of soot and grime. Only the backs of his hands, blistered from the fire that had engulfed him, welcome this cold.

When he is clean—or at least as close to it as he can manage in these conditions—he puts on his one set of new clothes and places the dirty ones in the pack. Then he hikes south, passing quickly across the trail within sight of no one, and wends his way to the paved road that skirts the lake and the dam.

By early afternoon, Otto is seated in a diner housed in a converted gas station, devouring a hamburger and French fries set before him by a matronly server who introduced herself as Karen.

"You been on the trail long, sweetie?" Karen asks.

"Ma'am?" he says through a mouthful of food.

"People come in with backpacks, eatin' like that, lookin' like you do, they usually been on the trail for a while."

Otto looks his arms and hands over. Is it still that obvious? He decides he'll give himself a more thorough cleaning in the men's room before he leaves.

"Couple weeks," he tells the woman.

"Out there in all that snow the last few days?"

He nods.

"It's a wonder you hadn't froze to death. It's a strange time of year to try hiking the trail, you know. You want some coffee? We just brewed a fresh pot."

He does want it, but he also knows he must conserve his money. "How much is it?"

She waves away the question. "On me, sugar. We got a lot, and you look like you could use it."

A minute later, she returns with a steaming mug and sets it down on the table.

He blows to cool the surface and takes a sip. It's the greatest taste his mouth has known in months. "Thank you, ma'am."

"Such a polite boy," Karen says. "Don't hear too many people using good manners like that anymore, even around here. Your mama and daddy must've raised you right."

He hesitates. "Yes, ma'am."

He sips again.

"What happened to your hand?"

He looks at her over the ceramic mug, his eyes wide.

"Your hand." She brushes the back of her own to demonstrate. "What happened to it? And your eyebrows, too."

"Oh," he says. "Burned them. I used too much gas on my fire. Stupid."

"Ouch. You really must have gone wild with it."

He nods. "I was cold."

"Well, you might as well get cozy," she says. "You may not have heard, but there's been a whole lot of mess going on in the park the last few days."

Otto's pulse picks up. "What kind of mess?"

"Sounds like some crazies were tryin' to live in there somewhere," she says. "Can you imagine? Looks like they maybe killed some people, too. I don't know. Think they found some bodies up at the old fire tower. And then there was an actual fire a ways away. Some people told me this morning the trail's closed for several miles." She stops long enough to take a breath and shakes her head emphatically. "Whole world's gone crazy."

"Yes, ma'am."

"Except for nice boys like you," she says with a wink. "Oh, look. There it is now." She nods to a television mounted in a corner of the room near the ceiling.

Nausea washes over him. On the screen he sees his father's driver's license photograph. The stolid face seems to be staring at him and him alone, disapproving his presence in this place of convenience. He can hear his father's voice: *How weak. You couldn't make it out there on your own.*

Then the photo is replaced by overhead video footage of a scraggly, limping man in familiar winter gear standing on a snow-covered bridge. He raises his hands, the black form of a gun in one, as a half-dozen police officers surround him. He seems to be balancing on one leg, and a moment later, prostrates himself to the ground. A banner below the video reads: "MASSACRE SUSPECT IN CUSTODY."

It strikes Otto how strange his father looks on the video, how foreign but for the clothing. Perhaps it's the distance at which the video was taken that makes him hard to recognize, or the image's cinematic quality—a swooping overhead view, like in the action shows he loved to watch on television—that gives it the feel of fiction. Or perhaps it's because, for the first time, he's seeing Harlan Miles clearly. Seeing him as the rest of the world will know him. Not powerful and defiant, as Otto had always believed, but a desperate and hobbled man, capable of harm but also of being harmed. Willing to lay down his weapon to the people he called his enemies when he had sworn to his sons he never would do so and neither should they.

The man he thought he had understood with such clarity now blurs in his mind. He sees the same facts—the stirring tales he'd told them since they were young children of wrongs committed and future acts of bravery; the accumulation of months spent in the park exploring, scouting, planning; the braided grapevine by which lessons were etched on their backs; his willingness to kill those he saw as threats, and his inaction as Joseph lay dying—and suddenly they add up to an entirely different person. Someone inexplicable and grotesque. This man he has feared and loved in equal measure—who was he really? And how much of Otto's own life had been wasted on the man's lies?

Otto feels, at once, unsettled and free. He has worshipped Harlan his entire life, has devoted his own mind and body to pursuing his cause. For the first time, Otto allows the possibility that he was wrong about the man. That he owes this stranger nothing further.

But if that's true, what now?

Karen sets a small plate down on the table.

"Pecan pie," she says. "Last slice."

He looks up at her, puzzled, and she shrugs.

"You'll be doing me a favor. I need to make room for a new one in the cooler."

"Thank you, ma'am."

Minutes later, she brings him the bill for the burger and fries only. "Take your time," she says. "Nobody's in any rush, and I'm sure you'll need a while to figure out what you're going to do about the trail being closed."

"Actually, I think . . . I think I might be done with that," he says. "Maybe this mess up the trail is a sign."

She smiles as though genuinely considering the possibility. "Maybe so. But then what are you going to do?"

"Change of scenery, maybe," he says. "Got no reason I have to be here. I've heard Alaska's nice."

"I'm sure it is," she says. "But that's an awful long way off. Don't you have a home somewhere with someone waiting for you?"

"No, ma'am. Not anymore."

Otto stares down at his coffee cup but can feel Karen studying him.

"Well," she says, "I get off in a couple hours and I live just this side of Murphy. It's not Alaska, but it's west of here. If you need a ride, I can take you that far."

He smiles. "It's a start. I'd be grateful."

Otto finishes the pie and sets down cash enough to cover the bill and a generous tip for Karen. Then he locks the door to the men's room and washes himself as best he can. When Karen's shift is over, he follows her out to her car, throws his pack in the trunk, and settles into the passenger's seat.

All the way to Murphy, Otto basks in the pink light of dusk and the warm air blowing from the car's vents and wonders how far he'll get before someone figures out he's still alive.

TSULA

CHAPTER FIFTY-TWO

December 29

Tsula has finally settled into a comfortable position on the living room couch, blistering toes propped up on a pillow, when her mother walks into the living room. She wears a coy smile on her face. Her hand rests on Tommy Weathers's arm.

"Mom," Tsula says, throwing a blanket over her legs. "A little warning, please."

"What? I'm sure Tommy doesn't care about your feet. You can spare a few minutes for the man who saved your life, can't you?"

Clara Walker winks at him, pats his shoulder, and shuffles away before her daughter can answer.

"I'm sorry to intrude," he says when they're alone. "I did ask Ms. Clara if you were up for visitors before coming over and she said yes. I would have called you directly, but I realized I don't have your phone number."

She shakes her head. "It's fine. She's right."

"May I?" he says, motioning to a seat near the couch.

"Please."

"For the record," he says, sinking into the chair, "you survived two days alone outside in that weather before I ever laid eyes on you. I'd say you saved your own life."

"Wouldn't have mattered if you hadn't come along when you did. I owe you."

"Well."

He casts his eyes around the room until they settle on a small Christmas tree standing unplugged in the corner. Neither Tsula nor her mother has bothered to light it since they got home.

"I tried to visit you in the hospital, by the way. But they had things locked down pretty tight. Sounds like you had to contend with some pretty rough people out there."

"Some of them were. The others…" She sighs and picks at a loose thread on the edge of her blanket. "I don't know. I like to think the young ones were just misled."

"That's charitable of you, considering."

She gestures toward the bereft tree. "'Tis the season, right?"

Weathers nods. "How are you feeling?"

"Well, my toes are blistering now. They tell me my hands will be next. So that's fun. But they think I'll be able to keep most everything."

"That's good news."

"Also, I've decided I never want to see snow again as long as I live."

"I'm afraid you live in the wrong place for that." He chuckles, then adds quickly: "Not that I'm suggesting you leave."

Tsula studies the bandages on her hands for a long moment. "Can I ask you something?"

"Of course."

"What were you doing out there on the road when you found me?"

He leans forward in his chair, his expression now flat. "You already know the answer to that."

"I'm sure they have security cameras down there. If someone sees you—"

"The storm had knocked out the power up that way," he says. "Trees and power lines down everywhere. Internet, too. A real disaster. I had some reliable information—please don't ask me how—that it would be a while before they got things up and running again. It wasn't great driving conditions, let me tell you, and it took us a long time to get there. But I figured it was the best opportunity I was going to have for quite a while."

"Best opportunity to trespass without getting caught."

Weathers shrugs. "My grandfather's eighty-two, and his health isn't great. He should be able to see the cavern before he dies. It's our history. So when I heard about everything going down, I loaded him up, put the snow chains on the four-by-four, and away we went. We parked a ways off at the Sinks and started walking. If anybody came along and asked, we were just two crazy guys out for a stroll when we shouldn't be, tired of being cooped up in the house. At some point, I realized I'd forgotten one of the flashlights in the truck. Couldn't see anything in there without them, I figured. So I turned around to go get it, and there you were in the middle of the road, taking off your damn clothes and mumbling nonsense."

"Have you been charged with anything? I can make some calls."

He leans back and shakes his head. "I'm sure we're the least of their worries. Plus, we hadn't even had a chance to 'trespass,' as you put it, before we saw you. After that, it was just a matter of getting you next to a fire the fastest way we could."

"What did your grandfather say? About the cavern, I mean."

A toothy smile stretches across his face. "Neither of us can stop talking about it. There's something about seeing the writing up close. Gives it . . . I don't know, 'weight' is the only word I can think of."

"Do you know what it says?"

"Ah." He removes his wallet and pulls a tightly folded sheet from it. "I'm not good with the syllabary, but my grandfather knows it. We only got to see a little of what is written in there, because . . . well, you know. But I took pictures of what we did see, and he translated it for me later. It says: 'We are the ones who will not go. We are the ones who hide with tears in our eyes.'"

He stares at the words for a moment, clears his throat, and returns the paper to his wallet.

"I understand there's more like twenty feet up the wall. But you'd have to climb up there to see it, and neither of us was really up for that."

Sirens sound in the distance, and a dog's howl joins the chorus.

"I haven't really been able to sleep much since," he says, his eyes growing distant and glassy. "I just keep thinking about who they were, what they went through. Did any of them ever make it out of that cave? Maybe their descendants are some of our own neighbors and they don't even know this is part of their story."

Tsula sits quietly, her brain grinding on something he said. "I may have an idea," she says finally. "If it works, it could be a win-win."

He cocks his head, grinning cautiously. "Tell me."

CHAPTER FIFTY-THREE

January 8

"Did you make it through the protestors alright?" Park Superintendent Bradford Hall hands Tsula a mug of coffee. "Careful, it's hot."

"It's fine," Tsula says. "I still haven't gotten feeling back in these fingertips. One of the perks, I guess." She sips and recoils from the mug. "Nerves in my mouth still work, though."

He sits down behind his desk and holds up his hands. "I did warn you."

Tsula nods toward the window. "How long have you had the company outside?"

"Not long after they arrested Mr. Miles, I'd say. When word started trickling out about who he was, what he was trying to do, people started showing up. Just a couple at first, but it seems like every day they double. The story seems to have woken a bunch of kindred spirits."

"I guess it'd be too much to hope he was unique."

The superintendent turns toward the window. "I've been thinking a lot these past few weeks about all that's gone on in these mountains. Not just the recent events, but, you know, over time. Would this park even be here if that hadn't all happened? And I do mean all of it." He sighs and looks at her. "It's an uncomfortable inheritance. But if we own it, we own all of it, you know? The beauty, yes, but the conflict and the hurt and the anger a lot of people feel, as well. And we have to do our best to manage all of it. We owe that to everyone."

"You think Alex Lowe felt the same?" Tsula asks.

"We didn't talk about it in those terms," he says. "But yes, I suppose he would agree. What he did helped us try to keep up our end of the deal."

The superintendent drifts off for a moment. Tsula blows the steam from her coffee and listens to the chants coming from outside. It's too soft for her to make out what they're saying, but she can imagine it.

"So," the superintendent says at last, snapping out of his distraction. "What brings you here, Special Agent?"

"Actually, I'm on leave," she says. "I'm just here as a member of the public."

"I don't owe many members of the public the kind of debt I owe you."

"Even so."

"Okay, then, Tsula Walker, average citizen. What can I do for you?"

She takes a deep breath before answering. "I'd like to talk about the cavern."

"I see," he says. "What about it?"

"It's not what you think. I meant what I told you when we met before. I'm not taking sides. But my mother . . ."

"The mother you chauffeur to the community meetings."

"That's right. It's a huge deal for her, the cavern."

"Huge deal for a lot of people. No question."

"I know I'm not telling you something you don't already know," she says. "But the thing is, Mom's dying."

He straightens himself in his seat. "I'm so sorry to hear that."

"I don't know for sure how much time she has left. But based on what the doctors are telling me, it's not a lot. Certainly not as long as it'll take to figure out what happens with the cavern or when the public will be able to get in there."

"Unfortunately, those wheels do sometimes grind slowly. Lots to figure out first."

"I get it," she says. "I do. But in the meantime . . ."

"Yes?"

She hesitates, and then: "I need a favor."

CHAPTER FIFTY-FOUR

January 15

Aweek later, Clara Walker sits in a wheelchair, reading the inscriptions on the cavern wall with her own moist eyes. Superintendent Hall is directly beside her, directing a flashlight beam at the wall. Tsula stands behind her mother, holding the wheelchair handles and her own breath.

Up close, it's the imperfection of it that strikes Tsula most: some symbols written larger than their neighbors, some strokes lighter than others where the medium had worn away against the rough limestone. This is not a work of art practiced and fretted over and intended for display. These are the words of frightened people, written with the knowledge they might not survive. Written, perhaps, so someone would know they had been there, that they had resisted a grievous wrong. She feels a tightening in her throat, her own eyes aching and growing hazy, and is thankful to be standing behind the others.

Her mother weeps openly, telling the man next to her between labored breaths, "Thank you, thank you so much." He bends to put his arm around her in response, and in the reflected light, Tsula sees a tear roll down his cheek as well.

When they return home that afternoon, Tommy Weathers's

car is parked out front. He rushes over to assist Clara from the passenger's seat and into her wheelchair. She smiles at him, and her eyelids droop heavily. He rolls her up the newly constructed ramp and inside the house, neither of them saying a word. She pats his face softly as he helps her into her recliner.

After her mother is situated comfortably and nearly asleep, Tsula walks Weathers out.

"Well?" he asks when they're alone on the porch.

She smiles. "Well what?"

"'Well what,' she says. You know what. What happened?"

"It was amazing. You're right—seeing it up close is a whole other experience. It didn't really click with me the last time. Maybe because I was nearly dead."

"Yeah, yeah, yeah," he says, waving his hand impatiently. "It's amazing. I told you that. But did *he* say anything?"

"Better than that," she says. "Mom cried. And then he hugged her and he cried."

"Really?" Weathers whistles and boxes the air, his feet dancing.

"Now, remember what we agreed," Tsula says. "He did this hush-hush as a favor for me. This never gets mentioned. Ever. I'd be willing to bet that what happened today is better for you than a hundred meetings and faceless petitions. But you say anything about this to anyone, we both lose."

"I know, I know. Still—"

"No 'still.' I'm serious. You say one word about this, I'll hunt your ass down."

"I promise."

"Alright, then."

He smiles at her but says nothing.

"What?"

He shakes his head and turns to go. "You're something else, Special Agent."

"You can call me by my name, you know. You've almost seen me naked."

"I have indeed." He opens his car door and swings his hand in a courtly flourish. "Perhaps I'll see you around?"

She shrugs and turns to go inside. "If you're lucky."

CHAPTER FIFTY-FIVE

March 5

Tsula watches from across the small room as Harlan enters, catches her eye, and pauses. His limp is stark, and even standing still he gives the impression of a buoy listing on choppy water. His hair has grown long and gray, his beard a patchy mess. Tsula has heard he's refusing to eat, and it's evident in his face and arms that he has lost significant weight.

He turns and says something to the sheriff's deputy escorting him. The deputy shakes his head and holds out a hand as though to guide Harlan to his seat. Harlan turns back to Tsula, his face now stony, and hobbles to the chair opposite her. The deputy nods to Tsula, she returns the gesture, and he recedes toward the door.

The week prior, Tsula had received a call from an investigative journalist based in Atlanta. "I've been doing some digging," he said. "I have information I think you'll be interested in." When he told her what he'd learned, she initially didn't believe him. Two days later, he drove up to Cherokee and showed her the evidence himself.

"How did you find this?" Tsula asked, staring at the papers.

"I'm good at what I do," he said.

"Does Harlan know?"

He shrugged. "Not from me. Story won't run until next week."

"Can I tell him first?"

He smiled and narrowed his eyes. "How would you manage that?"

The answer: she knows one of the deputies at the jail where Harlan is in custody awaiting transport to prison. The same deputy who now, a week later, presses himself against the back wall of the room just to make sure she doesn't do anything to Harlan that will leave a mark. Strictly speaking, she shouldn't be permitted contact with the man accused of trying to kill her. But Harlan has already pled guilty to that crime plus several others, fired his court-appointed lawyer, and been sentenced to life in prison. All that remains is his imminent transfer to the federal penitentiary where he will die. So perhaps the jail's rules could be relaxed just a little for a friend. Perhaps no one would miss ten minutes of surveillance video.

Harlan sits and stares at Tsula across the table. "You know I'm not talking to any cops without a lawyer present." His voice is strained and has lost its baritone timbre. It's as though he's aged two decades in a matter of months.

Tsula breathes in deeply and leans back in her chair. Despite her outward bravado, she wasn't convinced she could actually face the man voluntarily. When she'd blinked awake this morning, her heart already was pounding, and she vaguely recalled a dream in which she'd been running from something or someone in the dark. Her pulse did not calm as she drank her coffee and buttered the toast she ultimately couldn't eat. A dewy perspiration slicked her skin as she drove to the jail. But so pitiable is the condition of the man sitting across from her now that he appears an entirely different person from the one who'd chased and assaulted her. Gazing at him doesn't result in the wave of memories or panic she'd anticipated.

"What lawyer?" she says. "I heard you got rid of yours."

He turns his head, gives a wet, hacking cough, and releases a turgid stream of phlegm to the floor. "He was an idiot. But I'm sure the court would gladly appoint me another one if they knew the cops were still coming by, circling me like vultures."

"No badge here," she says, holding her hands up. "I'm still on leave."

"Is that right?"

"Scout's honor," she says. "Nearly dying earned me quite the vacation."

"You should be more careful out in those woods," he says. "There's more danger out there than people realize."

"Is that what you told Joseph?"

Lightning flashes in Harlan's eyes, briefly and then gone. "I was sorry to read about your mother in the obituaries," he says. "I would have sent flowers for the funeral, but the papers get to us kind of late in here."

Tsula's face flushes, and she clenches her hands into fists in her lap.

Behind unkempt whiskers, the corners of Harlan's mouth curl into a smile. "Why are you here, Special Agent? I doubt your bosses would approve of you fraternizing with the likes of me, even in your off-time."

"I've brought you a gesture."

"What kind of gesture?" he says. "I'd like to know how to return the favor."

"Of friendship, of course. What else?"

When she reaches inside her coat, Harlan swivels in his chair as though he might break for the door.

"Easy, Harlan," she says. "It's just documents."

He settles slowly back into his seat, his eyes narrowing. "You came up here to bring me documents?"

"Well, not just any documents. Historical documents." She removes a small, folded stack and lays it out on the table, smoothing it flat with her hand. "You know how there's been all this interest in our story?"

"I get letters every day," Harlan says. "Tons of them. I guess sometimes it takes a martyr to wake people up."

"Oh, it's woken some people up, alright. In particular, it got the attention of this one journalist who apparently has a thing for research. A real nerdy kind of guy. He came to town, and he started doing some digging through these old records archives. And do you know what he found?"

"I'm on tenterhooks."

"That's the spirit." She removes the top several pages from her stack and slides them across to Harlan. "The first thing he found was this old deed. I'm no expert at reading these things, but this reporter is. And it's been looked over by some other people who know what they're talking about as well. It's a deed signed by one Lowell Miles—that's your great-grandfather, right?—transferring ownership of his farm in 1929 to a gentleman by the name of Benjamin Owenby. Now, who is Benjamin Owenby, you might ask?"

She slides the next dozen pages off the stack over to him.

"Mr. Owenby was the owner of a grocery and a feed store in a nearby town, one of those that's now at the bottom of Fontana. At least, grocery and feed store is what it looked like on paper. Rumor has it that he also ran a speakeasy, maybe some cards, maybe some betting and some other stuff we won't mention. The local law never did seem to mind much. Looks like he was a big wheel in the town, so they didn't touch him. You know how that goes."

"Where is this going, Special Agent?"

"You in a rush to be somewhere, Harlan?" Tsula says. "I'm getting there. Turns out your great-granddaddy Lowell was a big, big fan of 'groceries and feed.' He racked up quite the bill over time, and he got to where he couldn't pay Mr. Owenby back. Between what he owed and the interest he was accruing, it was close to ten thousand dollars, which in 1929 was . . . well, it was a lot. So Mr. Owenby filed liens on Lowell's property for what he owed for 'groceries and feed.' And then . . ."

She slides over more papers from the stack.

". . . the liens were canceled the same day that deed was signed transferring the property to Mr. Owenby." She sits quietly for a moment, watching the gears in Harlan's mind turn. "You get where this is going now?"

The whole of Harlan sags then, as though some internal scaffolding has collapsed. He flexes his fingers slowly on the table, scraping his long nails across the surface, and pulls himself upright again. "Lies," he says. "Some reporter forges documents so he can sell newspapers. Nothing new there."

"See, I wondered that, too," Tsula replies. "But they're real alright. He found the documents in the archives. Original seal and everything. You can feel it. And he'll tell anyone who wants to verify all this exactly where he found them, so they can go take a look for themselves. But I haven't even told you the best part, Harlan."

She places the last five pages on top.

"The next year, 1930, Mr. Owenby turned around and sold that land to the government for the park. He made a tidy five-thousand-dollar profit. Which, again, in 1930 money is a good day's work."

Harlan stares at the stack of documents but doesn't touch them.

"I came to tell you, Harlan—since you and I are in this thing together, whether we like it or not—that this nosy reporter's article is going to run tomorrow. Maybe you'll get to read it when the paper finally gets to you in a month. Maybe you'll see it on the TVs they have inside there or the prison where you're going next. But everyone—all the people who write you fan mail and send me death threats, all the protesters outside, all the guys in the jail who think you're some kind of badass—*everyone's* going to know the truth. The righteous cause you killed people and sacrificed your own son's life for, the one you tried to kill me for, which is the part I take *very* personally, was all a lie. Some bullshit story your family told each other from generation to generation to cover up the shameful truth. A story that you were too stupid to confirm before you dove in headfirst."

Silence envelops them for several delicious breaths, until Harlan says, "Doesn't change anything. The government took thousands of people's land, didn't give them a choice. One less would be a drop in the bucket."

"Where'd those people get that land in the first place, Harlan? You really want to get into what got taken from who?"

Tsula slides her chair back and stands.

"You leaving me all this?" Harlan asks, gesturing to the table. "I do like reading the funny papers."

"You know I can't leave you anything, Harlan." She gathers up the documents, folds them neatly, and returns them to her coat pocket. "But the story will run soon. I'm sure you'll be seeing this stuff plenty."

She has nearly made it to the door when Harlan calls after her. "Otto?"

She pauses and shakes her head but doesn't turn around. "No one has found him. With any luck, he's gotten thousands of miles away from your dumb ass by now."

For a long while afterward, Tsula lingers in the lobby, gathering herself. Her hands, she sees, are shaking. The deputy who had escorted Harlan enters the lobby alone, the heavy secured door clicking shut loudly behind him. He approaches her, smirking, and she stuffs her hands into her coat pocket to conceal them.

"You should have seen him when I left him back in his cell," he says. He droops his shoulders low and allows his face to sag in imitation. "That was good shit."

She pats his shoulder and turns to go. "I owe you one."

Outside, a throng of protestors gather on the sidewalk sandwiched between the jail and a bordering four-lane road. Some hold signs that read "Free Harlan Miles, political prisoner," "The Govt takes: taxes, land, guns, life," and—her personal favorite— "They can have their cave, give us back our homes." A gray-haired man with a bullhorn shouts inscrutable words to a small collection of passersby who have stopped to listen and to the traffic whizzing past on the road. All protesters are armed except the children, who squat in a narrow strip of slowly greening grass in search of insects. Disconcerted deputies take turns, four at a time, standing sentry just inside the complex's fencing.

As Tsula approaches the exit onto the neighboring road, the protestors catch a glimpse of her SUV. En masse, they turn and direct their shouts toward her. She's not certain if they recognize her, or if they've simply decided that anything resembling an unmarked government vehicle will do. She wonders, too, how many will gather tomorrow after the news story runs. She considers driving back up just to take a look.

In a moment, she sees an opening in the traffic and steps lightly on the gas. As she does, she rolls down her window, honks her horn, and gives the shouting crowd a wave.

CHAPTER FIFTY-SIX

April 12

One late Sunday afternoon, as the spring beauties and trillium climb the nearby hills, Tommy Weathers pulls his car into Tsula's gravel driveway. She has parked herself in a rocking chair on the front porch to savor the warmth but stands when she sees his car approach. He emerges from the driver's seat holding a casserole dish.

"I was visiting Ms. Betty after church," he says when he reaches the porch, "and I mentioned that I was thinking of checking up on you. She made me promise to bring this by."

Tsula sits again, takes the dish from him, and sets it in her lap. "Take a load off," she says, motioning to an empty chair. She lifts up the foil over the dish and looks inside. She squints at the dish and purses her lips. "What is this?"

"No idea," he says. "She was too busy hurrying me out the door to tell me."

"Is it bad that I'm looking at it and still can't tell?"

"Not a great sign. But it smelled good in the car on the way over."

He settles into the vacant chair's creaks and groans and looks out at the yard.

"So," he says after a moment. "Are you back at work?"

"I am," she says. "I've been traveling a lot, which I guess is good. I think my boss is scared to send me back into Great Smoky, actually. Instead, he sends me to Acadia and Virgin Islands."

"Fancy."

"That last one's not bad."

"I'm sorry it's been a while since I stopped by," he says. "I've been meaning to, but I had this hunch you wanted some time to yourself after the funeral."

"You were right. I needed some time to think."

Weathers nods. "And if I may ask, what have you concluded from all that thinking?"

"Nothing concrete yet," she says. "My boss says he'd approve a transfer back out west if I want it. He knows I only came back for Mom, so . . ."

"Good for you." Weathers looks down at the hands in his lap and appears to be contemplating his next words. "Are you going to take it?"

She shrugs. "I haven't decided. I keep telling myself there's nothing for me here anymore. But then, every time I think of putting in the request, something stops me."

"We do have a lot to offer," he says brightly. "Great people, obviously. Lots of outdoor activities. A national park right on our doorstep." He turns to face her, grinning.

"You had me for a second there," she says, "but then you lost me."

"You'll come back around."

"I noticed you didn't say anything about any new historical sites."

Weathers gives a quick laugh—one short, withering tone. "I wouldn't hold my breath."

"I'm sorry," she says. For once, she means it.

He exhales noisily through his lips and nods. "At least they're talking about compromises now. Special access. Involvement of the tribe in interpretive and educational presentations. Stronger input on the official name. Small concessions."

"I know it's not what you wanted," she says.

"It's something," he replies. "But I'll never stop asking for more."

"That, I believe."

"You know," he says, "you helped get our foot further in the door than we would have otherwise. We probably wouldn't even be talking middle ground if it wasn't for you. I'll always be grateful for that."

Tsula studies an ant skittering along the arm of her chair. "Tommy, I've been meaning to talk with you, too," she says finally. "To thank you."

"For what?"

"For being so great with Mom."

He shakes his head. "I couldn't convince her about the treatments any more than you could."

"I mean in the end," she says. "When you visited with her so much. She lit up every time you came by. I'll always be grateful for that."

He looks off into the yard, blinks several times, and clears his throat. "She lit me up, too, you know."

A crow settles into an old white oak holding court in the front yard. The jet-black form seems to look directly at Tsula as it caws.

"I swear that bird's been here ever since the funeral," Tsula says, nodding in its direction. "When I get to missing Mom, I come out here, and by God, it always comes by. Just to give me hell."

"I'm imagining I've done something Ms. Clara did not approve of," Weathers says, closing his eyes. The bird reproaches him, and he nods in response. "That sounds about right."

They laugh, and the act reminds Tsula how long it's been since she's done so.

She lifts the dish off her lap and holds it out. "Are you feeling daring? I might as well put whatever this is in the oven to warm, but it looks like too much food for just me."

Tommy Weathers smiles. "I could eat."

ACKNOWLEDGMENTS

Thanks to Jon Gosch, Executive Editor at Latah Books, for believing in this novel. That someone with such talent would see something in my writing still leaves me speechless. I am likewise grateful to Kevin Breen, my editor, who showed this little story the greatest respect possible by working to ensure it was the best it could be.

I owe a debt of gratitude to everyone who gave me their time as I wrote this manuscript, from those who granted me the benefit of their unique experience, expertise, or connections, to those who read the manuscript and gave me feedback. Those include, but are not limited to, Christopher Smith, Special Agent in Charge of Operations for the National Park Service's Investigative Services Branch; Chelsea Saunooke, tribal council representative for the Eastern Band of Cherokee Indians; Roger Johns; Kathy Nichols; Michael K. Brown; Linh Pham; Danielle Herritt; Simone Ludlow; and Audrey K. Thompson.

Thanks, as well, to my parents for encouraging my love of books and writing from an early age. They were my earliest cheerleaders and remain some of the loudest.

And finally, to Cindy, Everett, and Marcus: You gave me the support, the time, and the space to chase this dream. None of this would be without you.

About the Author

    C. Matthew Smith is an attorney and writer whose short stories have appeared in and are forthcoming from numerous outlets, including *Mystery Tribune*, *Mystery Weekly*, *Close to the Bone*, and *Mickey Finn: 21st Century Noir Vol. 3* (Down & Out Books). He's a member of Sisters in Crime and the Atlanta Writers Club.

    When he isn't writing and paying the bills, Matt enjoys fly fishing, hiking, and backcountry camping. He holds a degree in English from Davidson College and a law degree from the University of Georgia. He lives near Atlanta with his wife, son, and father-in-law.

    You can reach Matt at www.cmattsmithwrites.com or follow him on Twitter (@cmattwrite).

CPSIA information can be obtained
at www.ICGtesting.com
Printed in the USA
BVHW072120161021
618822BV00001B/4

9 781736 012765